THE LAST
CHAMELEON

James North

Praise for Deep Deception:

"fast ... ng entertaining thriller, highlighting some of
today's real issues"
Basingstone Book Reviews

Discover us online:
www.crookedcatpublishing.com

Join us on facebook:
www.facebook.com/crookedcatpublishing

Tweet a photo of yourself holding
this book to **@crookedcatbooks**
and something nice will happen

For "T" and the Rug Rats

About the Author:

James North is a former U.S. Navy intelligence officer, consultant to the U.S. Government, political analyst, and university lecturer. He currently lives in Europe.

Acknowledgements:

I offer my sincerest appreciation to Alex, Ann, Carmen, Floyd, Hilary, Julie, Linda, Sarah and Sue who continue to take great pleasure in reading and commenting on my manuscripts.

Once again, I would like to add a special thanks to Jane Leigh-Morgan, Lorna Read and Maureen Vincent-Northam for their sharp eyes and editorial quip.

To Stephanie and Laurence Patterson at Crooked Cat Publishing, thank you for supporting the project.

THE LAST CHAMELEON

A Vanguard Novel

Prologue

London, England
St. James's Place, City of Westminster
Present Day

Caroline Dupré perched on the corner of her desk, staring out of the window, alternating her gaze between Queen's Walk and Green Park. Although her eyes were fixed on events below, she was reflecting on places far more distant than the ones beneath her fourth floor corner office at 320 St. James's Place. As she surveyed the world below, the expression on her face shifted, transforming her from inquisitive onlooker to distant, spellbound participant. She was captivated by the similarity and seemingly arbitrariness of the activities taking place in the park and along Queen's Walk. Spring had come early and both places were littered with people, milling about in the unusually warm weather. They moved unhurriedly—strolling casually along the pavements and footpaths and across the park's large, unfolding green. They seemed to be in a trance—moving about without intent and toward no particular destination.

After a while, she began to see their aimless movement as a metaphor—a crude allegory of the life she had left behind. She was a different person now, different physically, mentally, and emotionally. She had always been trim and athletic, but now she was leaner and toned. And although she still embraced her femininity, the bespoke black, two-piece Yves St. Laurent trouser suit and black Manolo Blahnik three-inch heel court shoes on her feet exuded a well-blended combination of strength, confidence and femininity. She was a product of Vanguard—a superb example of a successful transformation—an intelligence operative who was just emerging, but well-turned-out and perfectly tuned to play the dangerous game of espionage. She epitomized mental agility, intellect and strength and she possessed a killer's instinct. The latter, however, was something she was still grappling with. Subconsciously, she knew she could not forget who and what she was, but she also knew there would always be a lingering fear of what she had become.

The first steps in her metamorphosis had begun with the death of her husband, François. Yet throughout the tragic experience and her struggle against his faceless killers, she had managed to reject the tug of altruism and the adrenalin rush she felt each time she came closer to exposing them, or denying them ultimate success—her death and the elimination of a key witness to their dark conspiracy. Nevertheless, thoughts and feelings that she needed to do something, other than observe life's tragedies, had been growing and assailing her almost constantly by the time she met Vanguard spymaster Niles Peter Thornton aboard a flight from New York to Paris.

The encounter was a turning point. Only two months after meeting the elderly, but spritely and charismatic, man, she resigned her job as director of the organization her husband had died defending. The job had been a constant, and at times an unpleasant, reminder of his death, but she had convinced herself that it was his assassination, and not the intrigue, excitement, and danger that had seduced her into the dark world of covert operations—a world from which there could be no return.

Regardless of the questions that lingered in her mind about her motives, Caroline Dupré had no doubts whatsoever about her ability to assimilate, adapt, and even disappear. The desire to blend in and vanish was almost certainly the manifestation of her eagerness for change—a part of her struggle to move on.

It probably also explains why just two weeks after recruitment, she climbed aboard a small private jet for the U.S. Virgin Islands and underwent eight months of rigorous training in intelligence operations tradecraft, then allowed herself to be deposited in the sleepy former Central American British colony of Belize to master jungle and guerilla warfare, learn survival skills and acquire special weapons training. After the intensive molding and another full year of intensive Arabic language studies and a few more weeks of advanced tradecraft training the transformation was complete. She had become a part of the silent, dangerous struggle—she had become a part of Vanguard.

PART I

Chapter One

A dense cloud of dust trailed the white Toyota Land Cruiser as it punched its way through the already hazy air and sped north along the western fringe of the Ténéré Desert. It was headed toward the town of Assamakka, located in the northern part of the West African country of Niger. As the bulky 4x4 moved along the desolate road, Sa'id al-Bashir gripped its steering wheel firmly, leaned forward in his seat, and squinted to keep the vehicle's tires in the barely visible ruts. The road was already treacherous, but its condition had been made worse by the dry, choking *harmatan* winds that swept constantly over it, covering the tracks of each vehicle immediately after it passed. The *harmatan*-deposited silt caused the 4x4's wheels to shift, making steering feel like driving on ice.

Said al-Bashir had been driving hard for nearly ten hours and it had been slow going. He knew it would take at least two more hours to reach the Algerian border. Other than the three stripped-down bush taxi buses he had met heading south outside Arlit, the only other living creatures he had seen was a band of Tuareg tribesmen—dwellers of Niger's Aïr Mountains —who had crossed the road ahead of him. He concluded that because they were heading eastward, they were returning to

9

their homes in the mountains after a camel herding expedition. And judging from the sacks slung over the backs of several of their beasts, they had also been collecting salt.

He had set out from the Aïr Mountains three days earlier. The night before, he had camped not far from Tima, one of several towns in the interior of the Aïr Mountains, well known to foreign adventurers for its jade-colored oasis and breathtaking waterfalls. After leaving the mountains, he had stopped in the town of Arlit and filled up the vehicle's tank and two extra ten-gallon Jerry cans with diesel fuel. He had also bought food and topped up his fresh water supply before bedding down in the vehicle for the night just outside the once thriving mining town. Well before sunrise the next morning, he resumed his journey.

After sitting behind the wheel for several hours and with only thirty-five miles to go to reach the border town of Assamakka, he spotted an approaching vehicle about half a mile away. It was a light 4x4 pickup truck, painted the color of the national *gendarmerie*, Niger's paramilitary border security force. Seconds after he spotted the vehicle, it stopped and pulled off to the side of the road. It was obvious that its occupants had noticed him traveling rapidly toward them.

Sa'id al-Bashir had made the run between Arlit and Assamakka numerous times and he knew that off-duty *gendarmes* and regular soldiers garrisoned near Assamakka often freelanced in the area by setting up bogus checkpoints to extort money and valuables from taxis and their passengers and the drivers of private and commercial vehicles. For years, the stretch of road had been used by smugglers and was well known for military and border guard shake-downs. It was the ideal location for this type of 'unofficial activity', especially since anyone headed for Algeria from Niger by road had few other options. Despite the road's treachery, it was the quickest and most direct route from Arlit to Assamakka.

After observing the stopped vehicle, he reduced his speed

gradually. He knew the vehicle's occupants would be extremely cautious. They would observe him before flagging him down; they would be careful not to approach too quickly for fear that they might be stopping a military officer or civilian government official with sufficient rank to land them in the stockade. As the Land Cruiser drew closer to the stationary vehicle, three soldiers climbed out of it. One of them began walking toward the Land Cruiser with his arm outstretched, warning Sa'id al-Bashir to stop. By now, there was no doubt about the soldiers' intentions. The situation bore all the characteristics of a shake-down.

As the soldier closed on his vehicle, he surveyed the uniformed man's demeanor and assessed the lethality of the situation. He scanned the man's slight frame from head to toe and noticed he was wearing an olive-colored beret and the shoulder patch of the *gendarmerie*. He also noticed that the man wore the rank of a corporal and that he carried only one weapon, a French-made MAS 9mm pistol, a sidearm he recognized as somewhat antiquated, as it was no longer used by the French military. The other two occupants of the pickup truck were by now standing in front of their vehicle. They were also armed with MAS 9mm pistols, but in addition, they carried MAT-49 submachine guns slung over their shoulders. Their weapons were still pointed toward the ground, but if needed they could be quickly raised. Sa'id al-Bashir knew that their weapons could be trained on his vehicle at the slightest provocation.

His mind raced. *I'm alone, driving an expensive vehicle and carrying thousands of Euros in cash. How do I get out of this?* He knew he was a prime target not only for extortion, but outright robbery. There was no way to talk or buy his way out of the situation. The thoughts racing through his head were suddenly interrupted; his suspicions were confirmed when a smile swept over the face of the soldier who was walking toward him—a smile that suggested the man knew he and his friends had struck pay day.

Sa'id al-Bashir knew that if he resisted, the soldiers would detain him, probably beat him and take everything of value he possessed, including whatever fuel, water and rations he had. But with the large sum of cash in his possession and the expensive 4x4 he was driving, he would be lucky to survive at all, as victims of such situations rarely, if ever, lived to talk about their experiences. Leaving his fate to luck was not an option. He would not be detained, robbed, beaten or killed, because in three days he had to be in Paris. But first, he would have to cross into Algeria and reach the capital, Algiers.

By now, the soldier was walking on the road toward his vehicle and was directly in front of him. As his Land Cruiser drew nearer to his soon-to-be tormentor, Sa'id al-Bashir slowed to a crawl and lowered the heavily tinted driver side window. The vehicle continued to crawl toward the man; he stepped to the side of the road before it reached him. Sa'id al-Bashir could see that the smile on his face had dissipated and he had adopted the demeanor of a genuine military man. The face now staring at him was one of confidence and authority; when the Land Cruiser came to a halt alongside him, he greeted Sa'id al-Bashir authoritatively—with an air of officialdom.

"Good day!" the soldier said firmly.

"Good day," Sa'id al-Bashir replied politely.

"Your papers please…"

Sa'id al-Bashir reached into the compartment between the front seats and handed the man his Algerian passport, and employee identification card from Niger's national mining company, Société Mining Nationale de Niger (SOCMINN), and his driver's license. He watched as the man shuffled through the documents without really examining them. It was clear that he had no real interest in them. After a few more seconds of symbolic leafing and shuffling, the soldier looked up. "Where are you going?" he demanded more firmly.

Looking directly into the soldier's eyes, Sa'id al-Bashir replied, "I am on my way to Algiers to deliver some samples and to brief senior government officials. I hope this won't take long!" With a sense of urgency he added, "I am already running late!"

The soldier paused and stared at him scornfully, eyes searching for tell-tale signs that might contradict the story. A few moments later, the charade ended when the soldier commanded, "Please step out of your vehicle!"

"What is the problem?" Sa'id al-Bashir asked, looking genuinely perplexed. "You have examined my papers, haven't you? Are they not in order?"

"Yes, they are," the soldier replied.

"Then why not permit me to continue on my way? I have told you that I am going to a high level meeting in Algiers and cannot be delayed!"

"Calm yourself, sir!" The soldier was clearly annoyed. "This will take only a few minutes. I have orders to inspect all suspicious-looking vehicles traveling along this road. As you are no doubt aware, there has been an increase in cross-border smuggling and robberies, so we have been told to inspect all vehicles that may be transporting contraband."

Although well rehearsed, the soldier's explanation lacked conviction; this was made evident by the self-doubt, which by now had all but consumed his face. Recognizing the collapse of his enemy's confidence, Sa'id al-Bashir seized the opportunity to bolster the credibility of his own story. Keeping his eyes trained on the soldier, he reached into the space on the floor behind the front passenger seat, as if to retrieve the samples and exclaimed, "Look! If you will let me, I will show you the samples I am transporting!"

He halted and froze when the soldier shouted, "I do not wish to see them now! I will examine them in due course! But first, I must inspect your vehicle!"

Turning to face the soldier, he allowed his anger to erupt.

"Who is your commanding officer?" he demanded.

"Captain Hussein!" the soldier snapped. "He is at the border post at Assamakka. If you wish, you can speak to him when you get there. Now, will you please step out of your vehicle?"

Sa'id al-Bashir hesitated, which caused the soldier's anger to flare. "Why do you not want me to look inside?" the soldier barked. "Have you something to hide?"

Returning the man's gaze momentarily, he twisted around and reached behind the seat and again offered to show his samples. As he stretched across the center console, he kept the man's body in his peripheral vision. The soldier's right hand began to move toward the pistol, holstered at his waist. Realizing the man was growing nervous, Sa'id al-Bashir quickened his movement; his hand landed on the grip of the Ingram M10 9mm submachine gun he had placed on the floorboard before he set out from Arlit. Without skipping a beat, he swung the weapon up and over the back of the seat toward the open window and squeezed the trigger, letting out an efficient three-round burst.

Sa'id al-Bashir's movement was so swift and fluid that the soldier did not have time to remove his pistol from its holster. There was a tat-tat-tat as 9mm rounds exploded from the weapon's barrel and ripped into the man's chest. His eyes widened and a look of disbelief swept over his face. He fell backwards, arms outstretched, and collapsed.

After hearing the shots, the two soldiers, who had been standing in front of the pickup truck, raced toward him, weapons leveled. Within seconds, they began raking the Land Cruiser with sustained fire from their assault rifles. The bullets peppered the vehicle like fistfuls of pebbles thrown in rapid succession, but much deadlier. Glass shattered as Sa'id al-Bashir slammed the transmission into first gear, pushed the accelerator to the floorboard and popped the clutch. The heavy 4x4 leapt forward. He lowered his body across the front seat to escape the hail of bullets, which seemed to be concentrated on the windscreen and windows around him. As the Land Cruiser picked up speed, he shifted into second gear. He steered well to the left side of the road, stuck the barrel of the weapon out of the front passenger window and fan-fired from left to right. During the second sweep, he heard a scream. Two of his would-be assailants had been eliminated. Only seconds earlier, the odds were against him. Now they were even.

The Land Cruiser continued to accelerate. Sa'id al-Bashir peered over the dashboard through a hole in the near-totally demolished windshield and spotted the third soldier moving right to left across the road. He knew that if the man made it across the road to the driver's side of his vehicle, there would be little to protect him from the bullets when they penetrated the thin metal skin of the door. Moving to cut the man off, he changed direction, shifted into third gear, floored the accelerator and steered at an angle just ahead of the soldier. Taken by surprise and panic-stricken, the man squeezed the trigger and kept his finger pressed against it, generating sustained fire, instead of shorter, efficient bursts.

In a matter of seconds, Sa'id al-Bashir had gotten the break he needed. The soldier's selection of sustained fire had caused him to empty his weapon, but he kept squeezing the trigger. Nervous and surprised that the MAT-49's 30-round magazine had been emptied so quickly, he began fumbling with a full magazine he was trying to remove from the pouch on his combat belt. More luck. In the midst of the chaos, the soldier had forgotten about the 9mm pistol strapped around his waist. During the confusion and his struggle to reload, he had hesitated. He had stopped to remove the empty magazine instead of letting it fall to the ground and rapidly replacing it with a full one. The pause, as brief as it was, turned out to be a deadly error. It gave Sa'id al-Bashir enough time to get a bead on him with the vehicle.

After changing the magazine and chambering the first round, the soldier was leveling his weapon to resume firing. But when he looked up, the Land Cruiser's huge bumper was about to bear down on him. He tried to leap out of the way, but his reaction was too late and too slow. The winch mounted on the Land Cruiser's bumper plowed into him. His body jack-knifed at the waist; as if by reflex, he squeezed the trigger and let out an ear-splitting scream. But instead of being slammed onto the road, the tow hook at the end of winch's cable caught his web belt. He knew that he was going to be dragged and run over. He was right. Several hundred yards later, his belt came undone and the winch hook let go of him, leaving his mutilated, dust-covered body on the desert floor beneath a half-visible, baking hot sun.

Chapter Two

The dust-shrouded road that had lain stretched out before Sa'id al-Bashir earlier that morning had been whittled down to only a few miles. Sensing that his destination was just ahead, he drove the remaining distance as fast as the silt-covered ruts would allow the wheels of the vehicle to carry it and remain on the road. Less than thirty minutes earlier, he had engaged rogue border guards in a life and death shoot-out, but he was now on the outskirts of Assamakka. His pulse was still racing when he pulled the vehicle up along the side of the road and shut off its engine. After stopping, he glanced over his shoulder to check one last time that he had not been followed, and then turned his attention to Assamakka, now in front of him. The road was clear in both directions.

He took a deep breath, knowing that he had been lucky in more ways than one. He had managed to escape unscathed and none of his vehicle's wheels had been shot out. There was also no damage to the radiator. The fact that his vehicle had not been disabled showed that the assailants were amateurs and were unprepared for the way he had reacted. They had been taken completely by surprise.

It was now early evening and he could only hope that no other vehicle happened along, especially another military vehicle. If a vehicle did approach from the direction of Assamakka, he would have trouble explaining the condition of the Land Cruiser. If it came from the direction of Arlit, he would have an even greater problem explaining the condition of his vehicle and the three dead border guards. However, if a military vehicle came along from either direction his recent escape would have amounted to no more than a reprieve. He was certain there could be more trouble, and if it occurred, he would have no need to concern himself with an explanation because he would be arrested.

After a pause to collect his thoughts and calm his nerves, he started the Land Cruiser's engine and continued toward Assamakka. It was nearly nightfall when the vehicle crept into the southern end of the town. The sight of flickering lights ahead made him feel more relaxed. He knew he was well within reach of the Algerian border. All he had to do now was to get rid of the bullet-riddled vehicle before it attracted any unwanted attention. As he steered the Land Cruiser closer to Assamakka, he recalled a Tuareg man named Tar'iq Ibn Battutah from whom he had bought provisions on a number of occasions while traveling north. The man lived just on the southern edge of town and raised goats. If his recollection served him correctly, the man had a stable at the rear of his house which would be suitable for hiding the battle-scarred Land Cruiser.

As the 4x4 crawled forward, he scanned the road ahead, surveying the patchwork of mud brick buildings sprouting from the dusty, almost barren landscape. Well before entering the patchwork of structures, he spotted the dwelling belonging to the Tuareg trader. It lay some two hundred yards off to the left side of the main road, down a narrow track. He swung the vehicle onto the track and drove cautiously toward the building. A minute or two later, he pulled up behind it and a tall man wearing a flowing indigo robe and turban emerged. Sa'id al-Bashir climbed from the Land Cruiser and raised a hand. A smile broke out on his face.

After fixing his eyes upon Sa'id al-Bashir, the man roared with laughter, then belted out an enthusiastic greeting. Although accustomed to speaking Tuareg, his native Berber dialect, he let out a string of colorful greetings in Egyptian Arabic.

"*As-saláamu :aláy-kum, ya Sa'id! Áhlan wa-sáhlan! Káhyfa Háal-ak?* Hello Sa'id! Welcome! How are you?"

"*Ána bi-kháyr, al-Hámdu li-Láah, wa-ánta?* I am well, praise be to God, and you," Sa'id al-Bashir replied."

"*Ána bi-kháyr, al-Hámdu li-Láah!* I too am well, praise be to God," said Tar'iq Ibn Battutah. "But what has happened to your automobile?"

"I had some trouble with a few greedy policemen."

"Ah hah... I see!" the tall Tuareg said smiling, revealing coffee-stained teeth.

Sa'id al-Bashir stared momentarily into the man's jaundiced eyes and declared exasperatedly, "I am in need of a great favor, my friend."

The man's eyes shifted again to the embattled 4x4 and he nodded approvingly. "Whatever you ask, my friend, I shall do," he replied, an expression of joy consuming his face. The look was unmistakable. It was one of satisfaction. A blow had been struck, albeit vicariously, against the swelling number of ignominious vultures roving the lands.

"Come inside and sit down!" roared Tar'iq Ibn Battutah, towing Sa'id al-Bashir by the arm.

Sa'id al-Bashir followed for a few paces then halted abruptly. "But you haven't heard what it is I must ask of you."

"No, my friend, I have not, but you must have suffered a great peril if you are prepared to ask, and I of course will not pry, but I am at your service." The man smiled again and continued, "My brother, you are to me an honorable man. For years you have passed this way and done business with me; you have always paid me a fair price for the things you have taken. In fact, you often gave me more than they were worth. But what is most unusual and important to me is that you always asked about the well-being of my family. As you know, this is a place where men are accustomed to taking what they want and punishing those who dare to complain or, *Allah* forbid, try to stop them. This manner of yours is an honorable quality. For you, no favor is too great." Ushering Sa'id al-Bashir toward the entrance of his modest dwelling, he commanded, "*TafáDDaluu! Báyt-i báyt-kum.* Come in. My house is your house. We will drink tea!"

"*Shúkran.* Thank you." Sa'id al-Bashir replied, throwing his hand on the man's shoulder as they walked. He spoke softly. "What I ask of you then is that you permit me to place my vehicle in your stable. It will remain there for only a few hours, but we must cover it well. If you have a tarp or large shroud, we could use it to conceal its wounds from prying eyes. Later tonight, when the lights of the town have been doused and all eyes are shut, I ask that you take the vehicle south along the road toward Arlit until you come to the place of the attack. The place lies about thirty miles from here. You will know it when you reach it. You must leave the vehicle there. As soon as night has fallen, send your oldest son, Ali, ahead of you on horseback to this place and have him wait for your arrival. He should take two of your fastest and finest horses, one of which will be for you. After you have abandoned the vehicle, you will meet Ali and the two of you will return to Assamakka before the town awakens. I suggest that you stay well clear of the road during your return, as there is much danger if you are caught. Before long, the vultures will be seeking revenge. Are you still willing to help me?"

"Yes, I will do what you ask, *insha' Allah,* God willing."

"Good then," said Sa'id al-Bashir. "In the morning when you have returned, I shall leave you and catch a ride from the center of town with one of the vehicles heading north to Tamanrasset. When I reach Tamanrasset, I will contact a friend of mine and ask him to inform my employer that the vehicle was stolen while I was in Arlit. Thus, it will appear that the thieves encountered and tangled with the gendarmes, but managed to escape. *Insha' Allah*, all will go as planned."

"*Insha' Allah,*" the man smiled broadly, once again revealing his badly stained teeth. "As luck would have it, you are just in time for supper," he announced. "We are having roasted lamb. My wife Nagwa is the best cook in the whole world," he added. "But before we eat, we must drink tea and smoke the *hookah*. I have a wonderful *shisha* which I know you will enjoy."

Chapter Three

The hours passed slowly and Sa'id al-Bashir tossed and turned in a feeble attempt to settle down to sleep, at last succumbing to a semi-doze. When he finally awoke at 3:15 a.m., his eyes were fiery red and he could feel them burning in their sockets like pieces of glowing charcoal. After a few moments, he sat upright in the cot, swung his feet over its side onto the floor and sat there for several minutes, trying to collect his thoughts. Finally, he rose to his feet and began dressing in the darkness of the tiny room. Immersed in thoughts about what had to be done, he momentarily allowed himself to consider where he was and the hospitality that had been extended to him by his host. He was grateful, yet puzzled by the man's generosity. He had known Tar'iq Ibn Battutah for several years, but had never given him anything more than his deepest respect.

Still contemplating his future, he struggled to keep his eyes open. Once again, his thoughts returned to his host. After a while though he decided that the man's generosity and kindness were simply a reflection of his good nature and perhaps also an expression of gratitude for him striking a blow against his enemies—a vicarious blow, but nevertheless a small victory over rogues for whom people like him had increasingly become prey. From his own experience, he was left with no doubt that uniformed parasites had been preying on the likes of Tar'iq Ibn Battutah and other hard working, law-abiding citizens for years.

Sa'id al-Bashir sat quietly in the darkness of the mud dwelling. His eyes were still adjusting. As soon as he could make out the various objects near him, he reached out and took the cotton indigo robe, pants and turban the man had given him from the small stool near the cot. They were just what he needed for the role he was about to play. After dressing, he moved cautiously, careful not to make any noise. A few seconds later, his eyes adjusted fully to the darkness and he slid his feet into the sandals that jutted out from under the narrow cot. It was just after 3:30 a.m. After transforming himself into a city-dwelling Tuareg trader, he moved through the small mud hut toward the back door, trying to avoid waking the man and his son, whom he had heard enter the house only half an hour earlier. He knew they would be asleep by now—all three of them crowded into the other room—Tar'iq Ibn Battutah, his wife Nagwa, and his fifteen-year-old son, Ali.

He made his way quietly through the house. He was still groggy when he reached the small back door, but mindful enough of its low height to bow his head to pass through it. When he lifted his head, he saw his host standing in front of him. The man had either elected not to sleep and had been in the stable, or had gotten out of bed and left the house by the front door.

"So, you are leaving," Tar'iq Ibn Battutah said, smiling and looking unusually alert. "I have done as you asked, but it appears you are still in a hurry."

"Yes," Sa'id al-Bashir replied, "I must be off if I am to catch a ride north. It's a long journey."

"Yes, I know, but must you leave without bidding my family farewell?"

"I apologize, my friend. It was not my intention to leave like a thief in the night, but I did not want to disturb your sleep. You must know that I am indebted to you and I appreciate your kindness, hospitality and above all, your help. I hope you will convey this to your wife and son."

"I can do this for you and I shall, but when you pass again, you must tell them yourself. God be with you, my friend!"

"Thank you, my brother. I will see you again soon. I shall repay you for your kindness and generosity."

The two men clasped hands briefly, embraced, and bid each other farewell. Then Sa'id al-Bashir set off on foot toward the main road. There were only a few lanterns and electric lights flickering from the mud dwellings that peppered the roadside leading into town. Most of the inhabitants of Assamakka were still sleeping. He carried with him only a small satchel containing the Western clothes he had shed the night before.

Chapter Four

It was nearly 4:00 a.m. when Sa'id al-Bashir reached the center of town to look for transportation going north. His wait was only a brief one. Less than five minutes after he arrived in front of the bus and taxi depot, he spotted a vehicle heading north—a gray, late model and well-maintained, Land Rover Discovery 4x4. The vehicle projected an appearance of officialdom. He stuck out his arm and hailed the driver. To his great surprise, the vehicle slowed and pulled off the road. As luck would have it, and as he had suspected, the occupant was a mid-level Algerian government official. The vehicle's chauffeur lowered the front passenger side window. He bid the two occupants good morning then asked about their destination. The official, a somewhat sheepish man, leaned forward in his seat and announced, "I am headed to In Salah, but I will be making a stop at Assekrem to visit relatives. I can offer you a ride as far as the junction for Assekrem." The man then added, in his best attempt to show that he was not a snob, "It is only a few minutes on foot from the junction to the center of Tamanrasset."

The itinerary was perfect, Sa'id al-Bashir thought. The distance from Assamakka to Tamanrasset was about 180 miles, with In Salah another 270 miles. Barring any unforeseen events, they would reach Tamanrasset around 7:00 a.m. He would alight there and make his way to the airport and catch a flight to Algiers. If he failed to catch a flight from Tamanrasset, he would still be able to hire a car and driver and continue on to

Algiers. The drive from Tamanrasset northwards would be a long one, but at least the road would be significantly better than the one he had traveled on in Niger and he would be able to make good time. But, just as in northern Niger, there were risks associated with traveling by car in southern Algeria. He knew this, but he had little or no time to waste; taking a plane was the preferred method of travel. He smiled to himself. The future he had been working towards for so long was almost within his grasp. Just two flights stood between him and the future he'd sought—a future of wealth and influence that had eluded him, but he was now being guided like a homeward bound sailor following the North Star.

The driver reached across and opened the door to the front passenger side and Sa'id al-Bashir climbed in.

"*SabáaH al-kháyr*! Good morning!" Sa'id al-Bashir said once more.

"*SabáaH an-núur*!" replied the official from the back seat.

The man on the back seat introduced himself as Dr. Hassan Murad and immediately plunged into a diatribe about the ineptitude of Algerian workers and their attitudes of self-importance.

"You are quite fortunate," the bureaucrat said, almost smiling. "I work for the Ministry of Industry. I am on my way to In Salah to inspect a new small engine factory, but will call at Assekrem, not far from the camp site at La Source, beforehand for a brief visit with some relatives. The trip to the factory, of course, is one that I dread. This place has 'state of the art' equipment and highly skilled engineers and managers, yet it produces more than thirty percent below its capacity. I have not seen what is happening there, but I suspect most of the workers are lazy and it is the General Manager's fault they do not work harder. So, if he hands me excuses, I shall sack him on the spot. It is so difficult to find good executive managers these days. This is because they work for the government. They all want big salaries, big offices with big desks and a car and driver without earning these things."

Deliberately bastardizing his Arabic, Sa'id al-Bashir replied, "I am Tar'iq Ag Boti. I am a trader from Assamakka. I do not know these things you speak of."

"What sort of things do you trade?" the man asked condescendingly.

"I trade livestock."

"What kind of livestock?"

"Goats, sheep, chickens... I also trade salt and cloth and sometimes camels and camel meat, when they are available."

"So... What is taking you to the big city?" the man asked, raising a brow.

"I must travel to Algiers to visit my brother-in-law who is ill. Perhaps I will bring him back with me. He is the only member of my wife's family who is living and she has not seen him for many years."

"I see," the bureaucrat replied, seemingly unconvinced. "I wish you every success."

"Thank you," Sa'id al-Bashir replied.

The man's diatribe on work ethics and questions about commerce continued; after a while, Sa'id al-Bashir found them nauseating and feigned sleepiness. Nevertheless, he had gathered from the man's ramblings that in addition to working for the government, he also had a stake in a family-owned produce company that supplied fruit and vegetables to the Algerian army and a few towns in the south of Algeria, near the Nigerien border. He was mindful not to engage in too much more discussion about trade and business, as it would have exposed his thinly veiled cover.

When the government-owned 4x4 arrived on the outskirts of Tamanrasset, the driver passed with ease through the checkpoint that awaited all travelers moving north from the southeastern end of the city. Soon afterwards they turned and drove northwest on the city's ring road, away from the Oued River, bypassing the city center. By now, Sa'id al-Bashir was truly asleep. After a few more minutes, they approached the turnoff for Assekrem and La Source. The vehicle left the ring road, turned northeast and stopped. The driver announced, "Hôtel Tinhinane lies about a kilometer northwest if you are in need of a place to stay."

Having been roused from his sleep by the chauffeur announcing that he was leaving the city, Sa'id al-Bashir sat up. When the vehicle came to a stop, he climbed out,

duffle bag in hand. He stuck his head inside the passenger window, thanked the official for his hospitality and said farewell.

"*Shúkran.* Thank you," he exclaimed.

"You are welcome!" the man replied then instructed the chauffeur to continue.

Hôtel Tinhinane... he thought as he alighted. *It is in the middle of the city. From there I should be able to get transportation north to the airport.* He crossed the road and began walking northwest, toward Hôtel Tinhinane.

Chapter Five

North Africa
Algeria
Southern City of Tamanrasset

Sa'id al-Bashir strolled toward the heart of the city. Along the way he paused, then made a slow three hundred and sixty degree turn to take in the sights, which were by now bathed in sunlight that cascaded over the Hoggar Mountains to the northeast. When he entered the city proper, instead of going directly to Hôtel Tinhinane, as had been recommended by his travel companions, he turned north along the main street and entered Restaurant Le Palmier, which was located just opposite the city's main taxi stand. There he drank tea, ate soup and salad, and enjoyed freshly made *falafel* before crossing the road to the taxi stand.

It was not quite yet 8:00 a.m. and he was feeling anxious, but the prospect of the trip to the airport soon began to raise his spirits. His mood was further buoyed by contemplation of imminent good fortune. However, when he arrived at Tamanrasset Airport, his hopes were dashed. Because he did not know when he would reach Tamanrasset, he was not able to make a flight reservation; without a reservation, he could not fly to Algiers to catch a flight to Paris.

On arrival at the airport he learned that the only flights from Tamanrasset to Algiers with open seats were the next day in the mid-afternoon, which was of no use to him. He needed to get to Algiers this day, in order to catch the morning flight to Paris the next day. He sighed out of frustration. He knew that the only workable solution was to buy his ticket for Paris, return to the city, hire a car and driver and make the journey from Tamanrasset to Algiers by road.

After a short taxi ride of just over two miles, Sa'id al-Bashir was standing at the bus station in Tamanrasset. He was thinking how crazy it was to even consider such a long journey by car. But then the thought of a lavish lifestyle and abundant wealth entered his head and expunged all the self-ridicule.

It took only a few minutes to find a man with a good car who was eager to earn the extra cash he was offering for the 975-mile journey to Algiers. It was still only 9:30 a.m. when he found a car and driver for the journey. His optimism returned; he set out believing that if the driver was as skilled as he said he was and the car as fast as he boasted, and if there were no unforeseen delays, he might reach Algiers before midnight and leave for Paris the next morning.

Chapter Six

Algiers, Algeria

At 11:00 p.m., the chauffeur-driven car he had hired in Tamanrasset slipped into Algiers. It had been a high-speed, treacherous run from the southernmost part of Algeria to its northern coast. Surprisingly to Sa'id al-Bashir, the most difficult part of the journey was when they hit the crowded streets of Algiers. After negotiating the city's chaotic traffic, Sa'id al-Bashir instructed the driver to go directly to the Air France office, just off Boulevard Colonel Amirouche, even though the office was closed. He wanted to see the posters and other images of Paris that Air France had on display in the office windows for passersby. He wanted to be reminded of what Paris looked like before he arrived. A few minutes later, the driver pulled up just short of the airline ticket office and stopped.

After handing the driver four bundles of cash, each containing 5,000 Algerian *dinars,* he clambered out of the car and walked the short distance to the Air France ticket sales office, passing beggars and street vendors who had strategically set their sights on those whose fortunes permitted them the luxury of air travel. Holding a one-way business class ticket to Paris on the next morning flight, he strolled toward the city center. This time the smile on his face was broader and he was far more relaxed as he breathed in the fresh Mediterranean Sea air that permeated the night. He was anticipating the events of the next few days.

The long ride from Tamanrasset had left him feeling cramped and he needed to stretch his legs, so he decided to walk the two miles or so to Hôtel El Badr on Rue Amar el Kamar. He strolled along the boulevards near the waterfront and the streets of Algiers for more than an hour before making his way to the hotel. He knew from inquiries he had made in Tamanrasset that the hotel almost always had one or two vacant rooms. And at only 70 *dinars* a night, it was a bargain. But equally as important, it was clean, hospitable and close to the airport—all good reasons why it was so popular with foreign budget tourists.

Chapter Seven

After waking a slightly angered night manager and getting checked into Hôtel El Badr, Sa'id al-Bashir quickly showered and made his way downstairs to find a late meal at a nearby restaurant. But when he arrived in the reception area there was a man sitting in the hotel's small lounge, keeping a constant eye on the bottom of the stairs and the small elevator doors. As he made his way down the stairs, the man made deliberate eye contact with him. He seemed to know him, but he was not the driver of the car he had just taken from Tamanrasset. This man was North African, clean-cut with a serious look about him. He was even missing the usual five o'clock shadow associated with many men from the region. As Sa'id al-Bashir passed through the hotel's small lounge, the man rose from his seat and followed him. Once outside the hotel, the stranger called out to him in a calm tone.

"Sa'id al-Bashir?" he said, not giving anything away.

"Who is asking?" Sa'id al-Bashir asked, his thick brows knitted in a frown.

"A friend. Someone with important information to deliver to you."

"Who are you?" he asked suspiciously. "And what is this information that is so important that you have seen fit to seek me out here?"

"It does not matter who or what I am. You are Sa'id al-Bashir, are you not?"

"And what if I am?"

"I have a message for you. Please do not stop. Continue. I will walk with you. I take it that you are about to have your supper?"

"I am," Sa'id al-Bashir replied, failing to conceal his growing concern. "How did you find me and who told you I would be staying at Hôtel El Badr? I told no one of my plans!"

"That really doesn't matter," the man replied sharply. "All that matters is that you show up for your appointment in Paris. I am charged with seeing that you do just that. No more, no less."

"What have you to tell me?"

"That's more like it," the stranger said teasingly. "I can see now that you do understand the concept of cooperation!" The man's smile may have been teasing but his eyes were blank. Sa'id al-Bashir's apprehension grew. The stranger had been so careful to cover his tracks.

"I am listening!" Sa'id al-Bashir barked.

The man chuckled then began. "Upon arrival in Paris, you are to proceed to the Hôtel Esméralda on Rue St-Julien le Pauvre. After checking in, you must purchase a black leather briefcase, one with gold latches, combination locks and a black leather handle. Is that clear?"

"And what shall I do with this briefcase?"

"Patience, my eager friend!" the man said. "You must also buy a suit. Not too flashy... something conservative. Afterwards, you should return to your hotel. On the afternoon of the following day, you will receive a call. You will then get dressed and make your way to Café La Fontaine in the Quartier Latin. You must be there at 5:30 p.m. Not a moment later. And do not forget to bring the new briefcase with the goods inside. Your contact will meet you there. He will say to you, 'It's a beautiful day, isn't it? But then springtime in Paris is always beautiful, isn't it?' You will reply, 'Yes, Paris in spring is very beautiful, but the summers are dreadfully hot.'" He continued. "You will have only one chance at this. Screw it up and all bets are off! Do you understand?"

"Yes," said Sa'id al-Bashir. "But who am I to meet?"

"Don't worry about who you are meeting. Your contact will find you. Just be where you are supposed to be!"

The secrecy surrounding what he was about to do and the ease with which the stranger had found him caused a surge of fear. Sa'id al-Bashir suddenly felt as if his intestines were tied in knots. He was not only frightened, he was nervous. He wanted to go over his instructions again with the stranger, but before he could muster the courage to communicate his concern, the man dropped behind, broke off, crossed the street and headed in the opposite direction.

After the encounter, his hunger pangs and desire for lamb and couscous vanished. By the next morning his fear had grown and he was even more nervous. Nevertheless, he boarded the flight to France; upon arrival in Paris, he checked into Hôtel Esméralda, and purchased the briefcase and suit as he had been instructed to do.

Chapter Eight

Paris, France
Quartier Latin

Worried that he might be late, Sa'id al-Bashir arrived at Café La Fontaine just after 5:00 p.m. It was a beautiful day. The weather was sunny and warm. The slow-moving air wafted a mélange of smells from dozens of brasseries and restaurants that lined the boulevards and the connecting streets which formed a catacomb, filled with shops, theatres and clubs. There were hundreds of things for visitors with a taste for the avant garde to see and do, but Sa'id al-Bashir was not interested in these things. Café La Fontaine was the only place he wanted to be.

He took a seat at a table outside the restaurant; a few minutes later a young, energetic waiter strolled over to him. The young man wore a crisp white shirt, black bow tie, black trousers and a starched apron tied smartly around his waist.

"What would you like, monsieur?" the young man asked.

"*Un café noir et un eau minerale, s'il vous plaît,*" replied Sa'id al-Bashir.

"Perrier?" the young man asked.

"*Oui. Avec des glaçons,*" he replied calmly, as the young man spun on his heel and navigated his way back through the maze of tables toward the restaurant.

It had been years since Sa'id al-Bashir was last in Paris, yet he was no stranger to the city. Two decades earlier, he had arrived in Paris, a young man among thousands who had fled the post-election violence, bloodshed and poverty in his native Algeria. In search of sanctuary, he had achieved refugee status and gone in search of meaningful work. He had hoped that he would make his fortune in Paris. But after years of struggle, and even after earning an engineering degree, he had left Paris and returned to North Africa, empty-handed. However, this time he was under no illusion. He would not leave empty-handed and disappointed, because he had come to collect a large sum of money—money he had already made.

Seated outside Café La Fontaine, wearing a conservative two-piece suit and with a fancy black leather briefcase beside his chair, he looked the part of a Parisian businessman—a savvy, energetic entrepreneur relaxing in the evening sun after a rough day at the office. The image, however, was no more than an impressive deception. Just hours before he left his hotel, he was told that he would be met by a man named Mustafa at Café La Fontaine. No last name, just Mustafa. The problem was, and had been since the day before he left Algiers, he did not know who Mustafa was, nor had he ever seen him, not even a photo of him. He was told not to worry... that Mustafa would find him and that was all he needed to know.

Sa'id al-Bashir sat quietly, basking in the warm sunshine. Contemplating what lay ahead, he reached into his trouser pocket and fished out a packet of Gauloises, his favorite brand. He took a cigarette from the pack, tapped one end of it on the table, put the filterless stick in his mouth and lit it. He took several long, deep drags before bellowing out a cloud of blue-white smoke. He could hardly contain the excitement he felt about the prospect of certain wealth.

A few minutes later, the waiter returned with his order. When the young man left, he quickly grabbed the hot coffee and sipped it hurriedly. The full weight of the reality of what he was about to do suddenly hit him and the shock of it was like being doused with ice cold water. He tried to relax, but the thoughts that invaded his head—troubling thoughts—about the impending meeting with the stranger named Mustafa, would not leave. He then realized that he was putting his trust, and possibly his life, too, in the hands of a man about whom he knew nothing, except his name, and that was probably an alias.

His troubling thoughts were interrupted by the waiter, who had pitched up in front of him and was blocking the sun. The young man had returned to see if he needed anything else. For a moment, he was oblivious to the waiter's presence and only became aware of him when the young man called to him a second time and in a slightly louder voice. After the waiter had gained his attention, Sa'id al-Bashir looked up and eyed him quietly for a few seconds, then tossed a ten euro note on the table to pay his bill. It was an unmistakable gesture—one that said, *I do not wish to be disturbed again.*

When the waiter left, he raised his wrist and gazed at his watch. It was nearly 5:30 p.m. As he sat gazing at his watch, he noticed that his hand was shaking ever so slightly. He was not his usual cool, calm and confident self—not the same man who had dispatched three would-be assassins on a dusty desert road to permanent retirement. He was suddenly gripped by nervousness, which was causing him even more discomfort. He was beginning to think that people around him were aware of his anxiety. He was becoming paranoid, losing his composure. Panic-stricken, he surveyed the tables around him several times, before realizing that no one was paying him any attention. They were, in fact, oblivious to his presence. *Just nerves…* he thought, battling with the thoughts invading his head. *I'm just a bit jittery, that's all. But who wouldn't be? Who am I kidding? I'm out of my league.*

Seconds later, he glanced at his watch again. It was exactly 5:30 and there was no sign of Mustafa. He could feel his anxiety growing. His mouth was dry and he was beginning to worry that he had misunderstood the instructions. *What if Mustafa is waiting for me somewhere else?* He knew he was no expert at clandestine meetings. The only way he would be able to identify the man would be by the black briefcase he would be carrying —a briefcase exactly like his own.

To calm his nerves, he took out another cigarette. He was just lighting it when, out of the corner of his eye, he spotted a man moving towards him. The man was tall and trim and appeared to be in his late forties or early fifties. He was dressed entirely in black. Sa'id al-Bashir surveyed the man's upper body and face then shifted his eyes to his hands. Tightly gripped in the stranger's left hand was a black leather briefcase. He returned his gaze to the man's face, which looked sadistic. His exaggerated features looked as if his face had been formed from sculpting clay, even chiseled out of stone. The man had a surreal look about him. He was clean-shaven with oily, jet-black hair, which he wore pulled back into a shoulder-length ponytail. He looked every bit a mercenary, the sort Sa'id al-Bashir had seen on several occasions when he had acted briefly as a facilitator for some of Africa's most corrupt and autocratic political leaders.

He watched anxiously as the stranger approached. By now, the man's piercing dark eyes were trained on him as if he were a target for some unspeakable act of violence. As the stranger moved toward his table, he stubbed out the cigarette he had only just managed to light. The stranger made a quick check of the surroundings and came to the table. When he arrived, he paused briefly then asked, "Is this seat taken?"

"No. It isn't," Sa'id al-Bashir replied.

The stranger pulled out the chair and sat down. He eyed Sa'id al-Bashir with disdain for several seconds, then calmly resumed, guiding Sa'id al-Bashir into a carefully scripted dialogue.

"It's a beautiful day, isn't it?" he asked then added, "But then springtime in Paris is always beautiful, isn't it?"

Reciting the phrase he had been instructed to deliver, Sa'id al-Bashir replied, "Yes, Paris in spring is very beautiful, but the summers are dreadfully hot."

Sa'id al-Bashir's voice was unsteady and it cracked on the words. The stranger looked him up and down again, this time showing even more contempt. "I am Mustafa," he said calmly, then asked, "Have you been followed to this place?"

Sa'id al-Bashir paused momentarily to collect his composure then replied sternly, "No. I haven't!"

"Are you sure?" the man returned, half grinning.

"Of course I am sure!" Sa'id al-Bashir snapped. "I have been sitting here for nearly half an hour and I have not seen anyone who seems to be interested in me! Can we get on with this?" he asked, trying to present a firmer and steadier demeanor.

"Do you have something for me?" Mustafa asked.

Sa'id al-Bashir did not speak. Instead, he nodded and his right hand drifted from the table to the briefcase beside his chair. Seconds later, he placed a Michelin road map of Niger on the table. Mustafa unfolded the map to a manageable size and fixed his gaze on the place where Sa'id al-Bashir had drawn a circle in red ink. His unusually long, spindly fingers seemed to envelop the map, leaving only its center exposed as he studied the circled location. When he was satisfied, he re-folded the map and slid it back across the table. As he pushed it towards Sa'id al-Bashir, he began rattling off the plan to conclude their business.

"As agreed, I have with me one and a half million euros, half of the full amount of your fee. When the transaction is completed, the other half will be deposited in the numbered Swiss bank account you provided. You may verify the deposit after we notify you. Do nothing until you are contacted. Do not try to contact us. We will contact you. Is that clear? Do you understand?"

"I understand."

Using his left foot, the man pushed the briefcase he had been carrying across the pavement to Sa'id al-Bashir, who had by then collected the map and delivery instructions and put them back inside his case, closed it and slid it across the pavement to the stranger. Seconds later, Mustafa stood up, swapped briefcase in hand, and disappeared into the throngs moving along Boulevard St-Germain. When Sa'id al-Bashir was certain the man called Mustafa was gone, he fished his handkerchief out of his jacket pocket and wiped his brow. He was sweating profusely. His hands shook almost uncontrollably as he fumbled to put the sweat-soaked handkerchief back into the breast pocket of his jacket. He poured the last of the Perrier into his glass, gulped it down then sat quietly for several minutes, trying to regain his composure. When his nerves had settled, he looked around the area, got up and went inside the café in search of a toilet. He wanted to examine the contents of the briefcase. In his nervousness, he had forgotten to inspect the contents before turning the map and instructions over to Mustafa. He felt like an amateur.

Once inside the toilet, he put the briefcase on top of the sink and opened it. He gasped when his eyes fell on the neatly laid stacks of crisp 500 euro notes inside, packed in plastic. He took out a pocket knife, carefully slit the plastic wrapper at one end and eagerly picked up a stack of notes. He leafed through them then waved the stack under his nose, inhaling and savoring the smell of their newness as if admiring the bouquet of a vintage wine. The smell of the new notes produced a rush of adrenalin and near uncontrollable excitement. But the euphoric moment was cut short by several sharp raps on the toilet door and a loud, angry, gruff voice.

"You in there! What are you doing? Hurry up! Others are waiting!"

"Alright, damn it! Keep your pants on!" Sa'id al-Bashir shouted. "Give me a minute, asshole!"

He closed the briefcase, splashed cold water on his face and ran his thick fingers through his jet-black hair in an attempt to brush it back into place. He gazed momentarily in the mirror at his image and smiled. In a short time, he had been transformed from a frightened gazelle into a lion. He opened the door and gave the man outside a nasty look as he brushed past him. Still charged with adrenalin, he strode away from Café La Fontaine and merged with the flood of pedestrians moving toward St-Germain metro station. *It's over…* he thought. *The success of that meeting calls for a celebration.*

On the way to Rue St-Julien le Pauvre and the Hôtel Esméralda, he stopped at a supermarket and bought a bottle of Rémy Martin. Not wanting to take any unnecessary risks, he decided to have dinner in the hotel dining room. After eating, he would retreat to the sanctity of his room and open the bottle of brandy. The next morning, he would go to the *Gare du l'est* and board the train for Zurich as a millionaire.

Chapter Nine

Sa'id al-Bashir finished dinner at precisely 9:30 p.m. and went straight to his room. Once inside, he took the bottle of brandy and a glass from on top of the dresser and poured himself a generous drink. Staring at his image in the mirror, he noticed how badly he needed a shave, but decided it could wait until morning. Now was the time to celebrate his new-found, hard-won wealth. With the glass and open bottle of brandy in hand, he moved across the room, opened the window and peered out into the night.

Across the city he could see Nôtre Dame clearly; its spires were radiantly lit, bathed in floodlight thrown up from the ground below. He stared at the grand cathedral for several minutes. He sat the bottle and glass on a small table near the window then walked over to the bed, knelt down and pulled out the black briefcase. Afterwards, he took a seat in a chair near the window and placed the briefcase on his lap. His mood was buoyant and he smiled as he clutched the glass of brandy, pausing momentarily, closing his eyes to enjoy the breeze that flowed in through the window. Unknown to him, the man called Mustafa had been sitting patiently in a car across the street adjacent to his hotel. He had arrived there and taken up the position after being informed that Sa'id al-Bashir had left the Metro station nearby. He had waited for nearly two hours while the Algerian ate dinner. When the light in Sa'id al-Bashir's room went on, he knew his quarry was in its nest.

Upon entering the room, Sa'id al-Bashir had moved about

freely, unaware that he was casting a silhouette on the sheer curtains that revealed his every move. Mustafa could see exactly where he was and what he was doing at nearly all times. Seconds after his quarry had sat down and opened the briefcase, his mobile phone rang.

"Sa'id al-Bashir!" he answered confidently.

"All is as it should be," Mustafa declared at the other end of the line. "The location of the material has been confirmed. Your transaction was completed one hour ago. You may call Zurich whenever you wish."

Before Sa'id al-Bashir could reply, Mustafa hung up. For a moment, al-Bashir was bewildered, but his puzzlement dissipated when he returned his gaze to the contents of the briefcase. He grinned, took a gulp of brandy and ran the palm of his hand over the surface of the cool, crisp, neatly stacked notes. He felt on top of the world and was at the pinnacle of euphoria when Mustafa picked up the remote control and pressed the switch. The red button triggered a detonator that set off the Semtex packed along with small nails around the inside frame of the briefcase he had filled with counterfeit euro notes. Sa'id al-Bashir heard a faint click. A millisecond later, there was a deafening explosion. The blast and the nails, which acted like shrapnel, ripped through his body and devastated the room. The building's fire alarm went off; within minutes, Rue St-Julien le Pauvre was filled with guests and passers-by, eager to see what had happened.

The explosion had dismembered Sa'id al-Bashir's body. It had also destroyed the rooms immediately above and below his, as the supporting structures collapsed.

Shortly after the crowd arrived, police cars and fire engines converged on the hotel and police and gendarmes began moving the crowd away from the building, but not before dozens of onlookers had seen what had happened.

When the area was cleared of spectators, the police discovered for themselves the source of their intrigue—Sa'id al-

Bashir had been decapitated and his head had been hurled across the street. It had landed face-down in the crotch of a fallen mannequin in the display window of a small boutique.

Chapter Ten

London, England
Near Regent's Park
Present Day

28 Balcombe Street, also known as Suffolk House, was a three-story, well-apportioned, white-washed building, tucked away down a one-way street adjacent to Dorset Square. It lay only a few blocks southwest of Regent's Park and only a short walk from Marylebone rail and Underground stations. It was a tasteful, unpretentious building of Georgian architecture— suited to and in harmony with its surroundings. It reflected the area's prosperity. Surrounded by a wrought iron fence, its façade was accented by a glossy black door, complete with brass knocker, door handle and kick-plate. To the casual observer, it was one of many well-preserved buildings recently occupied by companies looking to capitalize on the exploding effort to resurrect and recapture the image of imperial British houses of trade and commerce of earlier centuries.

Unlike the hordes of international commerce predators increasingly being unleashed on the unsuspecting or apathetic world, for more than five decades, the Ashmore Foundation— the occupant's name on the brass plate—masked activities far above and beyond those described in pamphlets prepared by the non-governmental organization inside its walls, or those heralded by the newspapers. The Ashmore Foundation was in fact a long-established and highly elaborate cover for Vanguard —one of the world's most secretive intelligence organizations. It had been the brainchild of the aristocrat and philanthropist Lord Charles Tarquin-Ashmore at the end of the Second World War. It was set up to carry out non-attributable intelligence operations against the former Soviet Union. But after the Cold War, it shifted its focus and began dealing with the less conventional threat posed by terrorism and other international criminal activities.

Suffolk House was one of two London properties owned by the Ashmore Foundation. The Foundation also had offices in seventy-five other countries. The second London property was a four-story Georgian townhouse at 320 St. James's Place, a short distance from Mayfair and the world-famous Ritz Hotel. The St. James's Place property was the more modest of the two in appearance, but it was the real face of the Foundation, while Suffolk House was the heart of Vanguard. Since its opening, the Foundation had hosted more than a dozen high level dignitaries, including nine heads of state, three Secretary Generals of the United Nations, the Queen of England, and the Kings of Denmark, Thailand and Swaziland. On any given day, 320 St. James's Place was a beehive of activity. It ran dozens of humanitarian projects and within its spaces ideas were germinated, funded and propagated. Projects ranged from support to victims of landmines in war-torn developing countries, to forgotten soldiers, relief to drought-stricken countries, tsunami and flood victims, and micro-level fish farming.

For the past six months, 320 St. James's Place was where Caroline Dupré had begun to live a part of her new life.

Chapter Eleven

London
City of Westminster
St. James's Place

The death of Caroline's husband at the hands of hired assassins more than two years earlier had for a time demoralized her, but after finding his killers, it had taken her only a short time to decide to join Vanguard. The move to London had been only one of several major changes in her life since she had met Niles Thornton. She had been intellectually and psychologically transformed; her view of the world had become more pragmatic. Still, she had never abandoned her intrinsic ideas about what her life meant to her and others, especially her son. Staring out of the window of her fourth floor office, she was still reflecting on the state of her life some two and a half years earlier when Niles Thornton appeared outside her door.

He needed to speak to her urgently, but upon seeing her gazing outside at the world below, he stopped in the doorway and stood quietly, watching and contemplating the thoughts flowing through her mind. He surmised that it had been the earlier-than-usual arrival of spring that was resurrecting painful memories for her. Signs of spring were visible everywhere around the city, especially in the blossoming of horse chestnut and cherry trees. Watching her, he was reminded of her fondness for parks and gardens. Paris's Luxembourg Gardens and New York's Central Park were her favorites. She had once told him that, amid the chaos of urban sprawl and mankind's self-manufactured chaos, parks were oases of tranquility and sanity. Despite the urgent reason for dropping by, he decided to give her more time and backed quietly into the corridor as if conducting a reluctant military retreat.

Despite her intense focus on the world and the movement of people below, she had been fully aware of his presence. Her rigorous training had made sure that all her senses were fully alert at all times. With the addition of her strong feminine intuition, Caroline knew that anyone or anything approaching her would need to be as silent and invisible as air for her not to sense their presence. Without turning her head or leaving her perch on the corner of her desk, she asked softly, "Would you have said nothing and just gone away if I had not spoken to you?"

"No. But you seemed so far away. Deep in thought and I wanted your return to be of your own volition," he replied apologetically. "But now that you have rejoined us, I would like a word with you. Shall we take a stroll in the park while we talk? It's a lovely day!" He beamed.

"Sounds like a wonderful idea," she replied, moving toward him. "I could use some sunshine and fresh air." She stopped. Something lay behind his smile and his friendly words. Something in his eyes gave it away. "What's on your mind?" she asked.

"What's on my mind?" Thornton repeated, as if playing for time. "I suppose you could say that it's something peculiar, perhaps even troubling. It's a series of rather ill-fitting and incredibly perplexing events which may or may not be related to one another—one that occurred in the North African desert and another in Paris about six weeks ago. I'm not quite sure what to make of it," he added, then changed the subject abruptly. "How is your son, Nicolas? It's his second year at Monte Rosa, isn't it?"

"Niles, there has been no change since you asked about Nicolas three days ago. He's perfectly fine, and you of all people should know he's in his second year there... You arranged it, remember? Right down to his new identity. But I think I know what you're driving at and I appreciate your concern. He misses me, of course, but he's adjusting. I plan to visit him next month."

"Good!" he replied, showing genuine delight. "I'm glad to hear things are working out." After a beat, his demeanor shifted again. She knew from his less than smooth and unflappable manner that he was deeply troubled. "Shall we take that walk in the park?" he asked again, locking arms with her and towing her toward the caged elevator in the center of the building. It was an awkward moment, an awkward situation; they stood in front of the elevator, side-by-side, in silence. When it arrived, they boarded and descended to the ground floor.

Chapter Twelve

Although Caroline was fairly tall and lean, alongside her Niles Thornton's long, slender frame towered. Like an odd couple, they strolled through Green Park. It was a beautiful day and the sensation of the warm sun on her face and the breeze in her hair made her feel fully alive, with an almost erotic charge. The feeling was a sign that she had all but reconciled the changes she had made in her life and was moving on.

"So," she turned and stared at him, "what is this urgent business you wanted to speak to me about?"

He stared at her for a brief moment from behind a tired set of hazel eyes and an unusually ashen face. "I'm not sure where to begin with this, but I think we've got a major problem brewing. I can't quite make out whether the origin of this problem is in Africa or Europe. All indications, however, point to Africa. We're still sifting through the very scant bits of information we uncovered. But they're mainly scraps and a lot of rumor I'm afraid. Things are still pretty sketchy and I'm afraid it's too early to commit assets to any single course of action because if we're wrong, we leave the barn door wide open, so to speak."

"Are you saying that something is happening right under our noses and you've got no idea what it is?"

"In a word, yes! We're at a disadvantage for now, but we're playing a game of catch-up pretty damn quickly. And we'll do it because we have to!" he added, seemingly to convince her as well as himself. "For now, we only know that one of the guys we had under close surveillance for quite some time disappeared and we don't know why yet. But we should learn something by tomorrow when Paris reports back."

"What about the Brits... I mean MI6, or what about Langley? Surely MOSSAD or the French must know something!" Caroline's fast mind was racing ahead.

"I've been in touch already and they all know even less than we do. I do know one thing, though... we've got to work fast! I need to schedule a few important meetings for tomorrow morning. Once we've figured out where we think this is going, I'll have something more substantive for you. In the meantime, I want you to prepare yourself for a trip to Africa, either Algeria or Niger... maybe both. I hate to drop this on you this way, but if what I think is happening is in fact unfolding, we are going to need a fresh face. Someone nobody knows, but someone who is also good! You were top of your class in every area of training and your performance in supporting four operations since joining us has been nothing less than superb. Do you think you are up to the challenge?"

Caroline tightened her lips. This was the chance she had been waiting for, but... "Do you think I'm ready?" she asked.

"There's always a need for more experience, but if you're asking me whether or not I think you're good enough, I would have to say yes. It'll be a challenge, but you'll have the best support we can provide. You'll be working with a contact we've used many times, one of our local operatives, and possibly one or two contacts we've just started developing. My hunch is that whoever is behind this will be looking for one of the old pros. So, using you won't raise any red flags. We've probably got less than seventy-two hours to put this in motion. I'm really sorry, but it looks like you're going to have to cancel any plans you've made for the next week or two."

Chapter Thirteen

Amsterdam, Netherlands
Schiphol International Airport

It had just gone 8:00 a.m. when Thomas Broughton boarded the 8:30 a.m. London-bound KLM flight at Amsterdam's Schiphol Airport. With the one-hour time difference between the European continent and the United Kingdom, he would gain an hour, which meant that his 8:30 departure would get him into London's Heathrow Airport at 9:00 a.m. Niles Thornton had dispatched a Foundation car to pick him up. Having no checked baggage, he moved through immigration, then swiftly through customs and into the arrival hall. Tom Broughton was ruggedly handsome; at six feet three inches tall, with a well-toned physique, his appearance was striking. He looked as if he had been carved out of granite. He had piercing brown eyes, jet black eyebrows and high cheekbones, which gave his brown, thin face a regal appearance. He had often amused his colleagues with stories about his royal lineage, but had never bothered to identify the ethnic group, royal bloodline or African kingdom from which he had descended.

He was retired CIA, a veteran of North Africa and the Middle East and had spent nearly all his career working there. After twenty-five years in the game, he had left the Agency some eight years earlier and joined Vanguard almost immediately. He was in his eighth year with Vanguard and still the consummate professional—an operative who still loved adventure and a challenge. His energy and drive rivaled that of the most junior operatives and his interest in clandestine intelligence operations was still as strong as the day he was recruited. His was the kind of drive needed to take on complex, dangerous and time-sensitive issues.

After clearing immigration and customs, he exited the terminal and traversed the bus and passenger drop-off lanes to the waiting, darkened window, black Mercedes sedan. The driver was behind the wheel and the engine was running when he climbed onto the back seat. Within seconds his mobile phone rang. It was Niles Thornton.

"Are you on your way?"

"Yeah. I'm leaving Heathrow now."

"Good. I've asked the driver to take you to Suffolk House. I'll meet you there."

The black sedan pulled away from the curb, sped off from Terminal 2 and headed east on the airport's inner ring road. Minutes later, it turned onto the M4, leaving the bustle of Heathrow with its long queues of taxis and cars picking up and dropping off passengers to fade in the distance. Before long, the only reminders of the airport's proximity to the city were the high-pitched whine of aircraft engines and the seemingly endless stream of large aircraft ascending into and descending from the sky overhead.

After merging with the throng of congested traffic heading toward central London, the driver began negotiating his way past large trucks, daily commuters, and sports car enthusiasts in search of space to unleash the horsepower of their powerful engines, but finding only feet instead of miles. About half an hour later, the Mercedes turned off the M4 and negotiated the Chiswick roundabout—one of the city's busy and increasingly chaotic circular junction roads—and turned onto the dual-lane A4 roadway.

The traffic on the A4 also seemed to thicken with each mile, but the driver carefully wove his way through it toward Marylebone. Broughton sat further back in his seat and mulled over all the possible reasons why Niles Thornton had summoned him to London. The call from the ageing spymaster the day before had been cryptic, despite having come over an ultra secure line. But what had concerned him most was the knowledge that receiving instructions directly from Thornton to fly to London meant something somewhere had gone terribly wrong. A face-to-face with Thornton was a rare experience for any operative—purely a one-off if it occurred at all during an officer's career. But this was his second face-to-face meeting with the distinguished and highly regarded spymaster. His first was in 2005, the day after the July 7 terrorist attacks in London. The summons to London and the nature of that meeting led him to conclude that whatever was troubling Thornton was far beyond one of his 'tricky matters.' He decided that the current situation must be as bad as, if not worse than, the events of September 11, 2001 and July 7, 2005.

Chapter Fourteen

London
Marylebone

At 10:15 a.m., the black Mercedes pulled up in front of number 14 Balcombe Street and stopped at the gate. The driver lowered his window, entered a code and the gate slid open. When the car pulled up alongside the building, Tom Broughton opened the door and climbed out before it came to a complete stop. A few strides later, he was at the front door. But before he could press the buzzer, the door opened and he was face-to-face with Niles Thornton.

"Come in." Thornton beckoned, clutching Broughton's hand in a firm shake and slapping him on the shoulder. "I trust you had a pleasant trip?"

"I've had worse!" Broughton declared. "London traffic seems to get worse each time I visit. Why don't they install a tram system like Amsterdam?"

"Good question! And I'm afraid you're correct about the traffic problem. It's getting worse every day. As regards to your question about a tram system, I haven't the foggiest why one hasn't been installed. But I'll tell you this much… Soon, there'll be total grid-lock on the roads. Cars, lorries and the lot will come to a standstill and become static displays," Thornton said jokingly.

Broughton let out a deep chuckle; after the jovial exchange, both men fell silent. They strode briskly past the receptionist and a security guard, with Thornton leading the way. As they approached the rear of the reception area, Thornton motioned to Broughton before drifting off to his left and entering a narrow corridor. Halfway along the corridor, he turned right and entered an office. Once inside, he locked the door behind them. The door was at least two inches thick and made of solid oak with hinges inside and a cipher key pad on the wall. Inside, the room was tastefully decorated, but rather austere. In front of the back wall sat a large executive desk with a leather chair behind it. On either side of the room there were large, ceiling-high book shelves, filled with rare leather-bound literary classics, scientific works and histories. In front of and facing the desk were a large leather sofa, a table, and two large comfortable-looking leather arm chairs.

Thornton broke the silence. "I asked you to come here, Tom, because I wanted what I am about to tell you to remain between the two of us, at least until I am sure what we are up against. Compartmentalized, you might say!"

"OK… You've got my attention. Now what's happening?"

"Just a moment and I'll end the suspense," Thornton replied.

Thornton moved gracefully over to a round thermostat on the back wall near the end of one of the bookshelves. He adjusted the temperature dial several times, first to 20 degrees Celsius, then to 15, and finally to 24 degrees. A second or so later, the center of the thermostat opened, revealing a biometric retina scanner. He peered briefly into it with one eye and a second or two later, the center section of the bookshelf moved forward from the wall and parted to the left and right, revealing a metal vault door with a cipher key pad and a fingerprint scanner to one side. Broughton looked on as Thornton punched in several numbers, then pressed the index finger of his right hand against the scanner. After a beat, the once hidden door slid back into the wall and opened to the left. Thornton looked at Broughton who was watching intensely and with great curiosity.

"This way, please!" said Thornton. Broughton followed closely. Thornton looked back over his shoulder and added, "I think you'll find this interesting."

"Interesting…?" said Broughton. "That's an understatement if ever I've heard one," he mumbled barely audibly.

"Surprised…?" Thornton asked. "Well, don't be, old boy," he said smiling. "This is the part of Vanguard that none of the operatives know about, at least not its location. As you can see, it's an operations center. In fact, it's 'the' operations center. Its location is a very closely guarded secret. Knowledge of its location, beyond those of us who built it and the people who run it on a day to day basis, would have disastrous consequences. So I am sure you can appreciate the need to keep it that way."

Upon reflection, Broughton judged that for the seemingly modest size of the building, the room they now stood in was surprisingly large. It occupied almost one entire side of the building. It bristled with banks of computers and several large screens that filled one of the walls. In the center of the room there was an oval-shaped elevated area surrounded by a four-foot-high railing, packed to the gills with more computer monitors and telephones. Five people with state of the art headsets and microphones, fingers dancing busily about keyboards, were hard at work in the area. They seemed oblivious to Thornton and Broughton's presence.

Thornton pointed to the elevated railed area and explained that the place was called the Operations Watch Center, and that those working inside it were always poised to enter 'the game' at a moment's notice. He further explained that the entire area made up the Vanguard Operations Center for Analysis and Logistics Support or VOCALS, a name which Broughton was already familiar with. Within VOCALS, the Watch Commander was supported directly by four assistants, who monitored operations around the globe when they were underway. The remaining dozen and a half people in the room supported and monitored communications, observed activity at selected safe houses, and coordinated logistics support for operatives in the field, through support personnel assigned to each of the Foundation's international offices. Thornton then went on to explain that because Vanguard had its own resources, it remained autonomous and detached from any single government and had no discernible footprint in the world of clandestine intelligence operations. The fact that Vanguard operated its own communications and imaging satellites, gave it even more independence.

Still puzzled about Thornton's reason for summoning him to London, Broughton interrupted. "I am thoroughly impressed with all of this, but would you mind telling me why you brought me here? I know you didn't fly me in from Amsterdam just to show me this... to give me the VIP treatment!"

"You're quite right!" Thornton replied wryly. "Let me show you something."

He led Broughton over to a vacant work station and typed in his access and identification codes. The monitor sprang to life. He struck a few more keys and a map of North Africa and Europe, traversing the Mediterranean Sea, covered the screen and a directional line appeared on the map, along with the names of cities and towns, important events and dates. He began to explain.

"Six weeks ago, there was a terrible explosion at a hotel in Paris's Quartier Latin. You've no doubt heard about it. I believe we all did, but dismissed it as an isolated incident. A few days earlier, an Algerian mining engineer working in the uranium mines in Arlit, Niger, disappeared. His boss and colleagues said he left the facility for what should have been a two-week vacation, but never returned. A few days after he left work, his vehicle was found not far from the Algerian border, abandoned and shot-up. According to what we are getting from French intelligence services, the Paris explosion was caused by a lone wolf terrorist—a suicide bomber who accidentally blew himself up while making a bomb, which they say he was planning to use against an unidentified multinational company. Piecing together the fragments of information from several of our other sources, however, we now know that's not the case."

"What do you mean?" Broughton asked.

"Well… for one thing, the chap who was blown up was no terrorist. According to one of our oldest and best North Africa contacts, the fellow killed in that incident was Sa'id al-Bashir, the missing mining engineer from Arlit. Sa'id al-Bashir was a frustrated Algerian who left Paris in the late 1990s and returned to North Africa to work in the uranium mines. He has long been on our radar scope, not as a major player, but as someone worth watching. In fact, our man in Algeria was able to keep fairly good tabs on his goings and comings between Niger and Algeria for nearly four years. But the last time he saw him was two days before his demise. The contact said Sa'id al-Bashir arrived at a house near his place in a 4x4 that had seen heavy action. He later found out that he had tangled with rogue border guards and managed to escape. Something worth noting is that Sa'id al-Bashir said he needed to get to Algiers in a hurry. At first, I thought it was for a rendezvous with a contact and then a return to Niger. But he just dropped off the radar scope. Then yesterday, I learned from our own operative in Paris that he was in fact the intended target in the hotel explosion."

"So what are you saying? Some low level dreamer with unfulfilled ambitions made a bomb and was planning to use it to settle an old score with the French, because he failed to strike it rich when he was in Paris? Lots of North Africans have tried to settle scores with the French, for past policies and brutalities they acknowledged committing during the Algerian civil war. What makes this guy any different?"

"Now that's the sixty-four thousand dollar question! You see, another piece of the puzzle fell into our hands about forty-eight hours ago. Al-Bashir was not acting alone. Yes, he was on his own, but not alone, so to speak. Our operative in Paris stumbled across a small, but invaluable scrap of information which, if true, tells me this thing is bigger than I initially imagined."

"And this piece of information gives us what, exactly?"

"It tells us, or at least it tells me, that we may be dealing with one of the most sinister, power-crazed and dangerous characters alive on the planet. He's a former intelligence operative from Bulgaria's days as a Soviet satellite. His name is Alexandâr Ilaivo."

"I've heard of him," Broughton interrupted. "They call him the Chameleon."

"I'm sure you have," Thornton continued. "He's a master of disguise and uses a half dozen or so aliases: Kraasimir Irnik, Petâr Kroum, Nikola Boril and several others. Ilaivo is a real nasty piece of work. He was a clean-up man for the KGB. Took care of all the dirty work, especially targets the Russians couldn't get close to. He was, and I believe still is, nothing less than thorough!"

"I remember him now," said Broughton. "But he never turned up anywhere I ever worked."

"I know. That's because he conducted operations mainly against Western targets and suspected Eastern bloc assets recruited by the West in Europe and the Far East. I personally had two run-ins with him. He was young then, but he was no slouch! He's quite possibly the best their side had and probably still is as good as he was then, if not better. And it looks as if he has resurfaced and is open for business again. Doing what...? I don't know, but our man in Paris said he met with al-Bashir about four hours before the blast, in what looked to him like a business meeting."

"How does our operative in Paris know it was Ilaivo?"

"I knew you'd ask that question..." said Thornton. "It's amazing what 50 megapixel digital photography can do," he added. "There was a single but decent photograph taken of the cleverly disguised man who met al-Bashir in Paris. He had deep-set eyes and there was a very faint, tell-tale sign of a scar on his forehead—a scar that, upon closer examination, appeared to run from his hairline down to his eyebrow. I gave him that scar! For years, he wore heavy makeup to cover it. He never got over our little encounter. Said he'd kill me personally if it was the last thing he ever did. Another thing... al-Bashir had about a million and a half euros in counterfeit notes when he was blown up, which leads me to believe he was either a messenger, or was selling something to someone that was of awful high value to them. Ilaivo's style is, or at least was, to flush his quarry out into the open, expose any associated network and take the whole thing down in as short a time as possible. He usually accomplished this before any of the targets knew what was happening. Sa'id al-Bashir may have been part of a wider network, but in Paris the Algerian was working alone. Either way, Ilaivo knew that, because he would not have eliminated him before he found out all there was to know. Do you see now? This thing has the hallmark of something much bigger and I need you and our North African operative, Simon Mills, on top of it. I have watched the two of you for years and I have concluded that you two are the best we have. Ilaivo is good... bloody damn good!" he added, then paused momentarily. "And believe me, if you're going up against him, you'd better be better than him. If you're not, you're dead!"

Chapter Fifteen

Thornton continued his search, moving through Vanguard's intelligence data base with the dexterity, mental prowess and ease of a tech-savvy teenager. It was a sharpness that could only have come from years of experience and knowledge— knowledge of adversaries and allies, but most importantly, a knowledge of patterns. By the time he wrapped up the oral summary on suspicious activities in North Africa and Paris, which he masterfully provided as he searched, he had amassed a collage of images on the large computer screen. The images were of Alexandâr Ilaivo.

Thornton pressed a few keys and in a split-second, the entire array was transferred to a portion of the large wall screen. There were dozens of still photos of the Chameleon—some in which he was made up as an old man, an elderly woman, a neatly shaven conservative college student, while in others he masqueraded as a businessman, a day laborer, a street vendor, and a tennis bum. "Except for the single image from Paris, the most recent photographs we have of Ilaivo are two years old," Thornton interrupted. "It's not a good situation, but it's the one we've got."

The elderly spymaster paused. A second later he continued. "As you know, after the Cold War, a great many of our former East European adversaries found a thriving demand for their talents and skills and became businessmen, in quite lucrative enterprises, I should add. Some set themselves up as consultants, soldiers of fortune, or other kinds of specialists for hire. Most of these chaps can easily be found because they advertise widely. Ilaivo, however, is different. Clients seeking to enlist his services don't go to him or find him. They get word to him and he finds them. In this way, he remains virtually invisible. That's why he is our most immediate worry. He's not getting any younger. So I suspect he's up to something big. He's a high stakes gambler. A high roller who never works for peanuts! Whatever he's working on will move fast, which is why we have got to penetrate his operation. I'll bet you this is his 'swan song', his last act before retiring, which means it'll be something big! We need to know what he's up to and what and precisely who else is involved."

"What makes you think this?" Broughton interrupted.

"Good question. I was, in fact, building up to the answer, which is why you are here. I brought you here because I need you to be available… to be somewhere I can get to you within the next twenty-four hours with the most sensitive instructions. And when you leave here, I need you to be my eyes and ears, as well as my representative when things get more than a bit tricky. I also want you and Simon Mills to work together on this, but you must not make direct contact. Direct contact between you and Mills must never take place during this operation. It would tip our hand. You and Simon will work together, but you will use VOCALS to stay in touch with each other. Simon will leave his base in Casablanca for Niger and help you piece together al-Bashir's trail. I want you to remain in Europe, though, at least for now. I want you to stay there until we figure out what's happening. We can't risk exposing ourselves to Ilaivo. For that reason, you will only be contacted by me, Mills and one other operative, and that contact will come through VOCALS. That other operative, who will be at the center of this operation, is an unknown to the intelligence world. Her anonymity is crucial. She, like Ilaivo, is anonymous and therefore invisible. She can't be linked to any intelligence service and not to you or Simon. But you are to watch her back.

In other words, I need you to keep an eye on her. Look out for her... a kind of guardian angel, so to speak."

"You mean wet nurse her?"

"I wouldn't exactly call it that!"

"What then? Who is she?"

"She's a golden child, you might say. A newbie."

"It sounds like wet-nursing to me!"

Thornton sighed. He was becoming exasperated with Broughton. "Look, Tom... What we are facing is unique and I have no doubt that time is critical. We need someone new for this. A fresh face, a special person... You and Simon will still have an important role in closing matters, if we are successful, but I can't afford to have you out front until I know precisely what we are up against. I hold you and Simon in the highest regard. You know this! You are Vanguard's best operatives. But there is someone who is running a close third, and maybe even competing for first under the circumstances. What we have to do will require special qualifications, qualifications neither you nor Mills possess."

"Why not?" Broughton fired back. "You've never intimated concern about my qualifications before. Why now?"

"Hang on! Let's take a step back for a moment. I brought you here to run this operation on the ground because it has complications and requirements that go beyond your perfectly honed skills and talents. In particular, requirements at this stage in the game make our newbie an invaluable asset."

"What makes this newbie so uniquely qualified?"

"Well, first, this newbie is a woman and an unknown one at that. Second, she looks indigenous to the region and speaks Arabic and French fluently. Because you cannot satisfy these requirements, your role, aside from serving as Chief of Operations, will in the early stages be one of support. In other words, your role is crucial, and this won't work without you. Do you understand?"

"I'm listening." Broughton offered more calmly.

"Good! I'm glad that's settled. The person I have selected for this operation is a quick study. She's extremely intelligent, rational, and stays calm under pressure. But more importantly, I know her commitment is unrivaled. She's every bit as dedicated, if not more so, than any of our other Vanguard team members. She just lacks the years of experience the others have, but we don't have the luxury of waiting for her to mature in that department."

"Sounds like we'll be walking a tightrope! When and where do we start?"

"We start immediately!" said Thornton. "I'll make the introduction later today so you two can get acquainted. Afterwards, your contact with her will be limited, most likely intermittent. I will bring Mills up to speed separately. After today, there must be no physical contact between the three of you, at least not until we know what we're up against and where we stand."

Chapter Sixteen

Vanguard's spymaster sat on the edge of his chair. He was leaning forward, eyes darting from left to right and up and down, searching the pages as he scrolled through the documents displayed on the over-size computer monitor in front of him. Every half-minute or so his hands moved about the keyboard like a piano virtuoso, while Tom Broughton, his protégé, peered over his shoulder. On the well-lit screen in front of them was an electronic dossier containing dozens of images and multiple pages of biographical material and operations notes on Alexandâr Ilaivo.

Thornton moved quickly through the first dozen or so pages, then stopped abruptly. "Here we are," he declared excitedly. "Ilaivo's last official assignment with Bulgaria's *Drazven Sigurnostn*—or the DS, if you like. The operation was launched on 18 February 1989, about nine months before the citizens of West and East Germany started chipping away at the Berlin Wall. He was directed by the DS to intercept and terminate an MI6 asset brought over to the West from East Berlin. The target was Helmut Bernhardt, a big fish… a colonel in East Germany's State Security Service, *Stasi*. The British Secret Intelligence Service (SIS) had spent years and nearly a quarter of a million pounds sterling developing him. But little did they know that Mikhail Gorbachev's *perestroika* and *glasnost* were about to bring the Wall down and open up a flood of information at bargain prices."

"I remember the operation," Broughton interjected. "It was

a classic! Well planned and executed."

"Yes. The first part was indeed well executed, but it all went rather pear-shaped in the end. Bernhardt was MI6's first and only real successful penetration of *Stasi,* a big fish; they owed him a way out when things got too dangerous for him and his family. But instead of whisking him out of West Germany immediately after the cross-over, he was stashed in a safe house to cool his heels until things settled down. The safe house was an MI6-owned facility, a working farm not far from Koblenz."

"What went wrong?" Broughton asked.

"The official version of the story is that Bernhardt was terminated by the senior farmhand, an elderly German man vetted and chosen to run the place. There were only a handful of people who know what really happened; the farmhand was one of them. But he never whispered a word because he was eliminated—an apparent suicide."

"Let me guess. Ilaivo was there and Bernhardt was no longer a problem for *Stasi.*"

"It looks that way, doesn't it?" Thornton replied, still mystified. "My guess is he body-doubled the farm worker the day before they brought Bernhardt in, did the job, and dispatched the old man with a bullet through the mouth to leave a fresh corpse as a patsy. There was even a suicide note from the old man in his own handwriting. The bastard also took out an MI6 operations officer and two counterintelligence officers. Rather an impressive job for an old farm worker in his mid-70s, don't you think? You have to hand it to Ilaivo, it was a neat and tidy job and he got away cleanly. I mean totally clean!"

"How so?"

"When the Berlin Wall came down, the British government had hoped to get to the bottom of the mess. MI6 had learned that several senior *Stasi* officers had grabbed the files on *Stasi's* juiciest operations and squirreled them away, in hopes of cashing-in with the West. However, when the files were offered to the British government, the one on Bernhardt was conveniently missing. Rumor has it that Ilaivo offered the enterprising officials three times what Her Majesty's government was willing to pay and a guarantee not to kill them if there were no duplicate copies. It was an offer they couldn't refuse. And they didn't, but three of the four of them were killed anyway. Ilaivo doesn't like loose ends."

"Where's the fourth *Stasi* officer?

"I believe he's somewhere in Portugal, in the Algarve. New identity, new life and playing lots of golf, I hear."

Chapter Seventeen

Tom Broughton had by now realized that Niles Peter Thornton's stories about Alexandâr Ilaivo's exploits meant that the challenge facing Vanguard, although still not fully understood, could be the most difficult the organization had experienced to date and could have consequences unlike any others in more than half a century. Staying out of the way of a killer who apparently had a vested interest in whatever was unfolding, and who could surface anywhere, anytime, and probably unrecognizable, was frightening. A deep sense of worry came over Broughton and he stood motionless, peering intensely over Thornton's shoulder.

"What else do we know about this character?" he asked Thornton, after several minutes of silence. "Do we have any idea what he actually looks like?"

"There are no file photos of Ilaivo as himself, and surely not any of him as he looks today," Thornton offered disappointedly. "Most of the ones you've already seen and are about to see, are of him in various disguises. In fact, during each of my encounters with him his appearance was different. That is, except the last one. Naturally, he had the scar that was described by our Paris contact when I last saw him. But if he wears makeup, which he probably will, along with some other disguise, you won't recognize him. Nevertheless, you must familiarize yourself with his physique, especially his bone structure—his cheekbones, jaw, nose, and forehead. Also note that he has dark, Romanesque features and deep-set eyes. He can change the color of his eyes with contact lenses, but because they are deeply set in his skull, he won't be able to create a shallower forehead or move his eye sockets forward. And you can forget about studying his posture. It won't help much because he is as good a thespian as they come. He can look shriveled and bent over one time and upright and energetic the next."

"So what's next?"

"I need to bring you and our star pupil together."

"Alright, but I thought you said you wanted me to keep my distance on this one."

"I do, but I also think you need to see who you will be giving instructions to, working with and even protecting, if and when the time comes."

"When do we meet?"

"How about this evening?" asked Thornton. "We'll meet at St. James's Place, fourth floor at 7:30 p.m. Be careful. I know you are the consummate professional, but be sure to use the right protocols and procedures for making your way there and into the building. We can't afford to make any slip-ups. Tomorrow, both of you will have to depart London—you back to Europe and our new operative to North and West Africa."

"I understand the sense of urgency," Broughton interrupted, "but what about developing leads? And where exactly will she and Mills fit in? And who else…"

Anticipating a barrage of questions, Thornton cut him off. "I knew you would have lots of questions. But if you can hold them until this evening, I may be able to provide a few more answers than I can at the moment. In just over an hour, I should be receiving a dispatch from one of our assets in North Africa. I am hoping it will contain good news," Thornton said, then added, "I'll see you at 7:30 then."

Chapter Eighteen

City of Westminster
St. James's Place

The arrival at 320 St. James's Place of a tall, lean, black man wearing green coveralls, a service smock and listening to music on an iPhone, was far from an oddity, and it was therefore not likely to arouse suspicion, nor thwart the highly sensitive meeting about to take place. Tom Broughton's identity had been concealed. He had taken the necessary precautions by disguising himself as a member of the building's cleaning staff. After entering the building, Broughton made his way to where Caroline and Thornton were waiting. They were sitting in a small but tastefully decorated reception room on the fourth floor.

When Broughton reached them, Thornton and Caroline rose to their feet and Thornton introduced them to each other. As they shook hands, their eyes met and a powerful electrical impulse passed between them that couldn't be ignored. As one who rarely revealed his innermost thoughts and emotions, Broughton couldn't hide the fact that he was taken by Caroline's beauty and her strong, yet feminine demeanor. She too was transfixed—riveted by his height and handsomeness, especially his regal face. It was obvious to Thornton from the way Broughton held onto her hand, during what should have been a customary handshake, that they would have no trouble getting to know each other.

"If you'll please follow me…" Thornton said, interrupting their gaze at each other. He then spun on his heel and led them through the reception area into one of the fourth floor office suites. Once inside the spacious area, Thornton moved over to the wall-mounted thermostat and dialed in several numbers, just as he had done at Suffolk House on Balcombe Street. Afterwards, the floor-to-ceiling bookshelf to their left parted and revealed a hidden door. Thornton peered into a retinal scanner, keyed in a few numbers and the door slid to one side, revealing a metal cage elevator. They boarded the elevator in silence and descended to the basement. When the doors opened, they stepped off into another spacious area, except this one had a large structure in its center—a room inside a room. The structure in the center of the area was an ultra-secure zone for highly sensitive conferences. Thornton again worked his magic and seconds later, they were inside the structure. It was a relatively large conference room, fitted with security monitors that were fed by the same live video surveillance cameras the building's security guards were monitoring. In the middle of the floor was a long, clear, transparent conference table with several telephones on it. Computer terminals stood to one side of the room and a large screen monitor covered the wall at the far end of the room.

Thornton took a seat at the head of the table and invited Caroline and Broughton to join him. For several minutes he sat in silence, examining the files on the table in front of him. He was, however, already aware of what the files contained. Still he leafed through them, feigning an intense interest. He was studying Broughton's reaction to Caroline and hers to him with great care. It was obvious to him that they shared a chemical attraction for each other, but he knew there would have to be more. This was their first time in each other's company; he needed to know how they reacted, professionally, to each other. It was important, as there was a lot riding on their ability to work together. Before sending them off to face a plethora of unknowns, he had to know how they would respond to each other, particularly as Broughton saw his role as that of 'baby sitter.' He was looking for signs of negative chemistry, pronounced differences in their general attitudes toward each other—the slightest indication of psychological or biorhythmic incongruity. He knew that many of these things would be revealed within a matter of minutes, even if they didn't communicate verbally or directly with each other.

Caroline and Broughton sat on either side of the table, not far from Thornton. Assessing them had not been as easy as Thornton had expected. Their demeanors were unnatural. They were both quiet and rigid. Both seemed to be discounting, even denying what had happened when they met. Unknown to Thornton, however, the entire time, they had been sizing each other up. Before arriving for the brief, Broughton had reviewed Caroline's biography via Vanguard's highly secure computer network and had been impressed. She was almost perfect in every way. He knew she was confident and at times gregarious, while at others, a lone wolf.

As chief of the operation, he knew he had to make his desire for absolute control clear to her without destroying her initiative and creativity. He would also have to remind her to play to her strengths, while remaining aware of her weaknesses. After sizing her up, he could find no chinks in her armor and concluded that this was a good sign. He decided to open a professional dialogue with her, but not until after the briefing was finished and after there had been time for her anticipation to grow and her stress and anxiety levels to rise. This way, he could get some idea how she would react to mission objectives, which in this case would be fraught with unknown factors. He also wanted to see where she thought the mission lacked clarity and what further explanation or guidance she thought was needed.

After studying the two of them for several more minutes,

Thornton cleared his throat, placed the dossier he had been holding in front of him on the table and slid it forward. He tapped on the small control panel on the table and the lights in the room dimmed. Without speaking a word directly to either of them, he began the briefing.

"For the past few days, pieces of information about the events that culminated in the Paris bombing have been pouring in. We have had a crack team of counterterrorism and technical analysts—Vanguard's finest—sifting through, poring over and analyzing every scrap of information from our operatives, agents, satellite systems and liaison officers."

Thornton slid his index finger across the interactive images projected onto the table's surface from below and a dossier of Alexandâr Ilaivo with photos and half a dozen reports on his activities populated the large wall screen at the end of the room like stacks of playing cards. Then he continued.

"Both of you have been briefed on the broader aspects of this problem, but what you are about to see and hear now is the whole story, as we know it this very minute. It represents all the intelligence we have on the recent activities of Alexandâr Ilaivo, aka the Chameleon, Sa'id al-Bashir and Ilaivo's known associates."

As Thornton talked, signs of stress from the problem and the lack of critical information were beginning to show on his face. It was the first time either of them had seen his mild-mannered personality give way to worry. Thornton sensed that time was running out, but for what, he didn't know. He cleared his throat again, took a sip of water and continued.

"Although Ilaivo has in the past worked mostly alone, it looks as if this time he enlisted the help of a four-man team— one he hand-picked. As usual, on those rare occasions when he does use support, none of the team members know who he is, nor do they know each other and they never see him, at least not without a disguise. They get their instructions via e-mail, internet chat rooms, a courier, or the old-fashioned but effective way, through a dead drop. One of them," Thornton said, sliding the cover from one of the dossiers to one side to reveal a Middle Eastern-looking man in his early fifties, "is an Egyptian." He tapped his forefinger on the man's forehead in the picture. He pushed aside two more photos. "These two," he added, returning to two of the other dossiers and drawing photos, "are Bulgarian and Russian. This one, the Bulgarian, is Andrei Chervenkov. The other one, the Russian, is Branimir Baikov. Baikov is former KGB and Chervenkov is a former *Drazven Sigurnost* operative. Chervenkov was trained by the KGB in the mid-80s, and he's very loyal to Ilaivo. Ilaivo throws a lot of work their way... dirty work, I should add." Thornton continued and drew a photo from the last dossier. "And this one," he said, pointing, "the fourth one, is Dimitar Krastev... he's also a Russian. He was KGB and FSB until about five years ago. He's one of the best there is with a sniper's rifle. He's a long-range killer."

Broughton interrupted. "Where are these so-called associates? Do we know?"

"From what we can see," Thornton replied, "they are not static. They seem to be running interference for him. He uses them like pieces on a chessboard, like a naval picket ship—a screening and early warning mechanism all rolled into one. If one of them gets taken out, he will know someone or something is getting close to him and he will either go to ground, or adjust whatever timeline he is working against. As far as the whereabouts of these characters is concerned, we don't know. However, we think the Egyptian, whose name is Farouk Hamdi, is in North Africa, most likely Algiers. Our analysts believe the other three are still in Europe. I'm sorry, but under the circumstances, that's about the best we can come up with." Turning to Broughton, he said, "As you well know, we don't routinely keep tabs on these sorts, unless of course they're among the bad guys we're up against. When we needed updates, we simply reached out to our friends."

Chapter Nineteen

Caroline listened intently as Thornton briefed them. His warning about the dangers associated with Ilaivo and his henchmen were being embedded in her conscious and subconscious mind. She would not need to be reminded. Watching the images of Ilaivo and the other four men on the screen had made it clear that there was no margin for error—a mistake could end her life and almost certainly the lives of others. She absorbed every detail of Thornton's warnings. When she finally spoke, she was deliberate, succinct and only asked about missing details.

"Is Farouk Hamdi my main concern when I arrive in North Africa, or are there others I can expect to run into? Is Hamdi running a network, and if so, how well established is it?"

"All good questions..." Thornton waded in without skipping a beat. "To answer your first question, yes, you bet he is! He's your only target and we cannot afford to lose focus on him! Regarding your second question, he is Ilaivo's eyes and ears in North Africa; as far as we know, he has been for several months. He has already established a fairly robust network of paid informants. Notice that I use the words 'paid informants', because they aren't part of any big picture strategy. They are just observers, not even foot soldiers, but you need to be aware of them, to include who they are and their activities. That's where Simon Mills comes in. Four days ago, he left Casablanca for Niger to trace Sa'id al-Bashir's movements prior to the Paris blast. He assured me this evening that by the time you get to

Algiers, he will have Hamdi's entire network laid out for you. Does that clear up your concerns?"

"Yes, it does," she replied.

"Remember, no one knows who you are," said Thornton. "To any potential observer, casual or otherwise, you are just another Westerner working for a non-governmental organization in a region fraught with humanitarian problems. Let's make sure it stays that way and no one will question your comings and goings. You'll be free to move all around the Sahel, including inside Niger, Chad, or any other place you may need to go."

"There's a lot of information that's missing," said Caroline. "How long do we have to find and put all the pieces of this puzzle together? And how will we know if we're getting any closer?"

"How long…? Hours! Maybe days, if we're lucky! How will you know when we're getting closer to figuring out what they are doing? That's fairly simple. It will become more difficult for you to operate!" Thornton replied, then added, "But, Caroline, if your cover gets blown, you'll know straight away. Someone will eliminate you. And believe me, if it's either of these guys, they won't fail! Look," he added passionately, "I'll be honest with you. Somewhere out there inside millions of square miles of desert, there is hopefully someone who knows the reason behind all of this. But without knowing what Sa'id al-Bashir knew and what Ilaivo now knows, finding whatever we're looking for is going to be more difficult than searching for the proverbial needle in a haystack. We've got every resource available to Vanguard ready to bring to bear against the problem. But we need to know precisely who else and what is involved, where they are and what they intend to do! That's where I'm counting on the two of you and Mills. My main worry is that we may have less time than we need to find the missing pieces of this puzzle and put them all together. In the meantime, we have to be ready to counter whatever plan Ilaivo has devised with a flexible strategy—one we can change, if need be, as we go along."

"Talk about a race against time!" Caroline declared. "What do we do when we know who, when, what and where?"

"As soon as we know what we are up against, young lady, I want you out of there! You hear me? Tom will provide instructions for your extraction and on where to go and what to do next. As a contingency, I have overland, air and maritime assets set up for use at any and all phases of the operation, but first things first. Tonight, you will fly to Algiers and Tom, you will go back to Europe and find out what you can about an unidentified vessel that sailed from Antwerp to an unknown destination on the West African coast within the past three weeks. If possible, also find out what you can about Ilaivo and his associates and what they're up to."

Thornton paused. He was beginning to show signs of weariness from the task laid before the organization and its small team of operatives. "From now on, all communications between the three of you and Vanguard will go through VOCALS, the main communications and logistics center here in London, and will be handled by the field office nearest you. You will receive dispatches from and to each other, as well as those sent to VOCALS via Vanguard's secure internet site. As usual, all voice and data contact from you and between the three of you will be fully encrypted, so don't lose your equipment. The new wristwatches, fountain pens and phones you have been issued are pre-programmed. You only need to speak the name of whomever you are contacting and these gadgets will do the rest. They'll perform voice recognition, detect vocal stress and warn VOCALS of imminent danger to you. The wrist communicator in particular can identify you by matching your chemistry and biorhythmic data against that in Vanguard's database in a matter of seconds. And if you become separated from it, it'll cease to operate and will be of no use to anyone else. We can also initiate self-destruct to further reduce the risk of compromise. Any questions…?"

Caroline looked across the table at Broughton to confirm that they knew what had to be done, and Broughton replied for the both of them. "We're good!"

"Perfect!" the ageing spymaster declared behind a manufactured grin. "Off you go and good luck!"

"We're gonna need it!" said Broughton.

PART II

Chapter Twenty

Algiers, Algeria

The Air France Airbus A330 from Paris's Charles De Gaulle touched down at Al Houari Boumediene International Airport in Algiers at 2:30 p.m. Caroline collected her baggage and was met in the arrival area by a Vanguard field office representative and local driver.

"You must be Celia," Caroline declared, extending her free hand.

"I trust you had a good trip," said the girl. She had dark hair and looked as if she was in her mid-twenties.

"It was uneventful, if that's what you mean. We departed as scheduled and the food and wine were nice," she added, then changed the subject abruptly. "Is everything all set?"

"Everything has been taken care of. My specific instructions were to get you to the office and situated as quickly as possible. We'll go by the housing compound first. We can drop off your luggage and you can freshen up if you like. I'll send Hassan to collect you an hour or so later."

"That sounds fine! I expect to do quite a bit of traveling over the next few days. Have the necessary arrangements been made?"

"That's all been taken care of as well. We were instructed by London to make whatever travel arrangements you need to happen. They raised your support priority level to five, the maximum. Only one of us, Joshua, the communications chief, has ever seen that before. He says the base operations priority level has shot from a relatively steady state of level two to level five only once since he's been on the job, and that was on 9/11. Is something similar about to happen? None of us have the full picture."

"This isn't the time or the place for this conversation!" Caroline snapped. "I know you and the others are probably jittery, but you will have to stow the questions until later," she added, somewhat apologetically. *Better not alienate the girl*, she thought. She didn't know when she might need her, so it was best to keep her on side. "What about my travel requirements?"

"Two days ago, we sent letters to the Algerian, Moroccan and Nigerien governments and their security officials, informing them of your arrival and that you are the new programs inspector for worldwide operations. We explained that you would need short notice access to existing and planned project areas and sites, in order to assess the efficiency of our operations and to report your findings back to the finance officer and the comptroller. In short, we told them that you are a powerful woman, as your assessments will determine whether or not funding continues to flow into North Africa.

"We also told them that, as an inspector, you are charged with ensuring that the resources earmarked for each project are being used as intended. We got responses from all three governments within forty-eight hours. All three issued you a *laissez passé*, signed by their Foreign and Interior Ministers. You can move about with virtually no restrictions. If challenged, you only need to present the letter. You know," she added, "it never ceases to amaze me how much influence money buys, no matter where you are in the world! In this case, though, I suspect fear of not getting more funds and losing existing programs were as much of a factor as these guys' concern about not being able to get their hands on a portion of the money to line their pockets. Then again, I suppose no bureaucrat in their situation would want the finger wagged at them by their government for shutting off the flow of free money." *They've been pretty thorough*, Caroline thought to herself. *They've certainly tried to cover every eventuality.* But if there was one thing her training had taught her, it was that no matter how detailed a plan might be, it could never be completely foolproof. The unexpected was to be expected at all times.

Chapter Twenty-One

The mid-morning sun danced on the windscreen of the Land Rover Discovery and settled on Caroline Dupré's face. Even with the vehicle's air conditioning churning at full blast, she could still feel the pleasantness of its rays. The warmth felt good. Unlike England's unpredictable weather, northern Algeria was bathed in warmth most of the year; there was not a hint of the humidity that normally thickened the air of most cities that lay on or near the coast. As the vehicle pulled up in front of the Ashmore Foundation compound, she couldn't help but admire the understated appearance of the building and its location. The building lay in a quiet but prestigious suburb of Algiers, just off Rue Chemin Mohamed Gacem and near the southeastern end of Rue Des Mimosas. It was a modest but well-apportioned three-story building, not far from the presidency and the Ministry of Foreign Affairs.

To allay suspicion about the Foundation's activities, only a small number of security guards and a few drivers were employed. The office nevertheless relied heavily on local personnel to administer its programs and projects. To maintain security and protect the integrity of its covert activities, operatives and support personnel relied on a state of the art electronic security system, replete with ground motion sensors and continuous, high definition, live video camera feeds. Sensitive microphones added to the array, which made the security system impenetrable, even from the sky. Inside the building, compartmentalized, critical and sensitive offices had been placed behind false walls, or were hidden in the building's huge basement. The basement was connected to an adjacent property by a tunnel that provided discreet access for personnel performing sensitive jobs at the facility. The occupant of the adjacent property was a small, Vanguard-owned, dummy company, comprised of mainly technicians who supported the field office. Unwanted attention was further avoided by making only a few antennae visible on the roof of the building.

Caroline waited in silence for the gates of the facility to swing open. She was confident that everything needed was already in place. She also knew that she was about to embark on what might be the most important mission she would ever undertake. Her arrival had been low-key; when the driver dropped her off at the building's front entrance, only Celia, the young dark-haired girl who had met her at the airport, had greeted her.

"This way please, Mrs. Dupré. I'll show you to your office first, then we'll go directly to the conference room, which incidentally is accessible in this building only from your office."

"Thank you. That'll be fine," Caroline replied. Feeling guilty about her treatment of the girl at the airport, she offered up an apology. "I'm sorry for biting your head off back at the airport. I didn't want to discuss why I am here, at least not in that environment."

"I understand. You were right. We've all been jittery the past two or three days and I suppose I let the anxiety get the better of me. I can promise you it won't happen again."

"I'm sure it won't." Caroline smiled reassuringly. "By the way, call me Caroline."

***

Inside the building's basement, the walls and floors bristled with large screens and computer work stations. At one end of the basement, there was a small room with a transparent floor, walls and ceiling. It held a conference table surrounded by eight chairs. Large screens hung suspended on all four sides of the table. There were three people waiting inside.

"Welcome aboard," the older man among the room's occupants said, extending his hand. "I'm Leonard O'Boyle, but everybody calls me Lenny. This is Jeff and this is Cayce." O'Boyle made only a thinly veiled effort to mask his disappointment over his limited role in the operation, despite having received instructions from London stating that it would be one of support. Still, he pulled no punches when it came to clarifying who was in charge. The way he saw it, operation or no operation, Algeria was still his turf.

"I am chief of the site," O'Boyle said. "Jeff is the section lead for communications and logistical support and Cayce... well, she's in charge of a small but highly efficient technical support team. Her team flew in yesterday from the States, ahead of you. They came especially to assist you," he announced sarcastically. "How was the trip from London?"

"Not bad, but it's good to finally be here," Caroline replied, shaking hands with everyone. "There's a lot of work to be done and I'm ready to start as soon as you open the gates!"

"Be careful what you ask for, young lady," O'Boyle shot back condescendingly, through a forced grin. "You may just get it. Oh! One more thing..." he added. "They probably didn't tell you in London that for the better part of the next twenty-four hours or so, you'll be working with Cayce."

"Come again!" Caroline said, perplexed.

"I don't want to confuse you, not after the guidance you've been given by London, but don't be too overly dependent on the wrist communicator, the encrypted phone, laptop or any of the other gadgets they issued you. Don't allow them to become a security blanket, because they can't and won't always get you out of a jam! You need other survival skills. That's what Cayce is here for—to teach you a few more tricks that'll come in handy in this part of the world. You were introduced to some of what she does during your training, but you only scratched the surface. I know we're pressed for time, but she's going to teach you how to transform yourself into someone else. She's one of the best in the business and she has an arsenal of tricks. In fact, she used to be a Hollywood makeup artist," O'Boyle added, beaming.

Caroline raised an eyebrow. *Was he kidding? It would take more than a bit of celebrity slap-on to disguise me well enough so that Ilaivo, a master of illusion, wouldn't recognize me!*

"When she's done," continued O'Boyle, as if reading her misgivings, "you'll know how to use wigs, hair-dye, makeup, contact lenses, eyebrows and lashes, prosthetic noses, cheekbones, chins, foreheads... even full masks, to avoid recognition and blowing your cover, or much worse, getting yourself captured or killed. She'll even show you how to add a few years or even decades to change those good looks and that perfect posture of yours," he quipped, trying to make up for his earlier sour demeanor. "All kidding aside, I don't envy you one bit, young lady! Most of us have had years to learn and apply these skills. You've got thirty-six hours at best. And from what I'm hearing about your mission, you're going to need all the help you can get. Don't forget, it'll be a lot of what Cayce teaches you that'll help you stay alive," he admonished. "Not the gadgets! Remember that."

"I'll keep that in mind," Caroline replied coolly.

Chapter Twenty-Two

"Let's get started, shall we?" O'Boyle commanded. "You've already seen the locations we've set up for you to visit," he said, directing her eyes toward one of the suspended screens. "You're off to northern Niger first. You'll work your way up by road from Akokan, a small town southwest of Arlit, toward Algeria's southern border. The plan is to get you out of here the day after tomorrow and on your way to do whatever it is you are supposed to do. The plan we gave to the Nigerien government calls for you to review work on the projects near Arlit. This will include a visit to the project at Arhli, a proposed site just north of Arlit at Oubandawaki Makiani and one at Iferouane, about seventy-five miles to the northeast. You have only twenty-four hours on the ground at each place, if you're lucky.

"We—that is, my team and the additional special personnel —have been directed to give you whatever you need. Stated more succinctly, we will do absolutely nothing else but support you. Because your view of this operation is bigger than any of ours, control and approval of your specific activities will come from your established chain of command. I should remind you that, for security reasons, we don't know who is in that chain because the protocols and communications architecture were set up by London. We are to act, only if directed, as a relay and troubleshooter. In other words, none of the field offices, except this one, know where you are. As for the rest of your fellow operations officers, we have no idea where they are physically located for this mission. Only London has that information and it has sole authority for disseminating it. This is why learning everything that Cayce has to teach you is important. As the office supporting you, we know where you are going, but we can't send or tell anyone in another area to assist or rescue you. We can only assist with your extraction… that is, if you activate an escape and evasion signal.

"Any questions?" he asked. "If not, you can stay here and work on whatever unfinished details you need to tie up, or Celia can take you back to your office. Cayce is ready whenever you are, but I suspect you'll want to see whatever dispatches you have received within the past twelve hours."

"No questions," Caroline said. "But I do want to say thanks in advance for all your help and support. I wish I could share precisely what I have to do with you. In fact, I wish I knew myself. Much of this is being made up as we go… on the fly, so to speak. So I can assure you that the precautions being taken for this operation are not of my making. I am merely a tool, a unique one I am told, but a tool nonetheless. This much I can share, though. London believes that a series of very significant events have occurred during the past several weeks, or perhaps even months, that are part of a chain. If left unchecked, they could culminate in something even bigger and more evil than the events of 9/11. We don't know exactly what that is, but whatever it is, I have to help find it and stop it, no matter what the cost. I don't know what you think of my being here, but I am not the only important one in this mission. I know it sounds a bit trite, but everyone is important. If you weren't, you wouldn't be affiliated with the mission. I wish I knew what else to say, but I'm afraid there's nothing more I can add."

Chapter Twenty-Three

Amsterdam, Netherlands

Broughton's mid-afternoon visit to his Foundation office on Teilingen Street was brief. The only reason he called in was to clear his appointment calendar and check to see if Vanguard's communications and logistics sections had sent any new information that may have been urgent but too sensitive for him to receive at home. After checking and finding there were no messages, he instructed his administrative assistant to tell anyone inquiring of his whereabouts that he would be out of the office for up to a week, traveling around Europe to raise funds for various Foundation projects. Minutes later, he was behind the wheel of his Saab convertible, heading for Antwerp.

After only minutes on the road, he could see that the trip to Antwerp would take less time than usual. Shortly after hitting the A10 ring road, he entered Europe's auto route E35 to find only a sparse and rapidly moving flow of traffic. Although it was mid-afternoon on a work day, the route was surprisingly clear, which made the dark-colored Peugeot that had followed him out of the city and was now hanging about a quarter of a mile behind him easy to spot. Just south of Amsterdam, he left the E35, turned onto the A27 and continued southeast.

The dark Peugeot remained in his wake, but dropped a bit farther behind. Less than an hour and forty-five minutes after setting out, he crossed into Belgium and could see the Scheldt

River ahead. At just over thirty-five miles from the North Sea, the Scheldt was the gateway to Belgium's seaport of Antwerp, Europe's second largest harbor and the fourth largest in the world. Shortly after entering the outskirts of Antwerp, Broughton left the A27 and turned west on the E19 toward the Waaslandtunnel, which ran underneath the Scheldt. But before reaching the tunnel, he turned and headed southeast along the river, toward the office of the Antwerp Port Authority. This time, the Peugeot continued straight ahead and entered the Wasslandtunnel, causing him to wonder if he was becoming paranoid.

Chapter Twenty-Four

Antwerp, Belgium

Broughton swung the Saab into the North Port facility's main parking lot and pulled up on the west side of the building. As soon as the car halted, he clambered out and followed the signs to the complex's main building and the Harbor Master's office. Inside, he was greeted by a smiling, young, bespectacled receptionist.

"You must be the gentleman who rang earlier," the young woman declared. "Mr. Broughton, is it?"

"Yes, that's correct."

"Welcome to Antwerp, Mr. Broughton," she said, pointing him toward the security officer. "I understand you are pressed for time," she added. "The security officer will take you directly to the Harbor Master's office."

Responding on cue, a tall, gangly young man clad in a dark gray uniform, rose to his feet behind his desk. Except for a night stick, pepper spray, handcuffs and a hand-held radio, he was naked and unprepared for any hard-core intruder or group intent on wreaking havoc at the facility. The guard offered a thin, forced smiled that failed to mask his aloofness.

Walking alongside the young man, Broughton could see that he was inexperienced, but judging by his stilted behavior, he was no stranger to bravado. Curious about the nature of Broughton's business, he tried to strike up a conversation as they walked, in the hope that Broughton would say something about why his need to see the Harbor Master was so urgent and his visit so important. But after listening to the young man's conversation, which turned out to be more of a monologue about his own inflated role in securing the port against terrorist attacks and organized criminal activity than a dialogue, Broughton could see that his escort's demeanor reflected ignorance as much as it did youthful exuberance, inexperience and a lack of knowledge about the seedier, darker and more dangerous side of human nature.

As they waited for the elevator, Broughton could feel his confidence growing; for the first time since the meeting with Thornton and Caroline, he was sure that progress would be made. He knew that shipping agents at the port handled berthing arrangements for all arriving vessels and that a visit to the Harbor Master's office would save valuable time. If anyone could help winnow down the number of agents with possible links to the vessel he needed to identify, it would be the Harbor Master. The Harbor Master's familiarity with arrivals and sailings and his frequent contact with ships' captains could be useful in identifying vessels that plied the route between Europe and West Africa, as well as many of the shipping agents who handled them. He also knew that constructing a list of vessels and agents could not be done in an instant, but he needed it done efficiently and with specific results. If he succeeded in developing a list of likely vessels, it would bring him closer to identifying the mysterious ship he needed to find—a ship which Vanguard knew regularly transported used vehicles to West Africa.

While mulling over how he would take on the task, it dawned on him that whoever the owner of the special cargo was, he or they would want to avoid suspicion, and therefore would probably use the services of a captain and ship that moved regularly along the West African coast and between Africa and other parts of the globe.

Despite growing optimism, Broughton was realistic about the situation. Without hard evidence, his ideas were no more than theories. Apart from the basic knowledge of Alexandâr Ilaivo and his hand-picked killers' involvement and the still undetermined role of Sa'id al-Bashir, the view of the situation from where Vanguard sat was at best opaque. He hated clutching at straws, especially when progress was slow or nonexistent. But to tackle the task in front of him, he would have to take one measured step at a time. There were numerous sailings to scrutinize and he couldn't afford to overlook any of them. There was no partial solution and the luxury of time to sift through the haystack to find the needle didn't exist. He would either get it right, or catastrophically wrong. And as if the pressure of having only one shot at getting it right wasn't enough, there was the added problem of unfurling events that had already started and knowing that something would happen again soon, without a clue as to what and when.

***

After several minutes' wait, the elevator doors opened and Broughton and his talkative young escort boarded. They ascended as far as the elevator could go, which was the floor just below the Harbor Master's office. When the elevator stopped, they got off and climbed a short metal staircase that ended in the operations center—an octagonal room stacked atop the main building, with windows that provided a panoramic view of the entire harbor and the southern fringes of Antwerp.

The Harbor Master was waiting at the top of the stairs. He greeted Broughton with a convivial smile and a firm handshake. He was a tall, corpulent man, who despite several NO SMOKING placards placed strategically on the walls of the operations center, clenched a smoke-swirling pipe between his teeth. An austere and clearly serious man, he wore a white shirt and dark tie, a visibly worn windbreaker and out-of-season corduroy trousers. On his feet, however, were well-shined workman's boots, which Broughton surmised was a legacy of years of military service.

"Mr. Broughton! Come in, please!" he said jovially, extending his thick-fingered hand and grasping Broughton's in a vice-like grip. "I am Willem Van den Berg. What can I do for you?"

"Thank you for seeing me on such short notice, Mr. Van den Berg. I need your office's help with identifying a vessel that sailed from Antwerp."

Willem Van den Berg paused momentarily, drew deeply on his pipe, and then pointed its stem toward several large computer screens that formed a semi-circle along the low walls of the operations center.

"We should be able to assist you with your inquiry," he said. "Do you know the name of the vessel?"

"That's the problem, you see," Broughton replied. "I don't know the vessel's name, but it would have sailed from here during the past ten or fifteen days, bound for West Africa for sure."

"I see. Are you aware that arrivals and sailings are provided on the internet each day by *CALA* and other shipping news papers and websites?" He paused once more. "Never mind… It appears this would be of no use to you, anyway, as you are missing the most critical piece of information," he added, smiling. "But that may not be a problem," he said confidently, now cupping the burning pipe in his large fist. "I will hand you over to the section that keeps track of these kinds of details. They have an archive with all arrivals and sailings, including the declared or first port of call for vessels sailing from here. I believe they can help you find the ship you are looking for."

Willem Van den Berg turned and gazed out over the port, as if surveying the expanse of his kingdom. He picked up the telephone handset and issued a brief set of instructions in French and then in Flemish. He then took the small radio that was clipped to his belt and repeated another set of instructions, this time only in French. Afterwards, he turned to Broughton, gave him another firm handshake and wished him good luck. His manner of doing business had been just as efficient and professional as the organization he worked for and represented, Broughton reflected. A minute later, his spindly, acne-faced escort reappeared at the top of the metal staircase and led him to the Port Authority's administrative spaces, three floors down.

Chapter Twenty-Five

Broughton stepped off the elevator on the fourth floor and followed his escort into the Port Authority's administrative office. Once inside, the young man wished him good luck and headed back into the corridor and towards the elevator. By now, Broughton was composed, more confident and upbeat than before. But his outward, confident appearance veiled a lingering anxiety and determination that crested and fell onto a worrisome premonition of outright failure.

For half a minute or so, he stood inside the doorway unnoticed. With so much at stake, the image of an unusually worried Niles Thornton he had seen just twenty-four hours earlier suddenly invaded his head. In retrospect, he realized that Thornton had been in a semi-hypnotic state, deeply troubled and no doubt for good reason. On the few other occasions he had met the elderly spymaster, he had been the epitome of steadfastness. But this time, fissures, if not crevices, were visible in the very bedrock of his being. Thornton's face had spoken volumes about how troubled and helpless he must have felt; the weight of the current crisis was being piled on top of other experiences of high tension, each characterized by its own unique potential for peril.

The tiresome days and restless nights spent worrying about an operation, or one of his operatives, or an important asset, had been heavy and inescapable burdens which Thornton had borne alone. Over time, age and the strain from it all had etched long, deep lines in his face. But with or without the

101

lines, the nearly fixed expression on his face had, only hours earlier, said it all: *Time is running out and there are far too many questions for which answers must quickly be found.*

Still standing near the door, without anyone's awareness of his presence, he cleared his throat. The two women who had been working on the far side of the room looked up and saw him and hurried over. He was surprised to learn that Willem Van den Berg had detailed both of them to assist him. He introduced himself and warned the women that the work he needed to be done would be tedious, but he was counting on a bit of luck with what he described as an elusive quest—a quest likened to a search for the Holy Grail. The older of the two women, a reserved, curvy, yet slight-framed woman, introduced herself as Élisabeth Blauvelt and the younger woman, a new colleague, as Amélie Boevers, her assistant and the office's information technology specialist. In defiance of her outwardly reserved nature, she wasted no time. She weighed straight in.

"Where would you like to begin your query, Mr. Broughton?" she asked briskly.

"Can we go back two weeks?" he asked, before catching himself. "I'm sorry... That should be three weeks?"

"Of course, no problem," the woman replied eagerly. "Three weeks it is! Do you have any other special criteria for the query?"

"Yes. Can you set the search parameters to identify outbound vessels with cargo of mainly used vehicles destined for West Africa? And when you have identified those vessels, can you check to see how many of them have made multiple voyages of this type? It is only a precaution, but I would also like to know which ones were making the voyage for the first time."

"So far, your requirements don't seem too complicated," the woman replied, "but I should warn you that some vessels may declare other European ports in Portugal, Spain, France or Italy as their port of call, even though they may continue on to West

Africa."

"That's a good point," Broughton conceded. "Is there any way we can check with the port authorities in those places, to see if any of the ships with the kind of cargo I am looking for have declared a West African port as their outbound destination?"

"That is precisely what I was going to suggest," the woman said, unable to contain the self-congratulating smile on her face. "We will do this. But first, my colleague will run the first of your queries."

After twenty minutes or so, the middle-aged woman produced two separate print-outs—two lists, one consisting of all outbound vessels carrying used vehicles as their primary cargo during the last three weeks, calling at a European port, and the second, a list of similar profiled vessels which declared a West African port as their next port of call. Much to Broughton's surprise, the first list contained only sixty-eight vessels, however, to his disappointment, the second list contained twenty-nine. This meant that just over half the vessels with used vehicles as primary cargo, had declared for a West African port.

The woman cut in again. "I can send the first list to the other European ports, to see if either of these vessels were pier-side or at anchor there. I will also pass it on to North African ports, to see if any of the vessels arrived there. However, if you are correct about your three-week window, none of the vessels on either list would be able to make it to ports in the eastern Mediterranean and arrive in West Africa on schedule. All the same, I will send the query to all of them with a request for an urgent reply. I should caution again that these port offices might not be very efficient, which means that getting a reply from the eight ports I am querying could take anything from a few hours, to a couple of days."

"Is it possible that we could ask each of them to reply within twelve hours? I know that would be really pressing the matter, but could you do that?"

"I could, but there is no guarantee they will oblige. Let me see…" The woman paused. "If I can send it as a personal request from Mr. Van den Berg directly to the other harbor masters, it just might work! I will, of course, have to obtain his permission," she beamed, adopting the persona of a determined amateur sleuth.

"If you would do that, I would be extremely grateful."

The woman looked up shyly from her console, her big brown eyes displaying uncontrolled eyelash flutter, which was followed by a primal flick of her hair over her shoulder. Broughton reciprocated and smiled flirtatiously as she lifted the phone and punched in the number for Willem Van den Berg's office.

"You can take a seat in our break area while you wait. This could take a little while," the woman added. "You can help yourself to coffee or other refreshments while you wait. I'll let you know when we're done."

Chapter Twenty-Six

"Mr. Broughton… We've run and completed all the searches with the parameters you requested and the queries have been sent, thanks to Mr. Van den Berg," Élisabeth Blauvelt declared excitedly as she entered the break area. "If they respond as I have asked them to, you should have your answer not later than lunchtime tomorrow. Will you be staying in Antwerp this evening, Mr. Broughton?"

He had already considered where the woman's generosity and friendliness was leading, and he was right. "Thank you," Broughton said. "And yes, I am staying in Antwerp this evening. I didn't know how long this would take so I had my office reserve a room for me at the Rubens-Grote Markt Hotel."

"I know the place. It's a nice hotel. I'm sure you will be comfortable there," Élisabeth Blauvelt chirped, flicking her hair over her shoulder subconsciously again. "I don't know how well you know Antwerp, but your hotel is just a short walk from the Grand Place. There are lots of brasseries and quite a few good restaurants there. If you like, I could meet you there for a drink and perhaps show you the town?"

"That's a very tempting offer…" He smiled to sugar-coat the rejection that was about to come. "I'm afraid it has been a very long day for me and I still have dozens of calls to make this evening and lots of office work to catch up on. I'd like to take a rain check, that is, if you don't mind."

"Only if you promise that next time you are in Antwerp we'll have coffee, lunch or maybe dinner together," the woman replied sheepishly, with a slight sultriness in her body language. "By the way," she added smiling, "you can call me Lilli."

"Alright, Lilli, that's a promise I look forward to keeping."

"In that case, I think I'll stay a bit longer and catch up on a few things as well," she declared. "Hopefully, we will get some answers to your query earlier than expected." She sighed. "So, I expect we will see you tomorrow then, yes?"

"Bright and early," said Broughton. "And thank you again for all of your help."

"My pleasure," Élisabeth Blauvelt said.

Chapter Twenty-Seven

It was approaching nightfall when Broughton left the Port Authority building. A few minutes later his Saab rounded the corner of Korte Koepoorstraat and turned into a small parking lot, some 200 yards down and across the street from the Rubens-Grote Markt Hotel. Although he remained grounded, his optimism had grown by leaps and bounds. He was more buoyant after making what he determined to be progress with the Port Authority's administrative office. The next step would be to positively identify the missing vessel and its current location, which would enable Vanguard to track its movement. He knew that accomplishing this would give everyone involved in the operation a bit of hope, especially his beleaguered boss, Niles Thornton.

He parked the Saab, clambered from it and grabbed his overnight bag from the back seat. While tracing his finger along the remote control to lock the door, he dropped the keys and, cursing his clumsiness, bent down to pick them up. But it was that butter-fingered moment that saved him. While he was still bent over, he heard a noise that sounded like a pebble being thrown against metal. He ducked instinctively and just as he went down, something whizzed past his head like an angry mosquito. A moment later, he saw sparks fly from the front fender of the Mercedes parked beside his Saab. Then the Saab's windscreen and driver side window exploded, showering the ground around him with glass. He was someone's target.

Across the street, on the roof of the building next to the

Rubens-Grote Markt Hotel, Dimitar Krastev, the former KGB-trained *Drazven Sigurnost* operative and hand-picked associate of Alexandâr Ilaivo, had been in position in his lair for nearly an hour. He was resting on his stomach and elbows near the edge of the roof of the building, looking through the scope of a silenced Russian-made SV 98 sniper's rifle. Dimitar Krastev had done his homework. He had assessed and chosen his position and had conducted surveillance of the area around the hotel earlier that morning, anticipating the kill. While waiting for his target, he had gloated over his prey's ignorance of his presence. But he had been too impatient. Instead of waiting until Broughton was halfway across the street and fully exposed, he had fired hastily—an unconscionable act for any sniper. Not only had he missed the target twice, he had given away his position.

Realizing what was happening and that he was trapped in the parking lot, Broughton crawled along the ground, back to the driver's side of the Saab, opened the door and pulled his .45 caliber Glock 30 pistol from underneath the driver's seat. More bullets struck the Mercedes and ricocheted off it into the night. After a few more shots had been fired, Broughton could see from the trajectory that the shooter was on the top floor or the roof of the building next to his hotel. Because there were no sounds from the shooter's weapon, he knew the man was using a silencer.

Broughton knew he could not stay between the two cars much longer. If the shooter was a professional, he would do his best to make up for his errors and complete the kill. If he was on the roof, he could easily jump onto the roof of the hotel and acquire a more direct line of fire on a confined target. To avoid such a scenario, he crawled to the rear of the Saab and peered over the trunk toward the roof of the building next to the Rubens-Grote Markt Hotel. But instead of doing what logic dictated and moving to the roof of the hotel, he saw a silhouetted figure with an object slung over his shoulder scampering across the roof in the opposite direction. Ambient light radiating from nearby buildings exposed the shooter enough for Broughton to see that he was clad in black, with a balaclava pulled down over his entire head. After botching the mission, the shooter had given up and was making his way at full speed toward a ladder that ran down the side of the building.

Broughton moved back around to the driver's side of the Saab, grabbed the silencer for his Glock 30 and dashed across the street to intercept his would-be assassin. He ran as fast as he could, zigzagging in case he was being set up for a second shooter. After crossing the street, he stopped at the corner of the building where the roof ladder descended. He could hear feet clanging frantically against the rungs of the steel ladder. Someone was hurriedly descending. Only a few people were moving along the street; they were more than a block away from the building, totally unaware of what had just happened.

Broughton took a deep breath, stepped out from around the corner and tried to take aim, but the shooter had seen him and only a split second earlier he had swung the rifle from his shoulder and fired wildly toward Broughton. The rounds sparked as they ricocheted off the wall and the street, pock-marking the pavement near his feet. Broughton retreated around the corner to safety. Then suddenly, seemingly out of nowhere, a dark colored Peugeot, like the one Broughton had seen tailing him on his way to the Port Authority, skidded around the corner down the street behind him and fish-tailed its way past the hotel at high speed. Broughton heard the car and looked over his shoulder. As it moved past, he could see that the front passenger window was open.

The car continued to accelerate and sped past him. The sound of suppressed gunfire—a rapid pop-pop-pop—came from its front passenger side window. Broughton dove forward and pressed his body against the pavement. The car continued up the street and screeched to a halt. This was the best chance he was going to have to get a shot at his attacker. Making a split-second decision, he rolled over toward the edge of the street and came to rest on his stomach. With his Glock 30 in hand and arms extended in the direction of the vehicle, he saw the shooter from the rooftop dash toward the car. The man pitched his weapon in through the open window and was reaching for the rear door handle when Broughton squeezed the trigger. Pop-pop... two rounds in rapid succession and the darkened figure released the door handle, grabbed his hamstring, fell to his knees, then clutched his throat.

The rear wheels of the Peugeot spun violently and the smell of cordite and burning rubber filled the air and Broughton's nostrils. After several seconds of spinning wildly, the car's wheels gained traction and it leapt forward. Tires screeching, the Peugeot's driver rounded the corner at high speed and left the rooftop shooter's body in the middle of the street. A dozen or so curious pedestrians appeared from nowhere and stood over the crumpled figure, forming a circle around him, gasping in shock and disbelief at the lifeless figure whose blood was forming a widening scarlet pool on the pavement beneath him.

Chapter Twenty-Eight

The incident had exposed Broughton in the streets for only a few minutes, as the event, in its entirety, had taken little more than five minutes. Despite years of experience and his instinctive response, the unexpected attempt on his life had left him with a pounding heart and trembling hands. Nevertheless, he managed to recover and slip from the scene unnoticed. He was lucky. All the attention had been focused on the disturbance caused by the collapse of his would-be assassin and the dark Peugeot that had sped off and abandoned the man.

With everyone's attention focused on his would-be assassin, Broughton returned to the parking lot, collected the overnight bag he had left near his car and made his way into the hotel. He passed through the lobby of the Rubens-Grote Markt's, which was abuzz with chattering and craning-necked guests—all speculating and gossiping about what had happened in the otherwise quiet, up-market part of the city. Broughton took his key from the clerk at the reception desk, who was almost bursting to contain his excitement about what had just happened.

"What's all the excitement about in here and out in the street?" Broughton asked the young man.

"Ah, Monsieur Broughton... it's a good thing you didn't arrive ten minutes earlier," the man said excitedly, with widened eyes.

"Why is that?"

"You would have been caught up in a gun fight! You only

just missed a dangerous shoot-out about twenty meters down the street from the hotel. There was gunfire and screeching tires everywhere, like in the movies. It looks as if Antwerp's drug and prostitution kingpins had a go at each other. Unfortunately, it seems that they no longer restrict their deadly battles to the seedier quarters of the city. I was told by several of the guests that at least one of them was killed in the shootout. I will let you know when I learn more," the clerk added, twitching with nervous excitement as Broughton turned away and walked toward the elevator.

Chapter Twenty-Nine

As soon as Broughton entered his room, he checked in with VOCALS via Vanguard's high security communications network with his laptop, logging in under the codename 'ZEUS.' He reported the incident and provided an update on his activity at the port facility. But the Watch Officer had had news for him, too, which had just been received.

"Congratulations on staying alive! It's good to hear your voice! It sounds like you had a really close call," the Watch Officer declared, trying to make lighthearted humor about the dangerous incident. He continued, "If you're wondering what happened, we had the Peugeot that tailed you this morning under satellite surveillance, but it managed to evade us by going into an underground parking garage. To make matters worse, the occupants shut down their mobile phones and removed the batteries. They also disabled the car's anti-theft tracking device, which we could have exploited. As you probably have guessed, the car was stolen. We didn't pick it up and start tracking it again until it showed up near your hotel."

"Is there any good news in all this?" Broughton asked, trying to control his temper. "These guys seemed to know exactly where I would be!"

"I understand your frustration, ZEUS, and yes, there is a bit of good news, but I'll let the boss share that with you."

Niles Thornton chimed in. "Things are heating up," he declared, his image suddenly filling the screen of Broughton's laptop.

"No kidding!" Broughton returned. "What the hell happened?"

"What happened, indeed..." said Thornton. "Answering that question is simply stating the obvious... you've been made! And we have to assume that you've been fully compromised. It also means that we must be on to something important. I apologize personally for dropping the ball on keeping the Peugeot and its occupants under surveillance, but not knowing where and exactly what to look for is causing a bit of resource over-stretch at this end. We should've been able to warn you of what you were walking into and you should've been able to neutralize the threat before it materialized. I commend you for holding it together, but it should be of some consolation to you to know that the shooter you took out was Dimitar Krastev— one of the former KGB-trained *Drazven Sigurnost* operatives I briefed you about."

"Krastev! I don't understand," Broughton replied, surprised. "If it was Krastev, how could he have missed? He's one of the best, inside or outside the game!"

"It was Krastev alright! We have it on good authority. Our contacts inside Belgium's *Sûreté de l'État* and the Netherlands' *Algemene Inlichtingen-en Veiligheidsdienst* positively identified the man you killed as Krastev. He must have gotten sloppy, maybe even too confident. Whatever caused him to miss, you should consider yourself lucky! By all accounts, you should be a dead man. And as best I can tell, you surprised Ilaivo. You probably weren't even on his radar scope until this morning. Your visit to the Port Authority probably was an unforeseen event, a development that made him nervous. I think we're getting close to something. Preliminary examination of the incident tells me the move against you was put together in haste. Krastev is meticulous and usually takes his time. He earned a reputation for paying attention to the minutest of details. Speaking of developments, where do we stand with our mystery vessel? Any luck?"

"Not yet, but I've got a good line on it. I expect we'll get something soon. The Port Authority's office managed to reduce the list of possible vessels to ninety-seven, twenty-nine of which left Antwerp and sailed directly to West African ports. They're checking to see if any of the other sixty-eight are sailing to West Africa via other European or Mediterranean ports. I suspect we'll get hits on quite a few of those."

"I was hoping for something better, but as you're still alive and we've started the ball rolling, I'll accept that as good news for now. I suppose what you've found already is more than we had twenty-four hours ago. If my instincts are right, the attempt against you probably means one of the vessels on those two lists is the one we're looking for. But even if we identify and find it, we still don't know what it's transporting or planning to transport. We may learn something from Caroline when she checks in. She still has lots of digging to do and Mills is still providing counterintelligence support to her, albeit a bit limited. He is also helping her trace al-Bashir's movement around Niger and Algeria to give her some more leads. They're both working flat out."

"What else has Mills done? I haven't seen any dispatches from him. He should be giving her everything she needs to get her set up for her part of the operation."

"He has and he is," Thornton replied. "As promised, he has identified Ilaivo's Egyptian 'fixer', Farouk Hamdi's entire network. Hamdi has agents and a dozen other informant type assets spread throughout Algeria, Morocco and Niger. Caroline is being thorough. She's assessing the situation and exercising total caution in her movement, as well as in who she contacts. She's very clever, you know. She won't do anything to blow her cover. For now, she still has freedom of movement, as no one has linked her to you or Vanguard. As far as we can tell, there are no impediments to Mills' side of the operation, either. We have to keep it that way. By the way," he added. "Do I detect something a bit more than professional concern about our

115

young and very attractive new officer?"

"No, you don't," Broughton snapped. "Remember, you put me in charge of this operation and I intend to see that it succeeds. And that means each of us has a job to do. You yourself said that this is probably something bigger than we've ever seen before, which means the stakes are too high for the operation to fail. I intend to run the operation on that premise. From here on, I want to see all the dispatches from those two, not just critical alerts. In the morning I'll resume my search for the missing vessel and hopefully by this time tomorrow, if not sooner, it'll no longer be a mystery."

"Give them a break," Thornton said. "Like you, they've both just hit the ground with this within the last twenty-four hours. By tomorrow, you should be able to get dispatches directly from this site. Your critical alerts will come as usual via your wrist device and your secure mobile phone. All operations instructions involving changes will be sent from me to you via VOCALS, for you to pass on to the team. Just keep your head down," the spymaster cautioned. "And remember, you've taken out Krastev. They may be one man short, but they're on to you. Keep your eyes open. We know the Russian and the other Bulgarian are somewhere in Europe. I doubt that either of them were part of the failed attempt against you. Ilaivo wouldn't risk losing more than one of his attack dogs in a single operation. But you can bet your next pay check there'll be more attempts. In the meantime, we'll get a fix on the Russian and the Bulgarian, so we can warn you before they make another move against you. We have to assume that if they are aware of some form of organized effort to stop them, they'll be looking for other operatives. We can't let any suspicion fall on Caroline and Mills. After this incident, Ilaivo and his goons will be more vigilant and, without a doubt, more dangerous."

Chapter Thirty

Niamey, Niger

The Air France flight from Algiers touched down at Agadez, Niger's second busiest and second largest international airport, at 11:30 a.m. From Agadez, Caroline boarded an Air Algerie flight to the isolated mining town of Arlit. When she arrived at Arlit, a heavy Mitsubishi 4x4 and a Foundation driver were waiting for her.

"Bonjour, Mademoiselle Dupré," the driver announced in French, laced with an accent from his native Hausa language. "My name is Moussa dan Gogo, but please call me Moussa," he added. "I have instructions to take you to your hotel this evening and tomorrow morning, to projects located to the south and northeast of Arlit. I am also at your service this evening, if you should need to go anywhere. I have been driving for the Foundation for many years now," he added, in an attempt to ensure he had her confidence.

"Thank you, Moussa. I've heard that you are a safe, reliable driver. In fact, they say you are one of the best," Caroline added, smiling to cover the lightning fast check she was doing of his demeanor, stance and body-language. She thought he seemed a bit over-eager to impress her and that could mean more than mere good manners and nerves. She couldn't let herself become paranoid, but she knew that she needed to be observant at all times, and not let her guard slip once, not even for a second.

"Thank you very much, *mademoiselle. In shaa' Allah*, I will do my best to get you to your appointments safely and on time," the man said, switching to Arabic.

After collecting Caroline's luggage, they set out for the center of Arlit. Leaving the airport, they headed south toward the town, which was less than ten miles away. Arlit's population of around 80,000 was made up mostly of mine workers from across North and West Africa. There were also several hundred French nationals, some with their families.

The landscape between the airport and the outskirts of Arlit was barren, yet oddly picturesque. In most areas, the beige desert sands gave way to reddened earth, interrupted only by the silt-covered road that cut through the desert. Moussa made nervous small talk and asked about the rumor he had heard—a rumor started by concerned employees that, as the Ashmore Foundation's inspector for North Africa, she had come to shut down several projects in order to save funds, which everyone knew were increasingly becoming tight. Caroline reassured him that this was not the reason for her visit and that neither his job nor those of the other local Foundation employees were at risk. If this was the general view regarding her visit, she would have to watch her back. Being in danger from Ilaivo and his men was one thing, but she didn't want to be the target of nervous citizens out to protect their livelihoods. It was an extra annoyance that could muddy the waters of her main objective.

Wearied by her musings, Caroline sighed. "Moussa. After you drop me at the guest house, you can take the rest of the evening off and spend it with your family."

"Thank you very, very much, *mademoiselle*, but my family lives in the south of the country, just outside Niamey. I made the journey from Niamey to Arlit, as instructed, to support you. I therefore have no plans this evening. So, if you should need me, I am at your service."

"Thank you again, Moussa, but I want to have a bit of a

drive around the town on my own. I want to see and get the feel of the place."

"But you are a stranger!" he protested, showing concern.

"I'll be perfectly fine on my own. After all, I have your mobile telephone number. And besides, it's rather difficult to get lost, given the relatively small size of the town. You deserve an early evening," she added. "Have some dinner and relax. You've earned it after such a long and no doubt arduous journey. I'll see you bright and early in the morning."

"Then I will wish you a good night, *mademoiselle*," said Moussa. If you need anything, don't hesitate to call me. *Bonne nuit*!"

Chapter Thirty-One

Caroline checked in at the La Rochelle guest house at the north end of town and went straight to her room. Once inside, she set up her Thuraya satellite telephone-equipped laptop to report her arrival and receive the next set of instructions. She turned on the laptop and signed in under her code name, 'AMPHITRITE.' The fully encrypted program used to enter Vanguard's ultra secure site sprang to life, running in the background of the laptop's commercial software. The critical code containing its executable instructions had been cleverly dispersed across, and hidden in, several commercial applications. The program was quick and efficient. Even to a knowledgeable user or competent hacker, the fragmented code looked more like viruses or sophisticated spyware than a deliberately loaded, comprehensive, control program. Just as important as being inconspicuous, it left no evidence of access to the Vanguard site after the user had left it.

The ultra secretive but ordinary-looking laptop had been designed in every way to prevent a compromise, while providing the highest security for Vanguard operations. Even if stolen or captured, two failed attempts at the password would wipe the entire system clean, rendering the computer worthless. In the event of password defenses being successfully bypassed, an unauthenticated iris scan or an attempt to remove the hard drive would produce the same results. In an emergency, the field operative could also use the 'escape' key along with an iris scan, to get the same results. To speed up transmission and retrieval time, information sent to and from operatives, even though encrypted, was limited to 350 characters and simulated a lengthy text message sent from a mobile telephone.

After going through the first phase access procedure, Caroline entered another password and peered into the laptop's web camera for an iris scan. This was the final step for identity authentication. The entire process from laptop startup to full access took less than sixty seconds. Upon entering the compartmented area of the site, the latest tailored updates, including maps, photographs and graphics, appeared in priority sequence and instructions scrolled across the bottom of the screen, repeating only once before vanishing for good. The updates and her instructions read:

1. Chameleon associate Dimitar Krastev eliminated in Antwerp by ZEUS. Associate Farouk Hamdi and three subordinates currently in your vicinity.

2. Proceed to the Côte Bleu restaurant for 20:00 hours meeting with Georges Saint-Jacques, code name 'PAPILLON.' Look for middle-aged Frenchman in beige linen suit.

3. Ask PAPILLON if the food is any good. He will authenticate as follows: "I highly recommend the onion soup, especially on a chilly desert night."

4. PAPILLON has information on al-Bashir.

Chapter Thirty-Two

Caroline wasted no time. After reviewing the intelligence updates and instructions, she freshened up and headed to the center of town. Outside, the night was almost pitch-black. The moon was not visible and street lighting was intermittent. Once a booming town, Arlit had sprung up from the desert floor to support the uranium mining industry in the area. Now it was only a shell of its former self; a reduction in the demand for its high grade yellowcake, and the collapse in the world market price for uranium, had left the once thriving town almost bust. But French and Nigerien interest in production in Arlit had continued. In years past, there had been strikes and demonstrations by disgruntled workers over wages, safe drinking water and better working conditions, but they had subsided with the reduction in the global demand for uranium.

Alone behind the wheel of the 4x4, Caroline relied on the Global Positioning System (GPS) to take her directly to the rendezvous location. As she drove into the center of town, she slowed the vehicle to a crawl and caught sight of the Côte Bleu neon sign hanging over the balcony of a two-story French colonial-style building. Each time the sign flashed, its colors alternated between France's tri-colors blue, white and red. How odd a mode of advertisement for a French-owned establishment, she thought. But they are, after all, the colors of the French flag and must have been a decision inspired by patriotism, she thought.

She passed the restaurant and parked three blocks down and

across the road. She wanted to walk the fairly short distance to get a feel of the town. As she approached the Côte Bleu, she could hear clicking coming from the sign as it flashed and changed colors. From inside, she heard voices that sounded like the buzzing of bees and the occasional outburst of laughter. When she stepped inside, she was greeted by the *maître d'*, a tall, thin, effeminate man with a pencil-thin mustache who looked like a throwback to the gangster movie era of the 1930s and '40s.

The Côte Bleu was housed in an impressive and deceptively large building. Although modern, it had been built in the grand style of nineteenth century French colonial architecture, complete with long, shuttered windows and a sizeable second floor railed balcony. Surprisingly, indoor tropical plants adorned the room and several large fans hung from the high ceiling, lazily beating the air and swirling, almost in unison.

"*Bonsoir, mademoiselle*," said the *maître d'*. "Do you have a reservation?"

"No, I do not," said Caroline, making eye contact and bathing him in a warm smile, knowing he would be a pushover.

"Never mind," the man said, smiling back. "Will you be dining alone this evening?"

Before Caroline responded, she glanced down at her watch and her eyes darted around the room to see whether the beige-linen-suited Frenchman was there. There was no sign of him. Sensing her hesitation, the *maître d'* moved to assuage any concerns that may have been gathering in her head about the Côte Bleu.

"I can assure you, *mademoiselle*, there is no finer food or atmosphere in Arlit than at the Côte Bleu. I am sure you will be more than satisfied. After all, we have consistently been rated the best restaurant in town," he added, with a hint of arrogance. "And as you are probably aware, the *chef patron* has two Michelin stars."

"So I've heard," she replied. "I am dining alone this evening and I would like a quiet, secluded table in a corner, if that is possible?"

"*Oui, mademoiselle. Bien sûr,*" the *maître d'* replied. "I have just the table for you. If you would follow me, please…"

She walked briskly behind the man toward a long, highly polished mahogany bar. Seated near the middle of the bar was her contact. The *maître d'* led her past him to her table, which was just twenty feet away from the bar.

Chapter Thirty-Three

Caroline sat cross-legged at a small corner table adjacent to the bar, sipping a dry vodka martini. The day had been long and arduous, but she had gotten herself together and knew she looked the picture of elegant confidence, dressed in a soft white, classic shift dress with a thin black belt around the waist and a *crème*-colored cashmere cardigan draped over her shoulders. A pair of low-heeled black pumps adorned her feet, showing off her toned and shapely legs. By now, the Papillon had turned on his bar stool and was half-facing her. Behaving like the quintessential Frenchman, he was eyeing her legs and firm, womanly form. He tossed some West African francs onto the bar, gave a playful and anticipatory nod to the bartender, grabbed his glass, slipped off the bar stool and sauntered over to her table.

"*Bonsoir, mademoiselle*," the Papillon said, standing over her, swaying gently, with a hawkish grin on his face.

Caroline cringed inwardly. The drunkenness was something she hadn't expected. "*Bonsoir,* monsieur," she replied, making piercing, direct eye contact with him.

"Is this seat taken?" he asked, somewhat sheepishly. "I mean, are you dining alone?"

"Yes, I am."

"May I join you? I couldn't help but notice that you were alone when you came in," he said, sliding into the seat before she could reply.

"Why is that?"

"It's not difficult to notice a new face around this place, especially when it is as beautiful as yours."

"Do you always accost and try to pick up all the women who come into this place on their own?"

"Yes, I do. As I said before, it's not often that an attractive, sophisticated woman enters this place unescorted. Come to think of it, really attractive women like you never turn up in this place. Don't get me wrong," he added, "we get the occasional well-turned-out female businesswoman from Paris, but they're usually wearing rocks on their wedding ring fingers big enough to choke a camel. On the whole, I suppose, most of the ones who pass through—or, God forbid, stop and stay—are hard and bitter and have balls bigger than mine."

"I see… You're quite the observant one, aren't you?" There was something repellent about this man, she thought—something she couldn't quite put her finger on.

His eyes suddenly shifted. "One has to be, in order to escape the tediousness of this pampered, mundane, illusionary environment," he jibed. "Take the brunette over there at the table near the front door, for example," he said, dipping his head in the woman's direction. "The one with the two middle-aged guys," he added. "She wouldn't trade the dirt under her nails for silk fineries, Chanel No. 5 or anything! She's an engineer, you see. Drinks perpetually with the guys and loves it down there in the mines, but won't let any of them get close to her. Mind you, she hasn't been seen with any women either. What a waste!" he declared, then took a swill of scotch from the tumbler gripped affectionately in his spindly-fingered hand. "Were you planning on dining?"

"Yes. That was the plan," Caroline said wryly. "Is the food any good here?"

"Of course… Didn't the *maître d'* tell you? The *chef patron* has two Michelin stars," he returned sarcastically. "All kidding aside, I highly recommend the onion soup, especially on a chilly desert night."

"In that case, you may join me, or should I say you may stay, since you've already taken the liberty of seating yourself. And thank you. I think I will take your advice and start with the onion soup."

"An excellent choice," the Papillon replied, grinning.

She had initially thought the Frenchman was feigning his inebriated state, but she could see now that it was no act. He was quite drunk. *Who chose this idiot? He's clearly a burn-out and a regular fixture in this place—a lounge lizard who thinks he's a ladies' man, a has-been who is becoming increasingly delusional with age. With his kind of weak self-control, he could be... He probably is dangerous. He could jeopardize the whole mission.* Still surveying her from head to toe, the Papillon lifted his glass with what was left of the scotch, gazed into it momentarily and raised it in a toast. "*Salut!*"

Chapter Thirty-Four

A few minutes into the conversation and without warning, the Frenchman suddenly clawed back his composure. The transformation was instantaneous and nothing short of astonishing. He had managed a miraculous return to sobriety right before her eyes. After the startling at-will recovery, the Papillon fixed his bloodshot hazel eyes on hers, as if he were about to woo her. But before he could launch a full-on charm offensive, a very courteous, middle-aged waiter appeared.

"*Excusez-moi, s'il vous plaît*," the man interrupted. "*Mademoiselle...*" he paused briefly. "Are you ready to order? Will monsieur be dining with you?"

Caroline shifted her eyes momentarily to the Papillon. "Yes, monsieur will be joining me, but could you please give us a few more minutes?"

"*Bien sûr, mademoiselle*," the waiter replied. "When you are ready, just let me know."

"Thank you very much," Caroline said, then turned to the Papillon. "I believe you were about to share something with me."

"Yes, indeed I was," the Papillon said confidently. "Your boss has been racking his brain, trying to figure out what the Chameleon's relationship was with an Algerian national named Sa'id al-Bashir. Is that right?"

"Yes," Caroline replied.

"Well, this Algerian left Algiers about twelve years ago and moved to Paris, hoping to make his fortune. Instead, he had to settle for a hustler's life—one more among the 'dime a dozen' refugees flowing into Paris, eyes filled with hope. After pounding the streets for nearly five years, he lucked out as you Americans say and got into the Institut National des Sciences Appliquées and got himself a degree in mechanical engineering. Unfortunately, it didn't improve his life much so he packed up and moved back to North Africa—very bitter and disappointed, I should add. About three months after returning to Algiers, he got a job with Niger's state-owned mining company, SOCMINN, in charge of transporting yellowcake from the mine to storage and then on to the area that prepared it for shipment. The word is that he wasn't trusted enough to let him run things below ground, so management gave him something he couldn't screw up." Papillon snickered.

He paused briefly then continued. "About six months ago, he made contact with a couple of Arabs and a North Korean. According to my best contact, the Arab guys were not Arabs at all but Iranians and the North Korean was sent up here by his embassy in Niamey. Not a member of the North Korean Embassy staff, I was told. He was brought in from Pyongyang. The North Korean spent four days in Arlit and met with your man three times. One meeting took place here in the Côte Bleu. There were at least four meetings with the Iranians."

"What was the reason for all these meetings?" Caroline asked. "If your contact was right, why would al-Bashir have a meeting with these men? He was a mechanical engineer. Correction..." she added. "He was only a glorified transportation manager at the time."

"Good questions!" said the Frenchman. "There is no concrete proof, but I received several reports suggesting your man had been squirreling away yellowcake by the ton in fifty-five gallon barrels—drums, you Americans call them— somewhere in the desert, for a couple of years, if not more. If these reports are true, his contact with the Iranians and the North Korean must have been to make some kind of deal for that material. Either way, I'm sure it involved lots of money, or plans for lots of money to change hands. After all, it's always about money, isn't it?" The Papillon paused once more, then resumed. "Look…" he added, "I hope you have learned what you came here for, because that's all I could dig up."

"It's more than I knew," Caroline said. "By the way, not everyone is driven by greed!" she retorted, showing her disappointment with his apathy and cynicism.

"You are right! Sometimes power comes first. Then there's the money! You're naïve if you think it's about anything else. Let me remind you of something. Arlit is a small town in the middle of nowhere and the handful of local people who live here are too frightened to talk, especially to foreigners. There is no place to hide if someone finds out you've squealed on them. For example, after the last meeting with my contact, he went south to visit his family for a week. I haven't seen or heard from him since, which proves my point."

"Is it possible he's just lying low?"

"I doubt it. He was supposed to contact me two days ago. He's got a solid record for reliability. In five years, he has never missed a scheduled contact. Then yesterday morning, I received word from a friend of his family that he disappeared the day after he returned home. My gut instinct tells me someone got to him. You are an extremely attractive woman, and an intelligent one at that. You would be wise to leave Arlit as soon as possible. There are lots of bad people in this small and seemingly innocent town. Some of them are downright dangerous!"

"I guess I'll have to take your word for that, but I believe I can handle myself."

"I'm sure you can!" the Papillon replied, grinning. "After all, you are half French, aren't you? But all the same, you should allow me to escort you back to your hotel after dinner and tuck you into bed."

"Your deep concern flatters me," Caroline returned sharply,

breaking a slight smile, "but I think I'll be alright on my own."

"As you wish," he said calmly.

Just as the conversation ended, Caroline signaled the waiter, who rushed straight over.

"Shall we order?" she asked the Papillon.

"No, thank you," he replied. "Somewhere between your initial rebuff and that last *coup de grâce*, I lost my appetite. So, if you don't mind, I'll stick to the liquid menu I was selecting from when you arrived. *Bon appétit!*" he declared sarcastically. He pushed his chair away from the table, then rose to his feet and drifted back to the bar which, Caroline thought, seemed like his natural element.

Chapter Thirty-Five

Outside the Côte Bleu, a faint breeze had risen and the night had taken on a slight chill. Caroline slid her arms through the sleeves of her cardigan, pulled it snug around her shoulders and fastened the top two buttons. She was deep in thought— puzzled by what she had just learned from the Papillon—but still aware of her surroundings. *What did the Frenchman mean by lots of bad people in Arlit?* After walking about a block, her eyes had adapted to the near total darkness of Arlit's streets. Ahead of her and off to the right was the only light along the street. The arm that held it aloft was invisible and it seemed to hang eerily suspended in the dense night air like a dull, alien orb, encircled by a faintly glowing halo. As she walked back toward the 4x4, she detected a flicker of movement through her peripheral vision, just off to her right and slightly behind her. She turned abruptly to investigate. Nothing... There was only stillness. Aside from the hum of merry makers filtering from the Côte Bleu, which was growing fainter, the town was dead quiet.

A few more steps and she detected another disturbance of the stillness. Her steps quickened. Without looking down, she activated her wrist communicator, reached inside her handbag and eased out a Beretta Jetfire .25 caliber pistol and a silencer and fixed them together. The compact Jetfire wasn't her weapon of choice, but it was tiny, accurate, easy to conceal and with a nine-round clip, it offered reasonable protection—a kind of insurance when nothing bigger could be concealed or carried. Pistol in hand, arms folded in front of her, she slowed her pace to avoid exciting whoever was tailing her. Inside her handbag there were two more fully loaded clips.

A few more steps and across the street to her right and still slightly behind her, she detected more movement. Again, it was only a flicker. Her mind raced. *Damn it! There are two of them! Do I make a dash for the 4x4, or do I keep going as if nothing has happened and wait for them to make their move?* She recalled from her survey of the route on the way to the Côte Bleu that there was a narrow alley parting the low-level buildings, halfway down the block and on the left. Her training kicked in and her adrenalin surged. She did not know what lay in the narrow alley, but it was the best place to make a stand. She would duck into it and mount her defense. Then it dawned on her. *If this is a trap, there won't be anywhere for me to go. There will be a third member of the team in the alley. It's the perfect place! Change of plan. I'll approach the alley and appear to move past it, as if I am unaware of his presence. Without telegraphing my next move, I'll drop and squeeze off three shots—one at center mass, one low and the third slightly higher. The spread should help me hit something with blind shots.*

It was decided. The plan was set. She resumed a normal pace, eyes straight forward, now fully adapted to the night's near blackness. If there was no one in the alley and she made it past the gap, she would still have to cross the road to reach the 4x4. She turned slightly to look for signs of danger near the vehicle. As she turned, she saw a tall, thin silhouette, no doubt the second assailant she had detected earlier, dash across the road from his tailing position on the street opposite the Côte Bleu. *Damn it! Both of them are behind me now!* Her temples throbbed. Suddenly, she could sense the presence of someone only a few yards behind her. The entrance to the dark alley lay only a few yards ahead. The game had suddenly changed. The assassins hadn't changed the rules, the number of scenarios had simply increased.

Her heart pounded inside her chest; she knew it was too late to change strategies. Not wanting to give away her intentions, she continued walking, preparing to cross in front of the alley. As she approached the narrow gouge, the smell of Turkish tobacco, wafted by the faintest of breezes, trickled out of the alley and settled on her nostrils. A split-second later she caught a glimpse of a faint, red glow in the shadows against the building to the left side of the alley.

She stepped in front of the alley and went down without warning, exactly as planned. Four silenced shots followed in quick succession—pop, pop, pop, pop—but she hadn't fired. The figure with the lighted cigarette in the alley twisted to the right in a lazy corkscrew-like motion and fell forward on his side. Then, just feet behind her, she heard a thud on the pavement. She rolled onto her side and aimed at the tall figure now standing over her. His weapon was dangling at his side, non-threatening.

"Don't shoot!" the man said in a sharp, worried whisper. "It's me! Moussa!" he declared crisply.

"Moussa? What the hell are you doing here?"

"It's a long story, *mademoiselle*. I will explain later, but you must return to the hotel. You must leave now!" he commanded. "I will clean this mess up and meet you there in half an hour. Don't think! Just go! Go now!"

"Who are they, Moussa?" she returned angrily.

Pointing the barrel of his weapon at the man on the pavement, he said, "This one I believe you know."

Caroline rose to her feet.

With his foot, Moussa rolled the man over onto his back. His clothes were bloody, but she could tell he was wearing a beige linen suit.

"The Frenchman!" she shrieked, staring at his lifeless body. She fought back the urge to fire a few more rounds into him for good measure. "Damn it! That bastard!" she muttered, spun on her heel and walked quickly toward the 4x4.

Halfway across the road she stopped and gave one last look over her shoulder. She was stunned and angry about what had just happened, but she was also extremely grateful.

PART III

Chapter Thirty-Six

Antwerp, Belgium

Broughton finished showering and was getting dressed when the Rolex-like communicator on his wrist started to vibrate. Using its bezel, he dialed in a six-number code and a message immediately appeared and scrolled across its compact screen:

URGENT. ACTION REQUIRED. CONTACT VOCALS IMMEDIATELY!

Broughton flipped open the secure laptop, logged in, went directly to Vanguard's website and entered under his codename, ZEUS. Upon entering the ultra-secure site he found the following message:

PAPILLON CONTACTED. AMPHITRITE BRIEFLY ENDANGERED BY DOUBLE-CROSS TRIGGERED BY GREED. AMPHITRITE DISCOVERED AL-BASHIR MAY HAVE STOLEN SEVERAL TONS OF YELLOWCAKE FROM MINES. PAPILLON SET UP INDEPENDENT OPERATION TO STOP VANGUARD PROBE. NO EVIDENCE PAPILLON WAS DOUBLED. PAPILLON'S ACTIONS LIKELY TAKEN TO ENTER LUCRATIVE GAME WITH POSSIBLE NORTH KOREAN AND IRANIAN CLIENTS, BUT NO CONTACT BETWEEN

THEM WAS MADE. OPERATION EXPOSURE AVOIDED; PAPILLON AND ONE ASSOCIATE ELIMINATED BY LOCAL VANGUARD OPERATIVE. AMPHITRITE SAFE AND NOT COMPROMISED. NO SIGNIFICANT PROGRESS YET, BUT NO MAJOR SETBACKS. PROCEED AS PLANNED. UPDATE ON MISSING VESSEL NEEDED AS SOON AS YOU HAVE A BREAK.

Broughton signed off the site and was logging off the laptop when his hotel phone rang. It was Élisabeth Blauvelt, the enthusiastic head of the Port Authority's Administrative office, or Lilli, as she had asked to be called.

"Mr. Broughton!" she erupted with relief when he answered.

"Yes. This is he. Ms. Blauvelt?"

"Yes, it's Lilli. Thank goodness you're alright! I heard about the incident near your hotel on the radio in my office. For the last fifteen minutes or so it has been breaking news on all the TV channels as well. I'm glad you are safe. Amélie and I were worried about you. We knew you should have been arriving at your hotel about the time of the incident and we thought you might have gotten caught up in it. Thank goodness you are safe."

"I'm fine, thank you. I arrived only a few minutes after the incident," Broughton replied. "It's very kind of you to be concerned about my safety and it's equally considerate of you to ring."

"No problem," the woman replied. "It looks as if this is your lucky day!" she added, barely controlling her excited state.

"What do you mean?"

"You are safe and sound and I have some news for you. Good news, I should add. After you left, Amélie and I decided to carry on working on your query about vessels sailing from Antwerp directly to West African ports, or to West Africa from other European or Mediterranean ports."

"Have you found the vessel?"

"Not exactly, but we managed to considerably shorten the lists we started with. From the first list, we were able to identify three vessels sailing directly to West Africa and from the second, five sailing to West Africa after calling at European ports. All of the ones we identified called at Antwerp, of course, and are scheduled to spend only a short stay in port in West Africa. I hope this is of some help to you. I can pass the vessels' names to you now if you like."

Broughton paused for a beat. He heard several clicks on the line. They were barely audible, but he recognized what they were. Either his hotel phone or the phone at the Port Authority's Administrative office had been tapped.

"I have a better idea," he offered genially. "Have you and Amélie eaten dinner yet?"

"No, we haven't. Are you inviting the two of us to join you?"

"Yes, if you are free and interested."

"But what about all the work you have to finish this evening?" the woman asked, puzzled.

"Under the circumstances, it can wait," said Broughton.

"Hold on a moment," the woman replied. "I'll ask Amélie if she is free. I am almost certain she will decline, as she will want to go straight home. But I'll ask her, anyway."

The phone went muffled for several minutes, but he could still make out Élisabeth Blauvelt's voice. She seemed to be encouraging the young woman to call it quits and go home after their long day at work. After some back-and-forth between the two of them, she returned.

"Sorry to keep you waiting. But just as I suspected, Amélie said she can't make it this evening. She has a new fellow and they've been spending nearly all of their evenings together. New love," she added coyly. "She did say that she would be happy to have dinner another time, perhaps during your next visit."

"I see," Broughton replied. "In that case, tell her I would be happy to do that. How about you? Are you free this evening, or do you have somewhere you need to be as well? I know I said we would have dinner or a drink the next time I was in town, but I think we can move our dinner date forward on the calendar."

The woman responded nervously. "Yes... I mean no," she replied, fumbling for the right words. "I mean no, I don't have anywhere else to be. I have a cat at home, but I'm sure he won't mind if I'm a bit late getting home."

"Is that a yes?" Broughton teased.

"It's a definite yes! I would be delighted to have dinner with you. It'll make a nice change. Shall I meet you at your hotel?"

Broughton was tempted by the offer. As shy and naïve as she was, he still could not help noticing that she was signaling a strong desire to be with him. She was attractive, sensible and clearly had not had anyone special in her life for some time. She was lonely and he could see that his visit had created a spark of excitement in her life, if only a passing one. But he knew there was a possible risk of her growing attached too quickly. Her suggestion to meet him suddenly reminded him that he couldn't drive the Saab or allow it to be seen with its windshield and side window shattered.

"Actually, I think it would be better if you stayed where you are. I'll come by taxi and pick you up. This way, we can both have a few drinks. I'll see you in about an hour, if that's alright."

"An hour will be fine. But a taxi here and back to your hotel will be very expensive," she warned.

"No problem," he said, laughing. "I have an expense account."

Her comment about the taxi fare was another reminder that he needed to arrange for the Saab's windshield and side glass to be repaired quickly; the repairs needed to be done by mid-morning the next day.

After hanging up, he scoured the internet in search of an auto glass repair company that made call-outs. As luck would have it, he found two, one of them less than fifteen minutes from his hotel. He rang the company, left his details and arranged for the repairs to be carried out in the parking lot where the car sat at 9:00 o'clock the next morning.

Chapter Thirty-Seven

It had just gone 8:00 p.m. when the taxi turned into the North Port's main parking lot and pulled up in front of the entrance to the main building. Rather than phoning and waiting in the taxi, Broughton decided to go inside. He figured Élisabeth Blauvelt would be expecting him to come up to her office, so he asked the driver to wait while he went in and got her. On his way into the building, a tall and very fit security guard going off duty brushed past him in a hurry and nearly spun him around. The man did not apologize, which was unusual. He was still in his uniform and didn't even look up from under the cap that shielded his face. Because the man's build suggested he was fairly young, Broughton attributed his rudeness to the likelihood that he might have been rushing off to an arranged meeting or for a date.

Inside the building, the lobby was almost empty; the receptionist's desk was unoccupied. The bespectacled, courteous young woman who had sat there earlier in the day had departed with the rest of the building's regular daytime work force. The guard on duty at the security desk, a man much older than the acne-face, cocky young man he had encountered earlier in the day, had been expecting him. Élisabeth Blauvelt had rung earlier and left instructions at the security desk to send him up as soon as he arrived. Broughton showed the security guard his passport and the man decided there was no need for an escort, as the remainder of the building, except for the Operations Center and the Administrator's office, was dark and all doors to important offices had been locked and required a coded identification badge to gain access. The man sent Broughton straight to the elevators. "I believe you know your way to the Administration Office. It's on the fourth floor," he yelled across the lobby and returned to his auto racing magazine.

Broughton stepped into the elevator and pressed the button for the fourth floor. When it stopped, he got off and headed down the dimly lit corridor. Ahead of him and to his right, light spilled through the frosted glass of the Administrative Office's door and from along its edges where it had been left slightly ajar. He approached and knocked gently. When no one replied, he called to Élisabeth Blauvelt and entered. "Ms. Blauvelt! Ms. Blauvelt! Lilli! It's Tom Broughton! Where are you? Are you ready?"

The room was long and had an open layout with a couple of smaller offices to one side. At the far end of the room there were two poorly lit work areas partitioned by modular walls. From his visit earlier in the day, he remembered there were printers, filing cabinets and computer terminals in the area. He thought she might be there doing some last minute tasks. As he approached the work area, he called to her again, jokingly.

"Lilli? I hope you're ready for a big meal because I'm starved! Do you think you can tear yourself away from work long enough for a few drinks and some food? We can eat wherever you like!"

The office was eerily quiet. He approached the modular structure and stuck his head around it, only to find her in the far corner, slumped over the desk near a computer. A large, garnet pool of blood lay beneath her chair. He checked her wrist for a pulse. She was dead. He lifted her head to find that her throat had been cut. Her body was still warm; from the look of the scene, her attacker had come up from behind her. He had taken her by surprise, but she had struggled. There was skin and blood under her fingernails. *She had lost, but she had put up a damn good fight*, he thought, feeling a pang of regret and remorse for the part he had played in bringing this sweet woman's life to such a sudden, violent end. Her cat would go hungry tonight.

Then he suddenly remembered the security guard who had left the building in a hurry. *Why did he leave in such a hurry and why was he still wearing his uniform when every other security guard in Antwerp, including the ones at my hotel, seemed to be embarrassed about traveling to and from work dressed as rent-a-cops? Why was he wearing his cap and why didn't he look up and apologize after nearly colliding with me? Damn it! The son of a bitch had just killed her! That's why he was in such a hurry. That's why someone had been listening on the phone when she called the hotel.*

Élisabeth Blauvelt's handbag lay on the floor beneath the work table. It was open; a few of its contents were scattered about the floor, as one might expect. It had clearly been plundered. But the fact that most of its contents were still inside suggested that the killer had had little or no difficulty finding what he was looking for—the list of vessels Élisabeth Blauvelt was preparing to hand over to him. Being the thorough, organized employee she was, she had no doubt prepared the list on Port Authority letterhead and placed it in an envelope marked: URGENT and CONFIDENTIAL, Deliver by Hand to Mr. Thomas Broughton.

Broughton noticed that the woman had not had time to log off the computer before she was attacked. He was in luck. An intermittent flashing light on the network drive indicated access to the Port Authority's server was still open. There was a good chance the computer's screen lock was also not activated. To avoid suspicion of the woman's death falling on him, he needed to report the murder straight away, but if he did, he would lose valuable seconds and minutes and any chance there was to get his hands on the list she had prepared. He knew that once the police arrived, nothing would be released to anyone and Vanguard needed the list straight away.

Working quickly and carefully, he wheeled her chair slightly to one side, took out a pair of latex gloves and went to work. A single stroke on the keyboard's space bar brought the screen back to life and just one mouse click on the back arrow opened the previous screen and brought up the document she had been viewing when she was attacked. He was in luck. The names of all eight ships were still on the screen. The vessels' names were arranged in two columns—three in the first column, identifying vessels sailing directly to West Africa from Antwerp, and five in the second column, identifying sailings to West Africa from Antwerp via European ports. In haste, her killer had failed to delete the list from the file.

Broughton couldn't risk printing the list because a forensic examination of the computer files she had been working on would show that printing had occurred after her death. It would incriminate him for sure; such a result was unthinkable. He decided to take the names down by hand and if asked, he would explain the absence of a screen lock by telling the police that he probably struck the keyboard when he moved the body to see if the woman was still alive and needed first aid.

After taking down the names of the vessels, Broughton rang the security guard and asked him to call the police and come directly to the Administration Office. Within fifteen minutes, the police had arrived. They took a statement from him and he told them about the suspicious guard. As it turned out, the man was a last minute replacement for a guard who failed to turn up for his mid-day shift. He would have trouble clearing the woman's death from his head. *The killer must have been Ilaivo. The assassination bore all the signs of his work. But why would he have taken such a personal risk if the stakes weren't extremely high?*

Chapter Thirty-Eight

After returning to his hotel room, Broughton studied the list for the first time since leaving the Port Authority. The names he had scribbled hurriedly on the scrap of paper read like a 'who's who' in the murky world of suspicious vessels. It was no surprise to find that all were medium-size bulk cargo ships, already known or suspected of involvement in trafficking illicit arms, people, drugs and other contraband that found its way from places far from African ports and into conflict zones on the African continent. Many times they had also moved drugs and illegal migrants from Africa into Europe. Nearly all eight of the vessels on the list had started out transporting grain, ore or cement, but a decline in the movement of container vessels to Africa had created a transport bonanza for the owners of the vessels. They had stepped in and taken advantage of a growing demand for new and used luxury cars and 4x4s from a growing number of affluent Africans. The number of Africans willing to spend lavishly on luxury vehicles and to pay the exorbitant tariffs levied on them by governments, in order to show off their wealth, was growing at an absurd rate. Most were willing to forego cheaper and safer, although slower, delivery by container vessels. This meant there was always a large supply of new and used luxury vehicles at Antwerp or Rotterdam to fill out a vessel's load.

After studying the list, Broughton contacted VOCALS, as instructed, and sent in the names. Within minutes, VOCALS ran the names of the vessels against those in its data base. Three ships stood out on account of their frequent involvement in nefarious activities. These were the *Northern Celeste*, the *Louis Brevard* and the *Montserrat Star*. The *Northern Celeste* had sailed from Antwerp a week earlier and was ending a seventy-two hour port call in Genova, Italy, and was scheduled to sail to Freetown, Sierra Leone, on the West African coast. The *Northern Celeste* was followed out of Antwerp two days later by *Louis Brevard;* the *Montserrat Star* left a day after the *Louis Brevard*. Both ships were headed for the West African port city of Cotonou, Benin. Of the eight vessels profiled by Antwerp's Port Authority, only the *Northern Celeste*, the *Louis Brevard* and the *Montserrat Star* made frequent visits to Port Bushehr in Iran and the Port of Pusan in North Korea.

Broughton was beginning to feel that the odds were improving. There was now at least a one-in-three chance of identifying the vessel that would be involved in any activity that might be connected with the Chameleon and whatever plans that had been made for tons of stolen yellowcake. With the list of vessels narrowed down from dozens to eight, and now three, Vanguard could easily use its satellites to track the three vessels and the remaining six ships on the list. From now on, they could keep close tabs on their whereabouts.

Chapter Thirty-Nine

Arlit, Niger

About thirty minutes after Caroline returned to the La Rochelle, Moussa rang and asked to meet in the lobby. Before going downstairs, she decided to change her clothes. She had been too preoccupied with everything that had happened to notice the reddish dust that nearly covered her from head to toe. It also suddenly dawned on her that she had been dressed inappropriately for what had transpired. When she got dressed earlier, her intention was to tantalize and soften up the Frenchman by giving him the impression there might be other possibilities—possibilities beyond her contact with him to gather information.

She slipped out of the shift dress she was wearing and exchanged it for a pair of dark brown trousers and a gold, short-sleeve, silk top. She thrashed the dust off the cashmere cardigan, the only sweater she had brought with her, slipped it over her shoulders and went downstairs to wait for Moussa. She was still running on the adrenalin rush that had kicked in during the failed ambush. Despite being shaken up and confused, what had happened in Arlit's dark, dusty streets did not frighten her. Instead, it had steeled her nerves. The sudden turn of events and the close brush with death was proof that the situation was more fluid than even Niles Thornton had imagined it might be. The plot was thickening at a breakneck pace; for all her efforts, only a few leads had surfaced. To make matters worse, the number of players was growing exponentially. It was getting difficult to figure out who was in it to help and who had clambered onboard to make a fast buck.

Thornton knew the Papillon had gathered enough information to play both sides, but he had had no choice but to trust him. After all, a few years earlier he had been a fellow operative—a respected player of the game and a member of France's General Directorate for External Security or DGSE, who was still in good standing with the service. Thornton also knew the Frenchman personally and had used him and his informal North African network extensively. He had once even praised the Frenchman, declaring that his network had helped Vanguard pull off several of its most successful North African operations. Although the Frenchman had become a reliable asset, his services were not cheap. Rumor floated among Vanguard operatives that he was once paid more than a million dollars for services rendered in an operation against drug-smuggling terrorists.

Caroline wondered now why she had overlooked what was obvious from the outset. There had been signs—unmistakably, identifiable markers—statements the Frenchman had made which suggested that what unfolded in the dark streets of Arlit might occur. She knew that money was always a strong motivator for lies and deceit; it was clearly what was driving the Frenchman. He had told her as much and had called her naïve for thinking the game was about anything else. With the benefit of hindsight, she could see that his decision to play his hand as early as he did, showed that he had not been involved in the operation long enough to know that the Chameleon was calling the shots in whatever plan they were up against. If he had, he would have found out what the Chameleon's role was before he made his move. All operatives who had controlled or run intelligence operations during the last three decades knew the Bulgarian's reputation for extreme, terminal violence; if the

Papillon had known about the Chameleon's involvement, he probably would have been more cautious. But, like everyone else, he either did not have enough time to figure it out, or was unable to find all the pieces to put the puzzle together. But regardless of what he knew and did or did not do, there was little doubt that he had disposed of his informant because the man knew a great deal about what had been happening. The temptation to move in and wrest control of a nascent but lucrative deal between amateurs and highly trained professionals was irresistible. The prospect of unprecedented wealth had blinded the Frenchman to reality and he had let his own greed cloud his judgment—cancelling out years of training and experience.

After understanding what the Frenchman must have discovered, getting rid of the his informant after he found out about Sa'id al-Bashir's contact with the Iranians and North Koreans made sense, especially if he was planning to hijack the deal. The Papillon was a master of the game—a shrewd operative—a man who had even earned Niles Thornton's praise. He not only knew how to play the game, but when to play it. He must have figured that if he got it right this time, a deal with either side would be worth millions of dollars. It could have been his last operation, a final throw of the dice, and he had been ready to take the gamble. For the Papillon, it would have made sense to eliminate anyone who interfered with his plan, even a friendly operative if the operative was in a position to expose him. Caroline knew that if the Papillon's plan had worked, he could have killed her and blamed it on some unseen or unknown enemy and then played the game to its conclusion, even if he didn't know where the stolen yellowcake was hidden. It was clear that the North Koreans and the Iranians were the only people he had been interested in getting to know; he probably figured he could offer either or both of them a deal and stall them until he could find the hidden material.

As she waited in the small, claustrophobic lobby, other

thoughts crowed her head—more disturbing thoughts—problems with the operation that had created worries, far more than there should have been. The first challenge was how to find out whether or not the Frenchman learned from his informant everything Sa'id al-Bashir had been up to, and if he did, did it include what had been done with several tons of yellowcake? With the Frenchman and his contact dead, there was no way to know for sure. Perhaps he had known, but was only prepared to reveal it when the time was right, and for the right price. The location of the yellowcake was now the most critical missing piece of the puzzle.

A less critical, but more immediate concern, however, was the troubling feeling that she was losing the plot—that control of her part of the operation was slipping away from her. There seemed to be no way to keep up with events, especially with friends changing sides or spontaneously deciding to go out on their own. Added to this, and making matters worse, neither Broughton nor Thornton had mentioned Moussa's role as a minder. She was grateful that he had been there when she needed him, but from now on she wanted to know exactly who she could trust and count on and under what circumstances.

Chapter Forty

Caroline was still turning over a growing list of problems in her head when Moussa came into the guest house's lobby. He had changed clothes, which made sense because the ones he had been wearing were blood-spattered. He strode toward her with an air of confidence. The subservient chauffeur's demeanor had vanished; he was composed. He was a professional—someone who was well-trained and knew what needed to be done and was ready to do it when the time came. She could see that in addition to his new outfit, he had a strange look on his face— one that was markedly different from any she had previously seen. As he drew closer, she could see that he was sheepish about something.

"Good evening, *mademoiselle*," he said when he reached her. "I have taken care of everything," he said calmly. "The matter is resolved, but I must admit that I am embarrassed."

"Why so?" she asked sarcastically, behind daggered eyes.

"I am embarrassed about my actions. I did not mean to shout at you the way I did this evening, even though it was for your own good. I want to say how sorry I am and tell you that I offer you my deepest apology and hope you will forgive me. I also want to apologize for deceiving you and betraying your trust."

"In what way?" she asked, this time perplexed and genuinely concerned. "Were you acting on your own or were you following instructions?"

"I was following instructions," he replied.

"I see…" She paused.

"May I sit down?" he asked.

"Please do. But before you continue, I want… no, I *need* to know something. What happened this evening?" she asked, lowering her voice and trying to rein in her anger. "I don't mean the Frenchman's double-cross!" she added, to make sure he understood. "I mean what you did! Why did you do what you did and what are you supposed to do from now on?"

Moussa hesitated. "I understand your anger. You feel you were kept in the dark. I too would be angry, but the decision for me to serve as your chauffeur was not mine. Someone… one of your superiors, decided I should keep an eye on you. I was given no details. I was just told to 'look out for you', 'watch your back', as you Americans say. You should know that some time ago I too worked as an intelligence operative and I learned that the men in charge never sent an operative to do an important job unless they totally trusted that operative and felt he was fully capable. My understanding of this helps me understand you and the anger you now feel. You see, in the circles we move in, there is a common understanding that if an organization is forced to send an operative on an important mission and that operative is not fully capable, it will provide the best counterintelligence it can offer. Some see keeping an eye on an operative who probably will not produce the desired results as a waste of resources. They also believe such a situation increases the chances for failure, as well as danger to both operatives, because one or even both could be discovered and eliminated."

"That's precisely what I have been thinking! But tell me… Don't they trust me? And why did you know more about the Frenchman than I did? You knew he was up to no good! How did you know? You also knew about the double-cross. Were you planning to eliminate the Frenchman and take his place? Are you part of some plan to stop this operation or are you trying to help it succeed? Which is it? I'm not sure if you are aware of this, but until this evening, my superiors were convinced that the Frenchman was a trusted asset."

"This I cannot and will not dispute, and I will not try. But I believe your controllers knew there were risks. However, I am curious to know what the Frenchman told you about the fate of his informant, a man called Hassan," Moussa retorted. "Did he tell you that this man Hassan traveled to Niamey to visit his family and disappeared shortly after arriving there?"

"Yes, he did, but who told you?"

"The Frenchman lied, as it was thought he might do!"

"Who thought he would lie?" she demanded, raising her voice slightly, getting angrier by the second. She had been made to feel like a fool, and such a thing was alien to her nature.

"I will come to that in a minute, but first you should know that Hassan knew quite a lot about the missing yellowcake, probably except where it is hidden. Nearly two years ago, the man whose trail you follow enlisted the help of two local men from the town of Iferouane to help him with his thievery. It seems that this man carted the stuff off into the desert, perhaps with these helpers or with different ones. But what is troubling is that when the services of his two helpers from Iferouane were no longer needed, which was a few days before he disappeared, he lured them into the desert, somewhere to the northeast of Iferouane, and killed them. At least that's what he thought he had done. Miraculously one of them, a man named Salim Fa'izu Daoud, did not die right away. He clung to life for a few days. Salim Fa'izu Daoud was a friend of the Frenchman's informant. The Frenchman did not know this, at least not until a few days later. He also did not know that the day after this man Sa'id al-Bashir carried out his ruthless assault on the two men, Hassan left Arlit to visit relatives in Niamey, or so he told the Frenchman. But instead of going to Niamey, he went to Iferouane to look after his friend. He remained there for three days, leaving only after the man died."

Moussa paused and continued. "The Frenchman found out

about the relationship between Hassan and Daoud; somewhere along the way he learned that Daoud had shared what he knew with Hassan. The rest is not difficult to figure out. When the Frenchman put the squeeze on Hassan, Hassan cracked. But after being forced to confess, he foolishly thought he could get something out of the deal—he probably thought he was entitled to a share of any future proceeds, which was a dangerous idea. He threatened to expose the Frenchman to the national police or the *gendarmerie*. Hassan was convinced his knowledge and the Frenchman's cunning and connections could make him a rich man, too. The Frenchman did not see it that way. I am convinced that Hassan confessed a great deal to the Frenchman, but I doubt if he told him where the yellowcake is hidden, at least not its true location. Nevertheless, it appears the Frenchman was quite satisfied he had squeezed everything out of Hassan before he killed him. But by the look of things, he may have eliminated his man too soon."

"How do you know all this, and how long have you known it?"

"I was given this information this evening, only minutes after I left you."

"I see… But how?" she asked. "Who told you and who instructed you to do what you did?"

"I received word anonymously. It came from someone in Ahrli and was passed to me by a contact of mine in Arlit. As soon as I received it, I passed it to Vanguard and was given strict instructions. Your controllers felt there was no time to warn you about the trap you were walking into and they apparently did not want to risk making contact with you during the meeting, as it would have aroused the Frenchman's suspicion. It looks as if they had no other choice but to play along with him. They instructed me to keep a close eye on you and take whatever action necessary to prevent your assassination and any endangerment of the operation. The rest you know."

"I understand now. You were simply looking out for me as

you had been instructed to do." She paused. "Moussa, I am lucky and grateful that you acted when you did and I owe you my life. But I still don't understand why they assigned me a minder?"

"My English is not so good, *mademoiselle*, but I will try my best to explain. I do not know what you think I was suggesting when I said that an organization must trust and be confident in its operatives' abilities, but what I was trying to say is that being chosen to do this job is the greatest demonstration of trust in you your superiors could possibly show. It is a heavy responsibility—a responsibility that no one man or woman can accomplish alone. That is why I was assigned to assist you and assist you I will, even if it means giving my life. *Mademoiselle*, I wish for us to speak no more of this. I don't know all the details, but I can see from the sense of urgency and risks your superiors are taking, that what you are doing is more important than either of us and that time is precious. We must travel in the morning to Akokan, Arhli and Iferouane. I am confident we will learn more when we get there. But for now, we must both try to get some rest."

Tired though she was, Caroline lay awake for quite a while, unable to switch off, her mind buzzing with questions and alternatives. But when she let her thoughts drift to her son, she relaxed at last. Her last waking thought was: *Whatever the outcome of this business, I have to stay alive—for Nicolas.*

Chapter Forty-One

The trip from Arlit to the town of Akokan to visit a clean water project was a convincing decoy, but the two-hour drive back through Arlit to Arhli and Iferouane had cost valuable time— time they didn't have. Nevertheless, it had to be done to avoid suspicion about their movements. After the incident in Arlit, Moussa's demeanor had changed. Despite his explanation, which should have put matters straight between them, he had fallen silent and was more contemplative than before. He had spoken only a few times since they left the guest house. He drove along the road to Akokan, eyes fixed forward as if he were wearing blinkers. He was miles away and Caroline knew he would not be the one to lift the curtain of silence that had fallen between them. She was sure that he knew little else about the operation, which put him in an even more awkward position, but he was a fast learner. The situation was far too grave for the coldness between them to continue, and it was clear that he was not accustomed to a woman being in a position that relegated him to one of subordinate. She was worried that the events of the evening before had exposed the cultural divide between them and with it, his disdain and lack of confidence in her.

"You are a very brave and unselfish man," she offered graciously. "Anyone can see that. Your loyalty is unquestionable and your commitment unrivaled. I have given a lot of thought to what you said last night and it makes a great deal of sense to me. I want you to know and believe that I am pleased to be working with you. So if you don't speak to me, I am going to think you no longer like me. Moussa, I don't know what lies ahead, but I do know that without your help last night I wouldn't have made it on my own and I wouldn't be here now. I also know that I won't be able to do what I have to do today or tomorrow without your help. You are an important part of this, but I'm sure you already know that. So, I need to know if you still 'have my back'?" she asked, smiling.

Moussa managed a slight smile in return. "Of course! We are a team, are we not? You are a wise young woman, wise beyond your years. I can honestly say that I am proud to be able to support you. I don't know much about this mission, but I can see that it is an important one and I will play whatever part I am called on to play, no matter how big or how small it may be. I am at your service."

"That sounds more like the Moussa who met me at the airport!"

"Believe it or not, he never left your side. He has been here all along."

She could feel the iciness between them melting. *Maybe he was right. Maybe it had been normal all along and it was all in my head. Maybe I let the feeling of losing control and his intervention interrupt my focus. After all, it was his strong, but humble character that put things back in perspective.* His loyalty and humility did help remind her that what she needed to do was more important than any one person; it made her realize that whatever made her lose focus the day before couldn't be allowed to happen again.

"What should we expect to find in Iferouane?" she asked, changing the subject. "Is there something or someone there who can tie Hassan, the Frenchman's informant, al-Bashir and his co-conspirators to the yellowcake?"

"I am not sure, but I believe there is, and I am hoping that I am right. Iferouane is the one place all three of these men appear to have had in common, but it was from Ahrli that I received the information about the Frenchman. If we can learn why these three men came to trust and rely on each other, we may learn more about what happened in the months before they were murdered and what caused the trust between them to break down. Remember, al-Bashir set out to kill them in cold blood and I believe that before he did, they feared and grew suspicious of him. They may have suspected that one day he would double-cross them and for that reason they may have communicated this to someone. It is too bad they did not know where or when Sa'id al-Bashir would make his move."

"You're probably right. If the one he shot and left for dead was taken to the village and the Frenchman's informant went there to take care of him, someone else in the village may also know something. But if they know what happened to these men, won't they be afraid to talk?"

"They probably will."

"It seems unlikely that the Frenchman's informant was the only friend Salim Fa'izu Daoud had in Iferouane. His friend Hassan would almost certainly have had help in taking care of him. Besides, where did they take Daoud for medical attention? After all, shooting victims don't turn up in a place like Iferouane every day. It would have been difficult to keep it a secret. Do you think we can find whoever else may have helped look after Daoud?"

"I think we can, but you must leave this to me. I am an outsider, a stranger like you, but unlike you, I am a stranger these villagers are more likely to trust. You, too, are an outsider, but you are a foreigner. And... no offense... you arc a woman, which makes it almost impossible for you to approach them and make inquiries. The chances of anyone in the village talking to you about this are about as good as finding a camel skating on a frozen oasis in the middle of the desert," he added, grinning.

"Thanks for the vote of confidence! Go ahead... throw some more salt into my wounds," she said, smiling. "I can see that

I'm going to be very useful here!" she added jokingly.

"You are helpful! But don't forget, you are the rich Westerner who is assessing the village for possible irrigation and agricultural projects. Not only do you have money and influence, you also have the ability to bring employment to the village and I suspect every man, woman and child living there will turn up to see you. These people may be isolated, but they are nonetheless practical. This is about opportunity; for this reason, they will overlook the fact that you are a woman. They will be hoping that your meetings with government big shots and village elders will bring them a better way of life."

"To make sure they're not disappointed, I'll see that the Foundation follows through quickly with the wells, irrigation and agricultural projects and that a feasibility study is also done to see if a water purification and bottling plant can be set up and operated efficiently in Akokan. Regardless of why we are really here, these people deserve a helping hand and the Foundation is genuine in its efforts to assist them in these matters."

Chapter Forty-Two

The Mitsubishi 4x4 rolled into Arhli just before noon. Activity in the town's center was almost non-existent. A taxi, heading south along the national road, crammed with passengers and its roof rack piled high with bundles of market items, met them as they entered town. At the side of the road, a wiry, elderly man with a long grey beard walked alongside a donkey, swatting the emaciated beast intermittently as it struggled to maintain forward momentum under a three-foot-high pile of rugs. A few middle-aged men were perched on makeshift stools under the portico of the town's tea house, playing the board game *owari* and smoking *hookas* filled with aromatic *shisha*. The town's only gas station, a one-pump serve-all, offering auto repairs, tires, fan belts and locally made mufflers, stood unattended, barren of trade.

Entering the town, they sensed a strong presence of community—that belonging, unity and identity transcended Arhli and stretched beyond. This meant that even people from surrounding villages and towns probably knew about the deaths of the two men. But it was reasonable to assume that the amount of detail they knew about the circumstances was in all likelihood where reality started and ended. Each would have a theory or a version of events and each would no doubt declare that his or hers was the undisputed truth.

The ancestral home of Salim Fa'izu Daoud lay at the far end of the town, but they would not stop there. They would continue on to Iferouane, where the man had lived until the time of his death, to gather information. They, or rather Moussa, would visit his family home in the late afternoon when they passed on the way back to Arlit. In Iferouane, she would hold meetings with dignitaries and tribal elders to talk about the health and economic benefits new wells, a water purification plant, an irrigation system and an agricultural project could bring for Arhli and Iferouane. Moussa would move about the town asking questions, while searching for the home of Salim Fa'izu Daoud.

Chapter Forty-Three

Iferouane
Northeastern Niger

After leaving Arhli, Moussa swung the Mitsubishi 4x4 back onto the main road and headed northeast toward Iferouane. Before leaving Arlit, Caroline telephoned the mayor of Iferouane and a village elder to confirm her arrival. A day earlier, the Foundation had rung the provincial governor in Agadez, Abdullah Hafez, and notified him of her impending arrival. The governor promised he would be there when Caroline arrived.

Abdullah Hafez was a man who attached great importance to his post as provincial governor and had therefore elected to travel to Iferouane by plane, arriving at an airfield southwest of the town. Abdullah Hafez did not take well to long or arduous journeys; also, being a security-conscious man, he had his security detail deploy to Iferouane by road a day earlier so it could pick him up when he arrived at the airport.

As Caroline and Moussa approached Iferouane, they were greeted by a breathtaking view. In the distance, the Aïr Mountains rose from the desert floor against the sky like huge tents, throwing up a picturesque backdrop for the town. Visitors frequently referred to Iferouane as an oasis town, but its location, nestled in the Ighazar Valley, begged the question of how it had earned that title. Despite offering a captivating view of the Aïr Mountains, Iferouane was a dusty, wind-swept place with less than 600 inhabitants.

The journey from Arhli had been quick, taking just over an hour; Caroline and Moussa knew that if the roads remained empty on the way back, they could make a quick visit and an equally quick return to Arhli. The sites chosen by the Foundation for the wells and irrigation project lay on the outskirt of Iferouane, just to the east. To their surprise, they found Iferouane's transportation infrastructure to be in quite good condition. The roads were fairly good and while traveling north from Arlit, they had passed the airfield used by the governor. The airfield was no more than a speck on the vast desert landscape and oddly, its presence was marked by a single signpost, written in Hausa and French and located just at the turn-off to the entrance road. Driving past the airfield, they had seen a small, three-story building, presumably the control tower, from the main road. Like most of the country's infrastructure, the airstrip had been built to support or move French soldiers, military equipment, foreign workers, mining equipment and supplies in and out of the area and to protect and extract resources. At the height of mining activity in Arlit, personnel, supplies, spare parts and equipment flew in almost daily in order to keep the uranium mines and a large portion of some 83,000 inhabitants comfortable and working.

As Caroline and Moussa entered Iferouane, they discovered a town bustling with life. A lively, festive mood seemed to grip the entire place. Even the animals were moving about excitedly. There were goats as well as a few camels on hand; even dogs, which are generally not favored as pets, moved through the center of town. The sight of several whippets roaming about freely, with no masters in sight, was particularly puzzling.

As the Mitsubishi slowed and crept toward the center of town, a swarm of villagers descended on it. It seemed that all the women in the town had turned out—each dressed in a beautiful costume and colorful beads adorning her neck. As the vehicle rolled past the women, they broke into a tongue-fluttering, celebratory wail. Caroline's visit had clearly stirred attention not experienced since the outbreak of the second ethnic *Tuareg* rebellion against the country's government.

When the Mitsubishi came to a stop, Caroline clambered down and waded through the villagers, who had by now formed an unofficial welcoming committee. She cut her way through the crowd toward the front of the town hall where Governor Abdullah Hafez stood waiting. A small group of wailing women followed. The mayor and tribal elders formed a line across the hall's entrance. Everyone exchanged greetings and the group, including the governor, his entourage, the mayor, his cronies and tribal elders, moved inside for a formal welcome ceremony and refreshments. To Caroline's disappointment, her hosts were long on ceremony; after nearly two hours of welcome speeches, praise singing and well-wishing, the ceremony finally ended. The governor made a bee-line for Caroline, isolated her from his subordinates and insisted that she ride to the proposed project sites with him in his official car.

"Let me say again, *Mademoiselle* Dupré… welcome! We are very pleased that the Ashmore Foundation chose to come to our country," the governor said, beaming. "I am also pleased that the Foundation selected the Iferouane-Arhli area for these projects. They are a blessing and will bring prosperity to the people of the two communities, and maybe many more beyond the immediate area. As you can see, we are a poor people, but we are proud and generous. What is ours is yours."

"Thank you very much, your Excellency," Caroline replied. "I, too, am hopeful that we can proceed with the projects. But first we must determine the area's suitability. There are geological and other surveys to be conducted to assess the water table and the project will require lots of equipment, which will have to be brought in. We will also have to develop local expertise in irrigation and agriculture, if the projects are to succeed and have long-term benefits. As you have no doubt seen, in other places around the world with similar climate conditions, irrigating the desert and making it ready for food production is a highly complex endeavor. We must therefore look at this as a beginning."

Carolina and her host climbed into his 4x4. "You are quite right," the Governor replied, wryly. "And I agree with you one hundred percent," he added, trying to keep the tone of the discussion positive for all within earshot. "Shall we go to the sites in question?" he asked, placing his hand over the front seat and patting his driver's shoulder. "I understand that you are on a very tight schedule and I and the people of Arhli and Iferouane are eager for you to make your findings, deliver them to your headquarters in London and begin work."

Before the governor could finish his humble, but disingenuous diatribe, the lead security car, packed with armed bodyguards and flashing lights on, took off at high speed from the town hall. The governor's 4x4 did the same and the entire convoy catapulted itself toward the outskirts of Iferouane. Within minutes, the fifteen-car procession had reached the height of spectacle, as evidenced by a high rate of speed—a typical characteristic of official processions throughout much of the developing world.

Chapter Forty-Four

The governor's motorcade threw up a boiling cloud of dust as it left the edge of town and sped off into the desert. Moussa got to work as soon as the last vehicle trailed off. He left the town center hurriedly on foot, weaving his way through the maze of mud brick houses and a few white-washed, high-walled compounds. The high-walled compounds told him that he was entering the right part of town. They concealed the grander properties of politicians, senior bureaucrats, village elders, camel traders and prosperous entrepreneurs. Moving toward the east side of town, he soon reached the compound of the man named Salim Fa'izu Daoud—the brief survivor and sole beneficiary of Sa'id al-Bashir's carelessness. The compound was one of the newer and better maintained ones—a clear sign of new wealth, he observed.

Beside the gates, a man crouched near a small, open fire, making tea; beside him, a 12-gauge, single-shot, breech-loading shotgun rested against the wall. Upon seeing Moussa, the man sprang to his feet. Although he was startled by Moussa's sudden appearance at the gates of his master's home, he did not reach for the weapon. Moussa quickly realized that the man was a guard, one like so many others in the neighborhood employed by rich men to look after their families and the precious objects they had amassed, honestly and dishonestly. Moussa thought it ironic that the man Daoud had placed more importance on security for his personal possessions than he had placed on his own life.

"*Barka da yamma*," the guard said in his native Hausa language, as he rose to his feet.

"Good afternoon to you," Moussa replied in Hausa, also his native language. "Is this the home of Salim Fa'izu Daoud?"

"It is," the man replied suspiciously. "Who are you and what do you want?"

"My name is Moussa dan Gogo and I have come to speak to his widow. Is she at home?"

Through jaundiced eyes the man looked Moussa up and down. "Yes, she is, but this is not a good time!" he snapped. "She is still in mourning. Go away and come back in three months! What is your business with the widow, anyway? Did you not know she was grieving? Have you no respect for her and her family?" he scolded.

"I am looking for the man responsible for her husband's death. I am sure she will want to speak to me."

The guard paused. He looked as if he was thinking he may have overstepped his authority. After a minute or two, he told Moussa to wait. "Stay here! I will call one of the servants. He will carry your message to her. If she wishes to see you, you may enter."

The guard pulled the compound gate ajar and called to one of the servants. Seconds later a small, wiry, gray-bearded man arrived and took the message of Moussa's arrival to the compound's main house. Nearly ten minutes passed before the elderly man returned. When he did, he told the guard the widow wished to speak to Moussa.

Moussa was taken to a large reception room inside the main house. The room was almost dark, except for the splash of light that spilled in from an open door leading to what looked like a corridor. Heavy, velvet curtains were drawn together at all the windows. The widow was at the far side of the room, in a corner, reclining on a replica of a Louis XIV sofa. She was dressed in black, wearing an *abaya* and a *burka* that revealed only her eyes. A second woman, who appeared to be much older and dressed similarly, sat on a chair at the far side of the sparsely furnished room.

Moussa bowed from the waist and exchanged greetings with the widow of Salim Fa'izu Daoud, then apologized for his intrusion. "*Barka da yamma.* I am very sorry about your loss," he said. "I understand you are still mourning the death of your husband, so I will not take much of your time. I will be brief. I have come to see you because I am seeking the people responsible for his death."

The widow interrupted briefly to command the elderly woman on the far side of the room to bring tea for her visitor, then retreated into silence. Moussa resumed and she listened intently.

"I was told that before your husband died, a friend of his from Arlit, a man named Hassan whom he had grown up with in Ahrli, came to look after him and help attend his wounds. A few days later, however, Hassan was killed. I need to know if there was anyone else who may have attended or visited your husband in his final hours." Moussa paused, but there was only silence. He continued. "Madam, I beg you to consider this and to think carefully, as this is very important," he said. "Was there anyone else who spent time with your husband? I assure you no harm will come to you, your family or friends from your answers. So, if there is someone... another friend or business associate... you must tell me. Otherwise, the people responsible for his death will continue to lie, cheat, murder and who knows what other things and never be punished for any of it."

The widow looked on despondently as Moussa wound down his appeal. When he finished, an eerie silence fell over the room and lingered for several minutes. "His name was Agali," the woman said finally. "He is the other man who tried to keep Daoud alive. He would not leave him. The other one from Arlit you spoke of... Hassan. You say he is dead?"

"Yes, he is. Like your husband, he was murdered."

"Daoud had known Agali and Hassan since the three of

them were boys," the woman continued. "Agali always visited Daoud, but Hassan rarely came to see him. Agali was Daoud's best friend. He was always around… drinking tea and smoking *shisha* with Daoud. They were as thick as thieves… almost inseparable." She paused. "It was exactly the opposite with Hassan. When Hassan moved to Arlit, relations between him and Daoud seemed to grow cold. They still saw each other from time to time, but the friendship they had shared as young boys never returned. Even in the last few days of Daoud's life, they did not talk very much. I must say that I found it strange that Hassan seemed interested in talking to Daoud only when Agali was not in the room."

"You mean your husband did not initiate any of the conversations he had with Hassan? How and when did they speak, then?"

"As far as I can tell, he did not make conversation with Hassan. And when they did speak it seemed to make Daoud uncomfortable. Agali, on the other hand, except for times when he needed to attend to his personal needs, stayed at my husband's side until he drew his last breath. They talked a lot during those two days, but I am afraid that is all I can tell you."

"Thank you very much. You have given me much more than I expected and I am grateful for your generosity. I know it is difficult for you, but what you have given me will assist me greatly. I wish you and your family well."

The woman nodded in a show of acknowledgement. "One more thing," she said abruptly, causing Moussa to spin on his heels. "Daoud made Agali promise he would look after me and the children. He also asked him to take care of something he was unable to finish. Unfortunately, I never learned what this unfinished thing was, but Agali will know. He is an honest man. I am sure he will tell you."

Chapter Forty-Five

Algiers, Algeria

Abasi Abdel Mottaleb stepped forward from the line of waiting passengers and immediately began flirting with the three middle-aged Algerian women at the Air France check-in counter. They were clearly flattered. They could hardly believe their eyes. They even blushed and seemed to be struggling to contain their excitement. At nearly fifty, Abasi Abdel Mottaleb's muscular body, pharaoh-like looks, dazzling smile and his polished and almost perfectly enunciated Arabic had instantly won them over. After he had left the check-in counter for the departure lounge, the women debated furiously among themselves about which famous Egyptian film star he was.

As he walked away, Abasi Abdel Mottaleb smiled. His disguise had worked—he had caused a memorable stir among the women. *How little did the naïve know!* They had been completely wrong about him being a film star, but intuitively right about his acting talent. Abasi Abdel Mottaleb was no Egyptian film star and the name was one of several under which he performed as he moved about the world. Other names he had used included Gamal Ziedan and Ahmad Hamdan, but he was best known in intelligence circles as Farouk Hamdi—a name he had used for years. Lately though, he had become known for his association with the notorious Bulgarian, Alexandâr Ilaivo, aka the Chameleon.

Farouk Hamdi passed through security at Algiers' Houari Boumediene International Airport with ease and made his way to the departure lounge. There, he would anxiously wait to board the flight to Agadez, Niger. He was just over a day behind Caroline Dupré, but with each passing hour he grew hotter on her trail.

Chapter Forty-Six

Iferouane
Northeastern Niger

The high-speed, tight formation motorcade with the governor's 4x4 in the middle blew into town only minutes after Moussa slid behind the wheel of the Mitsubishi. When the governor's vehicle stopped in front of the town hall, Caroline did not get out. Moussa could see her and the governor's silhouettes through the vehicle's tinted windows. The governor was gesturing excitedly with his hands. The site visits had taken the entire afternoon and at times it seemed they would extend well into the evening. Governor Hafez was making a final pitch for the Foundation to move ahead with the projects. *The site visits must have gone well.*

After nearly ten minutes, the governor's gesticulations subsided; the driver got out of the vehicle, opened the rear door and Caroline clambered down.

Moussa pulled up alongside as if the transfer had been choreographed.

She bid Governor Hafez a final farewell and assured him she would start straight away on a feasibility study, and would dispatch engineers, irrigation experts, agronomists and other specialists to examine the sites she had been shown. When she climbed into the Mitsubishi, Moussa smiled.

"Governor Hafez is a very persuasive man it seems."

"He's persistent and determined, I'll give him that much!" said Caroline. "What did you find out?"

"We got lucky," Moussa replied. "There were two men who cared for Daoud. There was Hassan, who we already knew about, and Agali. According to Daoud's widow, Daoud, Hassan and Agali grew up together, but Daoud and Hassan were no longer close. Agali and Daoud, on the other hand, were life-long friends and Daoud evidently asked Agali to attend to some unfinished business."

"What kind of unfinished business?" Caroline asked.

"I don't know, but the widow was confident that Agali would tell us exactly what it is he was asked to finish."

"And what makes you so sure Agali will tell us?"

"He must surely know the danger associated with carrying around this information in his head. After all, it doesn't take a genius to see that this information killed his friends."

"Is there anything else?" she asked.

"Yes!" Moussa said, smiling. "Agali lives in Arlit. We can find him this evening, hopefully as soon as we return. The sooner we find him, the sooner we can leave this godforsaken place. It didn't take your friend the Frenchman long to put enough pieces of the puzzle together and I expect it won't take anyone else who's searching very long, either."

"You're right! The news about the Frenchman's demise must have the wires humming by now. It won't be long before others begin searching to see if they can collect the payday that eluded him. The sooner we find this Agali and get out of Niger, the better. Also, the longer we remain here, the more dangerous it's going to get!"

"My exact thoughts, *mademoiselle*."

Moussa and Caroline headed out of Iferouane. They turned first southwest toward the N25, then south toward Arhli and Arlit.

Dusk had nearly fallen; Moussa was hoping to arrive in Arlit before dark and in time to locate the slain man's friend, Agali.

Agali was the missing link—he was quite possibly the only person, other than Daoud, who had any knowledge of what Sa'id al-Bashir had been up to for nearly two years in the Sahara Desert.

Chapter Forty-Seven

Arlit, Niger

The sun was beginning to set when the Mitsubishi rolled into the north end of Arlit. A light haze hovered over the town. It would be dark soon. Both Caroline and Moussa were exhausted and anxious. The trip from Iferouane had taken them less than an hour; Caroline had had no time to contact Tom Broughton or VOCALS to notify them of the progress they had made. She knew that it was imperative that she make contact straight away.

But before they could make it to the guest house her wrist communicator started to vibrate. Using its bezel, she dialed in a six-number code. A message appeared and trailed across the small screen:

URGENT. CONTACT ZEUS AND VOCALS IMMEDIATELY.

The message scrolled across the screen twice, trailed off, then terminated.

"*Shit!*" she uttered under her breath, mindful not to offend Moussa. "We need to get to the guest house and we need to do it now!" After a beat, her wrist communicator vibrated again. It was another urgent message. This time from ZEUS.

I thought there was to be no direct contact. This must be serious.

STRONG POSSIBILITY YOU HAVE BEEN COMPROMISED! FAROUK HAMDI HEADED YOUR WAY. HE DEPARTED ALGIERS A.M. TODAY VIA AIR FRANCE TO AGADEZ. THREE MEMBERS OF HIS NORTH AFRICAN NETWORK ALREADY IN ARLIT. HAMDI NOT FAR BEHIND. USE ANY/ALL MEASURES TO EVADE.

"Moussa!" she shouted, looking worried. "Forget the guest house! We may have unwanted visitors waiting there. We've got to split up, but we also have to find Agali! I'll try to distract our visitors, while you find Agali. Drop me at the Côte Bleu. I'll be safe there. From there, I can see whoever and whatever is coming my way. I don't think they're stupid enough to move against me in a public place. Besides, they may not know about Agali yet, so you'll have to find him quickly. It probably was my arrival in Arlit that has them worried. They should be!" she added.

"Do you know how many of them there are?" Moussa asked, looking worried for the first time.

"So far there are three, but another one is on the way. Perhaps I'll get photos of them soon and will know who to expect. In the meantime, I'll keep an eye out for anyone who looks like he wants to kill me," she added, trying to inject humor into a dangerous situation. "Don't worry about me. I'll be alright. Just find Agali, debrief him and meet me at the Côte Bleu with whatever you learn! If there's a problem, use your wristwatch or the fountain pen, the ones that Vanguard contacted you on the other evening to warn you about the Frenchman. You can contact VOCALS, can't you?" she asked, half playfully.

"Yes! I should be able to do that using emergency procedures."

"Good then! I'll see you back here in about an hour," she added as she climbed down from the Mitsubishi.

Chapter Forty-Eight

Moussa turned the Mitsubishi around and headed back toward the La Rochelle guest house. But instead of turning down the road to the La Rochelle, he headed east, away from the section of Arlit inhabited by foreigners and toward the mud-brick dwellings of local residents. By now the sun had sunk well below the horizon. Dusk had descended and was rapidly giving way to darkness. The town's unlit eastern section was darker than the foreign inhabited section, which, despite its wealthy inhabitants, had only a spattering of street lights. Ahead of the Mitsubishi, hundreds of mud-brick dwellings lay scattered on either side of the narrow dirt road. In the distance, he could see a flickering light, just off to the right. As the 4x4 drew nearer, he could see that the light was spilling from a tea house—a small, mud-brick building with a tarpaulin flung over poles at the front as a kind of portico to shade *shisha* smokers and tea drinkers from the searing midday sun. Gradually, he could make out the figures of more than a dozen men perched on benches and homemade chairs under the tarpaulin.

He pulled the vehicle up on the side of the road, doused the headlights, climbed down and began walking toward the building. His ears were soon filled with the buzz of conversation and the occasional outburst of laughter. The men were joking and mocking each other, enjoying the end of a long day in the mines. When Moussa arrived in their midst, they fell silent.

"*Barka da yamma,*" he greeted them.

"*Barka da yamma,*" they replied, almost in unison.

"I am looking for a man named Agali. Do any of you know him?"

A moment later a tall, thin man stood up. "Who is it that seeks him?"

"It is I, Moussa dan Gogo. I seek him on behalf of Salim Fa'izu Daoud's widow. It is she who sent me."

"And why would a rich man like you be interested in the likes of a poor, run-down laborer? You have a fine vehicle and nice garments, and your pockets are probably full of money. Of what use would Agali be to you?"

"That's a good question. I bring a message for him from Daoud's widow. But first, my friend, I must disabuse you of your notions. I am not a rich man. Like you, I work hard every day. As for the vehicle, it is not mine. It belongs to my employer. I am here with a project manager to examine some development sites around the area."

The man fell silent. After standing motionless and quiet for about a minute, and with the eyes of the others fixed firmly upon him, he conceded. "I am Agali. It is me you seek. Come! We will walk and talk."

When they were a short distance from the tea house, Agali stopped. "I knew someone would come soon," he said. "I have been expecting you or someone like you, someone with lots of influence and a big, fancy car. You came to find out what Daoud told me, didn't you?"

Moussa nodded. "I knew as much," Agali said, seemingly relieved. "I am glad you came. The burden my friend cast upon me has been far too great to bear and too frightening to handle alone. But what is most troubling is what he asked me to do… Something I could not fathom."

"I understand your fear," said Moussa. "It's a very dangerous situation. Too many people have died because of the double-dealing and double-crossing that has happened already. But I hope that by telling me, we can put a stop to it and you will be safe. Maybe I can help you and your family move to Niamey.

That would of course be your decision to make."

Agali's eyes lit up. "Could you do this for me? Would you do it?"

"I will try, but I am almost certain I can. I give you my word. I will do my best. But you must trust and help me. Please believe that I am here to stop these evil things and trust me when I say that I will do everything in my power to see that you get safely away from this place as soon as possible."

"How soon can you do this?" Agali asked.

"I am hopeful that after a telephone call or two, arrangements could be made for you and your family to be in Niamey within forty-eight hours."

Agali became even more excited. "I am not sure why, but I feel I can trust you." He paused briefly. "A few months ago, Daoud's wife, Maha, sent a boy to Arlit to inform me that I needed to come to Iferouane right away. She did not say exactly why, only that it was urgent and that a most foul thing had happened. Naturally, I dropped everything and went there. Daoud was a boyhood friend of mine. He was my best friend. When I arrived in Iferouane I found him in a very bad way. He was seriously wounded. He had been shot several times in the chest and abdomen. He knew he would not last long. In fact it was a miracle that he managed to last as long as he did. Nearly four days he lingered. But he had always been a strong and determined man. Even after losing lots of blood, he managed to stumble and crawl nearly six kilometers from inside the desert to a dirt road, where he was found by a camel herder. The camel herder brought him to Iferouane." He paused again, this time to recover his composure. "For three days he lay barely conscious, knowing he was nearing death. On the fourth day, the day he died, he told me of a map—a map that marked a location in the desert that concealed 'buried treasure, bright yellow gold, a king's ransom' he said."

"Did he say where this buried treasure was?" Moussa asked, trying not to show impatience.

"No he didn't… Not exactly, but he did say the place was fifty miles southwest of Arlit."

"And what of this map he mentioned? Where is it now?"

"It was kept by the man Sa'id al-Bashir, the thief and liar for whom he toiled for nearly two years. Daoud said the treasure would soon be taken from its hiding place to the West African coast, where he believed it would be put on a boat to Persia or the Far East. By his own calculation and from what little he learned from al-Bashir, the treasure probably will be moved to the coast soon, possibly within the next day or two. I am afraid that is all I know. What bothers me is that this is more than Hassan knew and it cost him his life."

"Forgive me, my friend," Moussa said. "I know Hassan was your friend, but he was a greedy, selfish man who took risks and talked too much. He would have lied and cheated anyone. He could only see himself rising to the top; he would have stepped over and even on all of you to get there. He may have even killed to get his hands on the treasure Daoud described."

"Perhaps you are right," Agali said, pausing once more. "There is one other thing…" he added hesitantly. "Daoud was deeply sorry and repentant for his collusion with Sa'id al-Bashir and he wanted forgiveness for his sins. I believe this is why he asked me to track down this al-Bashir and the map and to use it to find the treasure and destroy it."

"Destroy it?" Moussa queried, perplexed. "Why on earth would he want to destroy a king's ransom in treasure?"

"I too found this strange. I asked him why he wanted me to do this, but he never got the chance to explain. Minutes after I swore to him that I would do as he asked, he drifted into a deep sleep and never woke up. That is all I know. Do you still wish to help me?"

"Yes, I do. I will begin making arrangements straight away for you and your family to leave Arlit. I am certain we can get you out the day after tomorrow. I will contact you tomorrow, after which you will take your family to Niamey. I will get tickets for all of you to travel by air. When you arrive in Niamey, you will be taken care of. You and your family will be resettled. You may remain in Niamey if you wish, or return to Arlit when all of this has ended."

"Thank you. Thank you very much! But I think we must return to the tea house now before they miss us."

Chapter Forty-Nine

During the short walk back to the tea house, Agali did not speak. Moussa was also quiet and pensive. As they approached the small shack's portico, a car sped down the dirt road toward them, bringing a cloud of dust behind it. The car skidded to a stop and three men with semi-automatic machine pistols sprang from it—two from the passenger side and another from the rear on the driver's side. Without warning, they began raking the men sitting in front of the building with a hail of bullets. Moussa instinctively dropped to the ground and rolled. As he dove for cover, he heard a muffled pop-pop-pop from the attackers' weapons and saw chunks of mud brick flying in every direction.

He lay on his stomach, body pressed against the ground, watching the unsuspecting men under the portico as they attempted to flee. Some of them screamed or cried out for help. He could see fear in their faces as they twisted, stumbled and fell one after the other. Blood spurted everywhere. Moussa managed to pull his Glock 27 pistol from the leather bag he carried and fired several rounds in the direction of the attackers, but the dust cloud shrouded them and he couldn't get a bead on either of them.

Suddenly, the driver's door of the car opened and a fourth aggressor slid from behind the wheel. The tall but lean and somewhat curvy figure, suggested a woman wearing what looked like a jumpsuit. She moved from behind the car and strode forward with determination and deliberateness, both arms extended in front of her. A split second later it was clear why. Muzzle flashes and the unmistakable sound of automatic weapon fire came from her direction. The tall, well-built woman was holding a compact Sig Sauer P556 SWAT semiautomatic pistol in each hand, each spitting bullets. *Why isn't she using suppressors like the others? Doesn't she care about the commotion?* Then, out of the corner of his eye, Moussa spotted Agali. He was trying to make his way around the corner of the building. His arms flailed gracelessly from his tall, lanky body as he stepped over his dead and wounded friends. He had just managed to make it to the corner of the tea house when he surged forward as if kicked by a mule. Two crimson circles suddenly appeared below his shoulder blades on each side; he slammed, face-first, into the wall and slid down it, leaving a wide smear of blood. His eyes were still open and his last expression was frozen on his face. It was a look of surprise, fear and disbelief. The woman's weapons had tracked him; after he fell, she lowered them, turned and retreated swiftly to the car. The car's three passengers continued their attack with choreographed precision. Having cut down anyone sitting or on their feet, they had begun raking the ground where the wounded lay writhing in agony.

For the victims, it was pandemonium. Everything had happened so quickly. Moussa was still on the ground, halfconcealed by corpses. His heart was pounding and his hands were shaking. His mind raced. Amid the cloud of dust and mayhem he had fired quickly and blindly and had emptied the magazine of his Glock 27 pistol. Now, however, the dust was beginning to settle; he could see all three assailants more clearly. They would also soon see him. Moussa knew that he would have only one chance to get it right.

He carefully and slowly reached down his leg and removed his backup weapon, a .38 caliber Smith & Wesson revolver, from his ankle holster. Without making any sudden movement, he drew a bead on the first attacker and squeezed the trigger. A small dark circle appeared on the man's forehead and his legs jackknifed beneath him. His weapon spurted bullets toward the night sky as he fell backward. The second gunman was quick to notice that someone among the pile of bodies was returning fire. He swung his weapon in Moussa's direction and let out a fusillade of bullets. Moussa dove in the opposition direction, rolled and squeezed off three rounds. The first caught the man in the knee and he let out a scream. His second shot missed and shattered the car's rear passenger window, but the third struck the man in the throat. The man dropped his machine pistol, grabbed his throat with both hands and began making gurgling noises. His legs buckled and he fell forward onto the ground. The third assailant was backing toward the open door of the car, still firing, when Moussa swung the .38 in his direction and fired. The man grabbed his groin and dropped to his knees. The next round found his chest and he keeled over to one side.

Behind the fallen assassins, the engine of the car revved furiously. The female killer behind the wheel whipped around in a donut-circle and the car sped off in the direction from which it had come, leaving Moussa prone on the ground, motionless and distraught.

Chapter Fifty

Caroline entered the Côte Bleu and headed straight for the ladies room. She was in luck. For the first time in her life she had stumbled onto an empty ladies' washroom. She locked the door behind her and instead of using one of the two comfortable chairs, she went into a stall. Perched on the edge of the toilet seat, she worked hurriedly. She pulled out a small notebook computer from her handbag, inserted a tiny hearing aid-size earpiece into her right ear, turned on the computer and entered her password. The small screen lit up and a customized desktop appeared. A click of the mouse and a fully encrypted program took over and directed her to an ultra-secret area of Vanguard's portal. She looked briefly into the computer's small camera lens for a retina scan and signed in again, this time under her code name, AMPHITRITE. The small device responded quickly. As soon as she entered the portal, a split screen appeared. The watch officer at VOCALS was on half of the screen and Tom Broughton took up the other half.

"I'm glad to see you!" said Broughton. "For a while you had us worried! I see you got my warning about Hamdi."

"Just in the nick of time," Caroline replied. "We were on the way to the guest house when it came through."

"We've been waiting for your report... anxiously, I should add. Any progress?" Broughton asked. "The old man is getting jittery. He's really worried. I've never seen him this way before, at least not at this level of intensity."

"I believe we made some progress, but I don't know how

much," said Caroline. "We picked up what looks like a good lead during the trip to Iferouane. Moussa is debriefing him now. The contact's name is Agali. He was a childhood friend and confidant of one of Sa'id al-Bashir's co-conspirators, a Nigerien named Salim Fa'izu Daoud."

"Why did you send Moussa?" Broughton asked, looking perplexed.

"I sent him because it was too risky for me to be seen with Agali. Fitting in might have been a bit difficult, to say the least, but going there could have blown my cover, assuming it wasn't already fully compromised. Besides, after I got your warning I figured I could help the situation by operating as a decoy, pulling them away from Moussa. We'll soon know if it worked. Moussa should be here shortly. I know we're not there yet, but I think we're a few steps closer to unraveling this," she added.

"I stand corrected," Broughton conceded humbly. "You made the right decision."

"It may well have been," the VOCALS Watch Officer interrupted. "But I don't think splitting up did much to throw your pursuers off track."

"What do you mean?" asked Caroline.

"If I may, ZEUS..." the Watch Officer said. "Less than ten minutes ago, we picked up an emergency signal then a short message from Moussa—it was very brief. He said he had been ambushed by four shooters, but managed to escape. The assassination team wiped out every living thing within fifty yards of the place. Somehow, their timing was perfect. They arrived just as Moussa and your contact, Agali, returned to the place where they had met."

"You worried me for a second," said Caroline. "When you said they wiped out everything, I thought you were about to tell me they killed Moussa. Did Moussa say whether he was able to debrief Agali?" Caroline asked.

Broughton took over again. "Yes, he did manage to confirm that he had successfully questioned the contact, but there was no time for any of the details. He'll make a full report when he sees you. Moussa is tough," Broughton added. "In the midst of all the shooting and chaos, he kept his wits about him. He took out three of the attackers. Unfortunately, the fourth got away."

"I thought you said there were only three of Hamdi's goons waiting for us! Where did the other one come from?" Caroline asked, infuriated.

"We're not sure," said Broughton. "But we think she is Alexandâr Ilaivo's girlfriend."

"*She*? What do you mean 'girlfriend'? What is she doing here, and how the hell did she pop up out of nowhere?" she asked, forcibly lowering her voice. So now a woman assassin had been added to the mix. It gave her a feeling she couldn't name, but one she certainly didn't like.

"Her name is Annushka Baikova and she's Russian," said Broughton. "She's the sister of Branimir Baikov, one of Ilaivo's four errand boys. She and Ilaivo go back a few years together. They met when he was in the Bulgarian Air Force. They became an item when they were going through air combat training together. Ilaivo left the Bulgarian Air Force a few years later for more glamorous and financially rewarding exploits with Bulgaria's state intelligence service. Annushka stayed in the Soviet Air Force and became a test pilot... flew the MiG-35 fighter. She finally left the military about three years ago and she and Ilaivo reunited about a year after that. Since then, Ilaivo has been using her to help set up and run safe houses for his operations." Broughton paused for a beat. "Strange thing though... there was an unconfirmed report a couple of weeks ago claiming that she was killed by a drug-crazed Russian arms dealer holed up in one of Ilaivo's safe houses in Finland. But if what Moussa reported about her being at the tea house is true, then the claim about her death was nothing more than a rumor."

Broughton paused again. He was worried. "Baikova is a damn good pilot!" he continued. "She can fly anything with wings or rotors. She must have piloted the chartered jet that left Morocco the other day with the assassination team. We know that two of the shooters who attacked the tea house came with her. The other one, a local, joined them after they arrived. Be careful!" he added, showing much more emotional concern than he was accustomed to doing. "Not only is she good with flying machines, she's pretty damn good with weapons and her fists. She's a female lynx and about as charming. I've heard that when it comes to martial arts, even Ilaivo struggles with her. They were made for each other!"

"Just what I need," Caroline interrupted. "A wonder bitch stuck in adrenalin overdrive!"

"One other thing," Broughton cut in again. "She personally eliminated Agali and I guess it's pretty obvious now that she's the one that got away. From what I gathered from Moussa's report, she enjoys her work. He called her the 'grinning killer' because she smiled the whole time she was filling her victims' bodies with bullet holes." Right on cue, the Watch Officer disappeared from the screen and four photos took his place. "This is the assassination team that hit the tea house."

"Thanks for the update," Caroline said, "but it looks like we no longer need three of these! What about Hamdi? Where is he?"

"Hamdi should already have arrived in Arlit," said Broughton. "Annushka Baikova and the assassination team arrived mid-afternoon and our contact at the airport in Niamey said Hamdi flew from Algiers directly to Niamey and from Niamey to Arlit late this afternoon. Watch yourself! It looks as if we've hit an exposed nerve. I think what you said might be true. We must be getting closer because they're throwing everything they've got at us."

"I'll be careful," Caroline promised. "I know who and what to look for now." *Especially the woman...*

"Just make sure you keep them in front of you at all times," said Broughton. "And don't forget, I need that report as soon as you debrief Moussa. We're almost down to the wire, so you'll have to make it short… just the essentials. Use your phone. I know it's not ideal, but it'll save time. Remember," Broughton added, "there's a hell of a lot riding on this. We can't come up short!"

"You'll get the report. I'll use my wrist communicator if I have to."

Speaking almost as if he were her father, Broughton reminded her of the growing danger. "Listen to me," he said. "As soon as you've debriefed Moussa and sent the report, I want you out of there! Do you understand me? I want you to leave Niger immediately!"

"Don't worry. You only have to say that once!"

Chapter Fifty-One

Twenty minutes after the tea house massacre Moussa walked into the Côte Bleu. He was disheveled. Despite his best effort to clean himself up, his jacket and trousers looked as if he had taken part in an urban warfare training course. There were large patches of reddish dust all over his clothes. He waited several minutes for the restaurant's *maitre d'*, who had wandered away from his post. He was embarrassed and growing increasingly impatient. He was not accustomed to visiting establishments frequented by foreigners. His eyes scanned the large dining area and bar as he waited nervously. After a few minutes, he moved forward. When he was halfway through the dining area, he saw Caroline sitting in a corner, across from the long mahogany bar. He made a beeline for her table. After learning what had happened from Broughton and VOCALS, she had a tall glass of ice-cold pineapple juice waiting for him on the table.

"Thank goodness you're alright," Caroline said, rising from her chair. "What happened?"

"I found Agali, but it all went wrong. It ended in a bloodbath, a massacre. They killed everybody at the tea house. I have never seen anything like it," Moussa said, visibly angered by what had happened. "It was a killing field! Those poor souls never stood a chance!"

"I'm sorry about those men, Moussa. I wish there was something I could do, but there's nothing… at least not now."

"You don't have to do anything! I am making it my business to do something. I will take care of it. I will find them, even if takes the rest of my life. I will find all of them and they will pay for what they have done!" His eyes glittered like black diamonds.

"I know how you must feel, but we have to finish what we set out to do. I know it's difficult for you but from here on it won't get any easier. For now, though, I need to know exactly what Agali told you. Don't leave out any details, no matter how insignificant they may seem. From now on, every minute and everything we do could determine whether we succeed or fail and probably whether we live or die."

For a moment, he looked at Caroline in silence. "He told me a lot," Moussa said. "Not much in the way of specifics, though. And a lot of what he said didn't make sense."

"What do you mean, it didn't make sense? Did he say what the chase and all this killing is about? Did he say what it is everyone is searching for and willing to deceive and kill for?"

"No, he didn't... not really. I suppose I just couldn't make out what he meant. He said Daoud and his friends helped al-Bashir bury treasure in the desert, about fifty miles southwest of here."

"What do you mean by treasure? What kind of treasure?"

"He said treasure, but he also called it 'yellow gold.' Said it was worth 'a king's ransom.' He said Daoud also told him about a map—a map which only Sa'id al-Bashir handled. He said the Algerian guarded the map closely, never let it out of his sight. He removed it from his pocket in front of them only twice. Once to mark something on it with a red felt marker and another time when he removed it from his jacket pocket, folded it and put it in his trouser pocket. After telling me about his conversation with Daoud, things turned a bit strange."

"Strange...? How? In what way...?"

"You know... bizarre! Agali said that Daoud made him promise to find al-Bashir and the map. Daoud told him to take the map and use it to find and destroy the treasure before it could be taken away."

"Taken away by whom?"

"He didn't know, but he did say the treasure would be taken from its hiding place to some unknown place on the West African coast and shipped to Persia or the Far East, possibly within the next twenty-four to forty-eight hours."

Persia or the Far East... "Did he say how he knew this?"

"No, he didn't. He just said in a matter of fact way that's what would happen."

"That explains al-Bashir's contact with the Iranians and the North Koreans." *Yellow gold, a king's ransom... buried in the desert.* "Moussa, I think Agali may have told us more than he thought he knew and I think we also know more than we thought we did. Moussa... you did great!" *Now I just have to pass this along to VOCALS. But it's far too much information for a short, simple encrypted text message.* "We have to get back to the La Rochelle. I need to pick up a few things we're probably gonna need, send a message to VOCALS and then we're gonna get out of town!"

"Have you discovered something?" Moussa asked, startled by the sudden change of strategy.

"You might say that... Finish your drink and go start up the Mitsubishi. I'll be right behind you."

"I'll pick you up in front of the restaurant," Moussa said, rising from his chair.

Moussa gulped the last of his pineapple juice; just as he started toward the door, a tall blonde woman came into the restaurant and began questioning the *maitre d'*. It wasn't long before the smiling and overly friendly *maitre d'* nodded and pointed in the direction of the bar, indicating that the person she was looking for was off to its left.

Caroline looked at Moussa and then at the tall, blonde Russian, who she recognized promptly as her nemesis. The woman was headed straight toward them. Bedecked in a light-weight leather flyer's jacket and a designer jumpsuit, Annushka Baikova strode confidently. Moussa recognized the look on her face. Her deep-set, blue eyes were empty, yet piercing. It was the same steely, determined look he had seen in them when she ended Agali's life. Caroline nodded to Moussa, signaling that he should continue toward the door, and he acknowledged. As Moussa approached the female killer, he quickened his steps with the intention of side-stepping her, but he had unwittingly telegraphed his intention. She had read him and moved directly into his path.

"You seem to be in a hurry," Annushka Baikova said in French, through a deep raspy voice laced with a Russian accent. "Do you always run out on beautiful women this way?"

Moussa looked at her scornfully, but said nothing. He was about to side-step her and move around her when she raised her left arm in front of him like a security barrier. "Look down!" she said, almost grinning. "Do you like being a man? Two shots and I could remove both your testicles! Do you believe me? Take a look! What do you think? Is my equipment as nice as your girlfriend's?" she asked, directing his attention to the silenced Beretta Jetfire .25 caliber pistol aimed at his groin. "Shall we go back and join her? She looks disappointed. Did she send you away? Couldn't you satisfy her? Is that why you are leaving? On second thought... perhaps it is more than that! She does look extremely disappointed! Now I am curious to know why."

Chapter Fifty-Two

Moussa's blonde, armed escort frog-marched him back to the table where Caroline was still sitting. Her pistol was pressed firmly against his spine as they walked. When they reached the table, Annushka Baikova instructed him to sit down. She remained standing, looking down on them, letting them know that she was the predator and they were her prey.

"I won't be as rude as your spineless lover here who ran away from you, so allow me to introduce myself. My name is Annushka Baikova, and let me see... you must be Caroline. I've heard an awful lot about you. Well, actually not an awful lot, just a lot of awful things," she said tauntingly. "You've caused quite a lot of upheaval, haven't you? Digging in places where you shouldn't be digging. Who are you, anyway? And this Ashmore Foundation... it seems to offer its employees limitless adventure. Is it some sort of front for a criminal enterprise? We have quite a few of those in Russia, you know. Or does it specialize in international espionage? You know... one of those 'do-gooder' organizations bent on righting wrongs and saving mankind from its self-destructive ways? There are so many questions I want to ask you, questions I am sure you are dying to answer, or should I say answer to avoid dying."

"Sit down, please," Caroline said calmly. "It's rude to stand when your hosts are all seated. Can I offer you a drink, or did shooting an unarmed, innocent man in the back not work up enough of a thirst?"

"That's very clever, but you see, he was not as innocent as

you think. Besides, he was fleeing, running away from me. No man walks away from me, let alone runs, when I want his attention. You wouldn't understand that. You are weak and don't know about these things. A life of private schools, nannies and trust funds taught you to snap your finger or ring a little bell to get the lesser social classes to do as you wish. But surely you must know that, deep down these people have nothing but contempt for you. I, on the other hand… whether they hate me or not, they just do as I command because they fear not pleasing me."

"Enough of the small talk!" Caroline interrupted coldly. "I thought communist totalitarianism was dead, or has the rest of the world just been in a catatonic state all this time? You know, you wouldn't be half bad, if you allowed yourself to be a real woman once in a while!" Caroline added, trying to undermine her challenger's resolve. "Why are you pestering me, anyway? And what's a Russian test pilot doing in this part of the world? There are no planes here to test-fly! Who's the puppet master pulling your strings? Surely there must be one. No one in their right mind would set an unbalanced, sadistic psycho of a bitch like you loose on the world and allow her to think for herself, let alone think for others!" she added, smiling.

"I see you have a sense of humor!" Annushka Baikova shot back. "And you have also done your homework. That's very good," the Russian said, pacing back and forth, first in a straight line, then half circling the table. "You are right about the control thing. You can't be a test pilot unless you learn how to control risk. Which leads me to your current situation," she added sadistically. "If you must know, there is no puppet master, but a colleague of mine should be along shortly. When he arrives, we can all have some fun, testing your limits. What's the matter with you?" she asked, turning to Moussa. "Cat got your tongue? You may not have the balls to keep your woman satisfied, but you handle your pistol pretty well! Did he tell you that he took out three highly experienced members of my team?"

"As a matter of fact he didn't. Apparently he's not as arrogant as you are!" said Caroline.

The Russian let out a faint chuckle. Moussa sat in silence throughout the exchange. He could see that Caroline's wit was grating on the woman's nerves. He had seen her in action only minutes earlier; he knew it wouldn't take much more to push her over the edge. Even in a busy restaurant, she probably wouldn't hesitate to draw her weapon and fire it into their heads. He was worried that he might soon be proven right.

Annushka Baikova sat down and steeled herself. Her face froze and her cold, deep-set blue eyes became even colder. For Moussa, it was reminiscent of the look he had seen on her face at the tea house—a precipitously troubling look that quickly gave way to a sadistic smile and a whirlwind of violence. Several minutes of silence passed. Then without warning she took the Beretta Jetfire she had trained on them under the table and placed it on top of the table. Caroline could not help but notice that the woman's long fingers and large hands completely enveloped the small semi-automatic pistol.

After placing her weapon on the table, Annushka Baikova instructed Caroline and Moussa, one after the other, to place their weapons on the table, butt first. Caroline laid her .25 caliber Jetfire on the table and Moussa placed his Glock 27 alongside it. The .38 Smith & Wesson was still in his ankle holster.

Annushka Baikova calmly raked the pistols across the table and let them fall into the handbag she had carried slung over her shoulder. To show her nemesis that she had taken all the necessary measures to minimize risk, she smiled and took her other hand from under the table. It, too, held a .25 caliber Beretta Jetfire. Annushka Baikova was where she was accustomed to being—in full control, or so it seemed.

Chapter Fifty-Three

Caroline accepted that for the time being, her jousting with the Russian had to end, but she had pushed enough to uncover a stress point in the woman's psychological makeup—a deeply ingrained emotional flaw that had manifested itself as an abomination of men. She had come to hate men, not because she thought them weak, but because she feared losing to them. Annushka Baikova learned from experience that everything she had gained had boiled down to competition, especially if she was pitted against a man. Because of this, she showed unwavering strength and control at all times—a perpetual desire to come out on top, whether competing against friend or adversary.

The game Caroline and Annushka Baikova had just played, although short and very dangerous for Caroline, had been necessary. Meeting for the first time, they had to size each other up. But Caroline still felt uncertain about who had won and who was mentally stronger. Unfortunately, the time for talking had ended and looks of contempt were all that passed between the Russian and her prey. Moussa tried to remove himself mentally from the situation by meditating. He was trying to clear his head, if only momentarily, of all conscious thought, but his efforts to commune with more serene and tranquil places was interrupted by Farouk Hamdi, who appeared suddenly next to the table.

"Aren't you going to invite me to sit down?" the Egyptian said, then smiled.

"I would, if I knew who the hell you are!" Caroline said angrily. "This place is getting a bit crowded! Don't you think so, Moussa?" she asked, knowing he wouldn't answer. "We've been here only a few minutes and already we've got uninvited and unwanted guests crowding our table."

"Let me guess… he is uninvited and I am unwanted," Annushka Baikova taunted.

"You're wrong, actually," Caroline retorted. "It applies to both of you! Neither of you was invited and neither of you is wanted! Is that simple enough?"

Immaculately turned out in a freshly pressed, khaki-colored linen suit, Farouk Hamdi pulled up a chair and sat silently for a few minutes, observing and listening to what was clearly a resurgent battle of wills between the Russian and the elusive hare he had been chasing. "Enough of this!" he barked after a while. "I'm sure you are aware that I didn't come to the Côte Bleu for entertainment, or the special dining experience it offers in this godforsaken place. And while I am sure that more than a few of the regulars in here would say the food is great and the place has a friendly atmosphere, I am not here to bask in its friendliness, either. I am here for intimate company… your company, Mrs. Dupré. It has taken me the better part of two days to track you down and I'm curious to know why you are here. On the surface, it all looks 'above board', as you Americans say. I know you are with the Ashmore Foundation, which makes some of your activities a bit difficult to understand… like meeting friends of a deceased mineworker and killing them in the process of tracking others down. I am sure that you will agree that these are interesting and unusual things, far too interesting and unusual to be discussed here, which means we should go elsewhere."

"I take it you're not open to suggestions," Caroline said sarcastically. "If you are, I know this wonderful little island in the Caribbean with palm trees and turquoise waters. We can all go there."

"It sounds absolutely fantastic," said Farouk Hamdi. "But I don't want you to get distracted by your surroundings. I need your full attention when I ask you some important questions—life or death questions, you might say. So, I suggest we waste no more time with these petty games. The sooner I find out what I need to know from you, the sooner you can get on with your business, which may in fact prove to be just as banal and unimportant as it appears. But it is up to you to convince me of that."

"You really don't expect me to believe that we're just gonna walk away after our little *tête-à-tête*? Take a look at your highly strung, deranged colleague!" Caroline darted the Russian a derisory glance. "She can't wait to end a few more lives! In fact, I'll bet she's already experiencing withdrawal pains because she hasn't killed anyone in the last half-hour. Look at her eyes. It looks as if killing has surpassed the thrill of screaming jet engines, flameouts, stalls, G-forces and inverted ejections."

"Don't worry about Annushka. You've got her figured all wrong," Farouk Hamdi said, smiling. "She may look strong and powerful, but she's as gentle as a lamb, if you stroke her the right way. But I get the distinct impression you've been tying knots in her ever-so-soft fleece. And that's not good for her and it's definitely not good for you. But I should warn you... she is the least of your worries. I assure you, you won't find me a pleasant adversary, either. So, if you and your strong, silent friend will come quietly with me, I have a car waiting for you out front."

"Where are we going? You rejected my suggestion to go to a Caribbean island, so the least you can do is tell us what fantastic spot you've chosen." Caroline paused, gauging the Egyptian's reaction to her sarcasm.

"You don't want me to spoil the surprise, do you?" said Hamdi, still smiling, obviously enjoying their sparring match. "I will tell you this much, though... First, we are going to take a drive, then a relatively short flight. I can assure you it will be a comfortable journey and you will be well looked after."

"Do you have any objection to me going to the ladies' room before we fly off to wherever it is we're going? Nature calls and I'd like to freshen up… you know, powder my nose and tidy my hair. A girl should look her best no matter what, especially if she's being taken someplace special!" Caroline said wryly.

"You have three minutes," Hamdi replied. "Annushka will go with you to make sure you don't lose track of time."

Once inside the ladies' room, Caroline headed for a stall, but the Russian stopped her from closing the door, which triggered an outburst. "Surely you don't expect me to use the toilet with you gawking at me!"

After thinking momentarily, the Russian conceded some ground. "You can close the door, but only halfway," she said.

Even with her minder watching her, Caroline managed to send an emergency signal using her wrist communicator. When activated in its emergency mode, the device sent out a high priority distress signal indicating that she was in trouble—in this case, captured. Things had moved much more swiftly than she had expected. She hadn't had a chance to send the update from Moussa's debrief, which meant Broughton and VOCALS were still operating in the dark. Annushka Baikova's arrival at the Côte Bleu had been unforeseen. There had been no time to ponder how the Russian knew where she was, let alone send an encrypted text message to VOCALS and Broughton.

At the first opportunity, Caroline reached into her handbag and turned the small laptop on in standby mode. Although not fully powered up, it emitted a low frequency signal which only VOCALS could detect and track. At least her whereabouts could be determined. Afterwards, she washed her hands and Annushka Baikova escorted her back to the front of the restaurant, where Farouk Hamdi stood waiting with Moussa close beside him. Whatever happened next, thought Caroline, she was going to try her best to anticipate it and, if possible, be one step ahead.

PART IV

Chapter Fifty-Four

Outside the Côte Bleu, a half-moon shone down over the desert. The temperature had dropped nearly 15 degrees Fahrenheit since nightfall and a slight chill had settled in the air. Farouk Hamdi had thought of everything. Before entering the restaurant, he had instructed his driver to take Caroline's Mitsubishi and dispose of it. Moussa would drive his vehicle and Caroline would sit on the back seat, between him and Annushka Baikova. Like Caroline, Moussa knew that if he climbed into the vehicle with Farouk Hamdi and Annushka Baikova, neither of them would ever be seen alive again. He had promised Caroline that he would sacrifice his life, if that was what was needed to complete the mission. He thought that he might as well find a way to take his revenge. He knew that Farouk Hamdi would not kill Caroline, at least not until he found out what he needed to know from her. But he, on the other hand, was expendable and could be disposed of at any time. He was worthless in the scheme of things and would be the first to be eliminated. He had to make his move—it was now or never.

Hamdi's Mercedes 4x4 with Moussa at the wheel picked up speed as it moved north toward the edge of Arlit. By now, Moussa was sure they were headed toward the airfield he and Caroline had seen on the way to Iferouane earlier that morning. Ever since they pulled away from the Côte Bleu, he had been studying how and when to make his move. Then he remembered the revolver strapped to the inside of his left leg.

The arrogance of these two idiots... their obsession with flair, drama and overconfidence has made them sloppy and careless, he thought. The pistol, a pearl handle .38 caliber Smith & Wesson, was a gift, presented to him by Vanguard, in appreciation for his support during several earlier highly successful operations in North Africa. The pistol and a sizeable sum of cash was Vanguard's way of expressing its gratitude. But instead of keeping the limited production weapon in its mahogany case, or putting it on display, Moussa had decided to use it; it had become his lucky backup weapon. It was fortunate for him that no one had thought to search either of them for other weapons.

Moussa thought about reaching down quickly and drawing the pistol, but realized that any sudden movement would result in closer and unwanted attention from his minder, Farouk Hamdi's driver, who was sitting on the front seat with a 9mm pistol practically thrust against his ribs. He also considered doing something irrational and unexpected, like running the vehicle off the road and escaping, with the expectation and hope that at least one of his captors would pursue him. After considering his limited options, he decided on the latter.

As the 4x4 plowed ahead, the town's edge became visible. The last mud-brick dwellings stood on both sides of the road. After passing them, the desert would unfold and they would be enveloped by its vastness. Moussa knew that if he stopped the vehicle in the desert and tried to run, there would be no cover, no way to evade anyone who gave chase. He would be an easy target. Then he remembered from their return journey from Iferouane and Arhli that the last mud-brick house on the very edge of town was abandoned. It was nearly a mile from the others... isolated... deposited rather oddly on the desert floor like a lone barrel cactus. It had caught his attention earlier because an abandoned house was unusual and meant one of two things: either its occupants had moved up the socioeconomic ladder, or they had migrated to a larger city with hopes of a better education for their children and a better way of life. Either way, it would not have remained empty, because a less fortunate relative would have seized the opportunity and moved in immediately.

Moussa pushed the accelerator gradually toward the floorboard and the Mercedes' speedometer moved up slowly. His passengers didn't notice the carefully measured increase in speed. The vehicle was nearing sixty miles per hour when it passed the last of Arlit's outermost dwellings. By the time it reached the isolated, abandoned house, they were going close to seventy miles per hour. Ahead, Moussa could see the silhouette of the lone, modest dwelling, sprouting from the desert. When the 4x4 drew parallel to the building, he slammed on the brake pedal, jerked the steering wheel sharply to the left and pulled up smartly on the handbrake. The vehicle leapt off the road. Its front wheels plowed into the desert sand, burrowing until the bumper made firm contact with the swelling mound of sand, bringing it to an abrupt halt. Just as Moussa had hoped, both front airbags deployed. He had judged the vehicle's response correctly. He opened the door and rolled out before the vehicle stopped. Once outside, he made the 50-yard dash toward the abandoned mud-brick house.

The passenger side airbag momentarily pinned his minder to his seat; he thrashed about for several minutes, trying to free himself. The abruptness of his actions and the rapid sequence of events temporarily disorientated and confused his captors, buying him enough time to get away and into the abandoned building. Moussa knew that if he reached the small house, he might be able to take out two of his captors, if two of them decided to pursue him. He had an advantage over them. They did not know he was armed. His only problem was that he only had six rounds of ammunition.

Chapter Fifty-Five

Inside, the mud-brick structure was cool and dark, except for where the moon threw funnels of subdued light onto the floor through the small, glassless windows. Moussa found a dark corner beside one of the windows facing the vehicle and stood quietly in the shadows. Before long he heard the plod of footsteps, muffled by the soft, powdery sand. Someone was moving rapidly toward the small house. Then came a shout; it was his front seat companion, beckoning him to show himself, to come out and surrender.

"Stop this foolishness!" the voice shouted in his native Hausa language. "There is nowhere for you to go. Make it easy on yourself! I won't harm you. You are a good driver. Hiding is of no use! What do you intend to do? You have no weapon! Come out, or you will leave me no choice but to come inside. And if I do that, I will have to kill you! Think of your family, your wife and your children! Do you want to die a coward's death? Shot in the head while hiding in this small, dilapidated place? I will give you exactly one minute then I will enter."

The man was standing about twenty yards away from the window, holding a compact submachine gun in front of him. "Come in and take me, if you are man enough," Moussa shouted. "You are right, you have the advantage! Why are you waiting?"

There was silence. After a beat, the man raised his weapon and trained it on the open window. He took two steps forward. He was about to take a third, but changed his mind and halted.

Moussa was hoping he would continue moving forward. *If he comes a few yards closer, I could kill him, charge out and take his weapon before the others know what has happened.* It soon became clear that the man was planning to lay down his own cover fire as he advanced. Moussa saw the barrel of the weapon swing upward toward the window. It was now or never. He sprang from the shadows, took quick aim through the window and fired two shots. The first hit his would-be assailant in the chest; as the man dropped to his knees, the second bullet hit him in his right eye and he fell forward with a dull thud.

Annushka Baikova heard the shots, which she knew were not from a semi-automatic weapon. She leapt from the 4x4 and ran toward the small building, zigzagging and releasing a hail of bullets as she charged forward. She was carrying two semi-automatic machine pistols, both spitting fire from their muzzles. For Moussa, it was *déjà vu*. He retreated quickly into the shadows in the hope that his attacker would charge through the door, but she remained outside. By now, it was obvious to her that her quarry was armed. A few seconds later, large pieces of mud-brick wall began to break away around him, shattering and flying through the air, the way they had done at the tea house in Arlit. Suddenly it dawned on him that the woman was firing full metal jacket rounds—armor-piercing. His physical cover was falling to pieces all around him and he had only four rounds of ammunition left. He knew he couldn't stay inside and wait for his executioner. He would have to take matters into his own hands by making a charge for the driver's weapon.

After firing dozens of rounds into the side and window of the crude structure, Annushka Baikova reloaded with full clips and started laughing. "You had better come out, you pathetic little man! Come out and die a dignified death! Surely you are not willing to allow yourself to be taken and executed by a woman?" she taunted. "I know now that I should have shot your balls off inside the restaurant. You don't need them! You are not a man! Hiding or running away from women seems to suit you well!"

Her taunting worked. Moussa was already angered by the massacre at the tea shop and was not thinking clearly. Nevertheless, he knew he would be killed sooner or later and he thought it better now than later—better now, when he had a chance to take a few of them with him, rather than let them choose the time and place.

"You are an evil, sadistic woman and you must die!" Moussa shouted, as he dove from the front door of the small building and rolled across the ground. After coming to rest on his stomach, he squeezed off three shots, the first of which whizzed past Annushka Baikova's head. The second grazed her shoulder and the third missed completely.

"You miserable little shit!" she shouted, then peppered the ground where he lay with bullets. Moussa rolled quickly to his left, but two of the rounds hit him in the front of his thighs, passing through and exiting at the rear. A third round pierced his right shoulder and shattered his shoulder blade as it exited, but worst, he had dropped his pistol, which now contained only one round. He tried to reach for it, but a heel came down hard on his right hand and ground it into the sand. He moaned uncontrollably.

"I knew you would soon be mine," the tall Russian *femme fatale* said, standing over him, fanning a machine pistol along the length of his body. "Prepare to meet your maker," she said, grinning. "But before you leave us, I want your very last thoughts to be of me and what I am about to do to you." Annushka Baikova trailed her weapon downward along his body and stopped at his groin. She smiled a familiar sadistic smile and fired two rounds. Moussa's body shuddered in agony, but he refused to cry out. "Don't bleed-out on me too quickly, you weakling!" she shouted, inching the weapon slowly and deliberately toward his forehead.

"You are a harlot and you will burn in hell when you die!" Moussa shouted.

"Yeah, yeah, yeah… but not today!" she gloated, changing her weapon to single fire. After a few seconds, the gloating turned to laughter and she pulled the trigger twice. Caroline heard the laughter, then the shots and saw the Russian jogging back to the vehicle. "I'll drive!" Annushka Baikova declared, climbing in behind the wheel. "This way you can keep a close eye on the little lady and maybe have a bit of fun with her as well."

"You sadistic bitch!" Caroline shouted. "You didn't have to kill him!"

"You are right," she replied. "I didn't have to, but I wanted to, so I did. He was of no further use, anyway. He was, however, more of a man than I originally thought!"

Chapter Fifty-Six

Annushka Baikova sat alone in front of the controls of the Dassault Falcon 900EX jet, making the necessary pre-flight checks before takeoff. Inside the executive jet's passenger cabin, Farouk Hamdi was rummaging through Caroline's handbag, as she sat quietly, wrists tied, in the seat facing him. It didn't take him long to discover the extra-small notebook computer inside.

"What is this?" the Egyptian demanded.

"What does it look like?" Caroline scoffed. "Haven't you ever seen a notebook computer before?"

"Don't be foolish! Of course I have," he retorted. "But I want to know what you do with it," he said, forcefully.

To dampen his fast growing, but still unconfirmed suspicions about her, she decided to speak openly. "If you must know, I use it primarily to keep in touch with my office. Project updates, changes in my itinerary, my whereabouts, those sorts of things," she added, smiling, knowing there was no way he could use the device the way it was intended to be used.

Suddenly, the whine of the small jet's three powerful engines rose as it taxied toward the runway. Farouk Hamdi gloated and tossed the handbag to her as he got up and headed toward the cockpit, notebook computer in hand. "I suppose I should tell you that you won't need this where we are going," he said. "Your employer will just have to wait and see where you turn up."

The Egyptian opened the narrow cabin door, stuck his head and shoulders into the confined space and handed the small, pearl-shell notebook computer to the Russian. "Take care of this as soon as it is convenient," he said to her.

As soon as Farouk Hamdi returned to his seat, the plane's engines rose to a steady high-pitched shriek and Annushka Baikova released the brakes. A split-second later, they were hurtling down the runway, lights zipping past the windows. After a few more seconds the Falcon 900 nosed up and started to climb. Shortly afterwards, the landing gear retracted into the fuselage and the plane continued upward. Soon, they would turn northwest over the Sahara Desert then head north for nearly an eight hundred mile journey.

The aircraft had just passed one thousand feet altitude when Annushka Baikova announced over the cabin intercom, "Ladies and gentlemen, this is your captain speaking. The estimated flying time to our destination is… well, we will know that when we get there. In the meantime, I ask that you sit back, relax and have a pleasant flight. Oh!" she added almost as an afterthought. "For our special passenger, if you will look out the window on the left side of the aircraft you will see that I am about to drop something off for posterity. So, if what they say about desert sands is true, it should make an interesting archaeological find in about five hundred years."

Caroline rushed to the other side of the cabin in time to see her small white, notebook computer spinning past the window. *That bitch is mad! It just barely missed the intake of the aircraft's aft engine.* She turned to Hamdi. "If she keeps doing these kinds of things, we won't live to see this special place you are taking me. Wouldn't it have been easier to put the damn thing in front of the wheels of the Mercedes 4x4 and run over it?"

"Yes, but that's not Annushka's style!" said Hamdi. "Besides, she knows what she is doing and I totally trust her. She knew exactly where that device of yours would go once it got caught in the airflow during the climb. She is a test pilot… remember? She is also a bit of a dramatist, so you should try to relax."

"She's also mental!" That too was an understatement,

Caroline thought. When it came to sheer, ego-fuelled derangement, the Russian was in a class all by herself.

"You should get some sleep," said Farouk Hamdi. "You've got a long night and possibly an even longer day ahead of you."

The Falcon 900 sliced through the air like a dart and climbed steadily to its cruising altitude of thirty-seven thousand feet. With the emergency signal from her notebook computer eliminated, Caroline took her captor's advice. She was beginning to feel woozy… as if she had been drugged, but she had not accepted food or drink from her captors. Yet she knew something was wrong because she was unable to fight off the sudden feeling of lethargy. She thought, *'Was it possible that he had gotten the waiter to slip something into my drink?'*

She could hardly keep her eyes open; she eventually succumbed, reclined in the luxurious leather seat and pulled a blanket over herself up to her shoulders. To her captors, it was a sign of subjugation, but for her, the struggle was just beginning. She would not and could not be a victim. Concealed underneath the blanket that shrouded her, she was still fighting against her captors. She resisted the intense drowsiness long enough to send a distress signal via her wrist communicator. She also made sure that the watch's locator beacon was activated and providing a clear signal for Vanguard's tracking satellite. She knew that once the signal was picked up, it could be relayed to Vanguard's analysts and technicians at VOCALS, the field operations chief or anyone else who needed to receive it.

Chapter Fifty-Seven

Amsterdam, Netherlands

Tom Broughton had dealt with the murder of the Antwerp Port Authority employee, Élisabeth Blauvelt, as quickly as the Belgian authorities had allowed him. He had been summoned to police headquarters for an interview around mid-morning. The police commissioner had decided to conduct the interview himself. But his fastidiousness and politically-driven motivation to lead the highly visible investigation pushed the interview late into the mid-afternoon. Because of this, Broughton did not leave the commissioner's office to return to Amsterdam until late-afternoon. He was behind schedule. To save time, he went straight to his office on Teilingen Street, instead of going to his apartment to get a badly needed fresh change of clothes.

He was still stinging from the woman's gruesome murder and he, more than anyone else, knew that he had made a mistake. He had committed the cardinal sin of an intelligence operative—he had allowed himself to attach more to his encounter with the woman than he should have. He had allowed her to become far too real, too personal too quickly, instead of treating her as the thing she really was—a useful acquaintance. This was uncharacteristic of him; he was finding it difficult to absolve himself of the feeling that he was partly to blame for her demise. Like a dedicated employee, Élisabeth Blauvelt had assisted him in dealing with a genuine and urgent appeal for help. She had been efficient, almost to a fault; but because of her efficiency and enthusiasm, she had unwittingly thrown herself into the oncoming path of danger. For her, the situation had undoubtedly been a simple, straightforward one —a *quid pro quo* arrangement. But it had been a naïve calculation, one in which she saw herself providing much-needed help in exchange for a rare and exciting opportunity for romantic frivolity.

Broughton urgently needed to set aside the niggling feeling of guilt. He needed more than ever to be focused. Pieces of the deadly puzzle were beginning to fall into place and time was not on his side. He had already concluded that of the three cargo vessels Vanguard had been monitoring—the *Northern Celeste*, the *Louis Brevard* and the *Montserrat Star*— it would be either the *Northern Celeste* or the *Montserrat Star* that would play a major role in the Chameleon's diabolical plan.

Chapter Fifty-Eight

Broughton was still studying the ships' movement reports sent earlier by VOCALS and waiting for Caroline's call with the results of the long-awaited debrief from her Nigerien assistant when the high priority message set off his wrist communicator.

URGENT MESSAGE… DISTRESS SIGNAL RECEIVED FROM AMPHITRITE.

Broughton picked up the telephone and told the receptionist that he was not to be disturbed until further notice. After giving the receptionist instructions, he locked the outer doors to his office and went into the high security enclave, which lay hidden behind a false wall at the back of his desk. Once inside, he logged into Vanguard's operations network and the entire message began to scroll across his monitor. He transferred what was displayed on the monitor onto a larger monitor on a wall with multiple screens.

The message read:

AMPHITRITE COMPROMISED AND CAPTURED. TRACKING SIGNAL FROM NOTEBOOK DEVICE ACTIVATED AT 19:45 GMT, TERMINATED AT 21:07 GMT. WRIST COMMUNICATOR DISTRESS SIGNAL ACTIVATED AT 21:12 GMT. DEVICE TRANSMITTING STRONG, STEADY SIGNAL, BUT MOVING AT HIGH SPEED, TRACKING NORTH-NORTHWEST TOWARD

ALGERIA OR WESTERN SAHARA. SPEED SUGGESTS OFFICER IS AIRBORNE.

As soon as the message trailed off, Broughton called the VOCALS Watch Officer, whose face appeared promptly on-screen. "I just read your update," he said. "It looks as if Hamdi and his minions got to her... but it also looks as if she's alive." He sighed, then added, "Thornton was right. Linking an officer's biometrics and stress physiology details to the new wrist communicator is paying dividends. Let's hope they don't wise-up to what its function is and remove it."

"Ditto! You're right. The communicator is our best chance of knowing where they are headed," said the Watch Officer. "As usual, though, trouble comes in pairs, which means I have some more bad news... We've lost Moussa. We think he's dead."

"Why do you think that? Are you sure?" asked Broughton.

"Sir... the signal from his wrist communicator terminated at 20:15 GMT, exactly thirty minutes after AMPHITRITE's notebook signal went active."

"But how can you be sure he's dead? Couldn't they have just removed it?"

"Yes, they could have... and there's a slim chance that this is what happened. And I emphasize 'slim.' As you indicated, the device won't work unless the officer to whose biometric and physiological profile it is linked is wearing it. The one Moussa was wearing is more modest in appearance than AMPHITRITE's, but if they took it from him and examined it, it might not take them too long to discover that there's something special about it. Remember... finding a highly sophisticated device like that on Moussa would cast even more suspicion on AMPHITRITE."

The Watch Officer paused, then continued. "My guess is that the termination of the signal from her notebook computer had nothing to do with the termination of Moussa's wrist communicator signal. The timing, however, suggests the situation eroded quickly for both of them, which probably gave them no time to coordinate a strategy. This led us to believe that getting rid of or destroying the notebook probably was just a precautionary measure. After all, anyone with a basic understanding of communications and computers could see that the notebook has a satellite connection capability. The Russian woman is smart in both of these areas... and she's also risk averse. If they had removed Moussa's wrist communicator, Annushka Baikova would have figured it out by now. And if she had, we wouldn't be getting this fast-moving signal from AMPHITRITE."

"I guess you're right." Broughton said.

"As long as that beacon keeps emitting, she's breathing and probably quite healthy. I don't know if they had time to tell you this when you were issued your new equipment, but the wrist communicators are designed to emit a distress signal that's triggered when an officer's physiological condition moves into a 'red zone' that's unique to him or her. The red zones were established by using empirical data taken from the officers' own stress load experience under dozens of intense and potentially highly dangerous situations. No mistake, sir, I'd say she's alive... for how long...? It's anybody's guess."

Broughton hesitated for a moment. "If Moussa has been eliminated, that means AMPHITRITE is alone with Hamdi and Baikova." *They undoubtedly believe she knows something... which she does. Maybe they've made a connection between her and me.* "We've got to stay on top of that signal!" he commanded. "We can't afford to lose it! I want to know exactly what that aircraft is doing at all times. I want updates every fifteen minutes. If it changes course, lands or falls abruptly from the sky, I want to know immediately. Has Thornton been told what's happening?"

"Yes, sir, he has," the Watch Officer said.

"I'm right here," said Thornton. "I'm always within earshot during situations like this. I didn't butt in because it's your operation. Having said that… what's our next move?"

"A rescue team… We'll move as soon as we know where they've landed. As long as the beacon in her wrist communicator keeps broadcasting, we'll be in good shape. But we don't have a contingency plan in the event it stops. As a backup, we'll just have to hang our luck on uninterrupted tracking of the aircraft. It's all we've got at the moment."

"We're already on top of that, sir," the Watch Officer said. "We know from its avionics and electronic signatures that the aircraft they're in is a Dassault Falcon 900EX. From what we can tell, it was sub-leased for Ilaivo three days ago from an executive aircraft company in French Guyana, by a small cut-out company based in Saint Martinique. If it hasn't been modified, and our research shows it hasn't, its range, when fully fueled, is 4,500 nautical miles."

"OK… that's good," said Broughton. "Now, given the aircraft's range and what we know about Hamdi's network and the operations he typically carries out in North Africa, where are they likely to be headed?"

"We thought about that too, sir… We believe Hamdi will head for Western Sahara. He won't go back to Algeria and he can't go to Egypt, because there's a price on his head there."

"Why go to Western Sahara?" Broughton pressed. "There's nothing there!"

"Precisely! Why Western Sahara, indeed… We think he'll go there because it's a simple plan. Lots of desert, it's isolated, which means searching for them will be like looking for a needle in a haystack. Why do something spectacular and complicated—which is what would be expected—when a simple plan will work?"

Thornton interjected, "He's probably right, Tom. It is the least expected course of action."

The Watch Officer continued. "Getting there undetected will be a bit tricky, though. But we believe that as soon as they cross into Mauritanian airspace, she'll drop low and fly under radar or through gaps in radar coverage in the area. We're almost certain that when they reach Western Sahara they'll stay in the northeast. There's an abandoned airfield northeast of Mahbés. I'm convinced they'll go there because it's out of the way and therefore a safer bet. They probably figure that if they can make it there undetected, they'll be safe."

"How confident are you about this?" Broughton asked.

"We're very confident," the Watch Officer said, after a quick around-the-room poll that drew nods from each of the analysts and technicians in the Operations Center.

"You'd better be right!" Broughton said sternly. "We're about to throw every rescue resource we've got in the area at these two targets. If we blow it, we don't get another chance! If we fail, we not only lose an operative, we lose an operative with valuable information that we desperately need. Do I make myself clear?"

"Crystal clear, sir!" the Watch Officer replied.

"Good then," said Broughton. "Notify the rescue teams, maritime assets and all operatives within a five hundred mile radius of the two locations to standby and be ready to do whatever they are instructed to do. Inform Simon Mills immediately that we are preparing to conduct a rescue operation and that, as the senior officer in the area, he's in charge. He'll take orders directly from me. Understood?"

"Understood, sir! The alerts and instructions have just been transmitted. We'll keep monitoring AMPHITRITE's signal and tracking the aircraft to see where it lands. As soon as its destination is known, we'll broadcast the information immediately."

Niles Thornton chimed in one final time. "The plan sounds perfectly reasonable, in light of the suddenness and urgency of these developments. I think you should proceed with haste, Tom. Good luck!" the spymaster added. "I have every confidence that we'll get her back, but I am worried that it may not give us enough time to act on what she has learned. But there's no need to worry about that now. We'll have to move one step at a time," he cautioned. "I'll leave you and the teams to get on with planning details. I will be in and out of VOCALS, but not out of touch. I have some favors to call in from Washington and a few other influential places across the Channel. Keep me posted."

Chapter Fifty-Nine

North Africa
Somewhere Over the Sahara

Departing Niger, the Dassault Falcon 900EX flew northwest over the desert of northern Mali, skirting the Algerian border until it crossed into Mauritanian airspace. After entering Mauritanian airspace, it descended sharply to an altitude of just one hundred feet, practically skimming the desert floor. Forty-five minutes later, it turned west and entered Western Sahara. Caroline woke up during the aircraft's quick descent. After opening her eyes, she sat up, twisted to one side and raised her seat from its fully reclined position. She threw back the blanket she had pulled over herself hours earlier and raised her arms in front of her to check the time. Her wrist communicator had been removed.

"You slept like a log," said Farouk Hamdi. "I don't suppose it had anything to do with that little something extra I had the waiter slip into that last martini you drank rather hurriedly..." He smiled at the puzzled look on her face. "Is this what you are looking for?" he asked, grinning and twirling her wrist communicator by its strap around his middle finger. "This is an interesting little toy you have. Does the Ashmore Foundation issue one of these to all its employees, or just the ones it sends out to spy? I removed and returned it to your wrist a couple of times. The funny thing is that it went on and off each time.

Why was that? What does it do?"

"Give me that back! It's only a watch, you moron!" Caroline shouted. "Your growing paranoia has you imagining things! That worries me. Paranoia can spawn violence in the most peaceful person. So who knows what it'll do to someone like you." She was clutching at straws and she knew it. She also knew that without the communicator, rescue was an unlikely prospect.

"It doesn't matter what it is used for," said Hamdi. "You won't need it where you are going. But I'm sure Annushka would love to have a look at it. She's a bit of a techno geek. She'll figure out whether you've been up to something you shouldn't be doing. In the meantime, just sit back and relax. We'll be landing in a short while."

"Forgive me if I sound flippant, but will I get to make my one phone call when we get there? After all, you've taken me into custody... at least that's what it seems like."

"Custody," Hamdi said tauntingly. "Why don't we call it what it is...?"

"And what is that?" Caroline asked sarcastically.

"Abduction! And in that case, the telephone call may not be a bad idea. Now that I think about it... you should make a call to your boss. Better still... we will arrange for something even better. So, I suggest you start thinking about what you are going to say to him as they could be your final words."

Chapter Sixty

Tom Broughton was still tucked away in the confines of Vanguard's secure spaces at the Foundation's Teilingen Street office, passing instructions to Simon Mills and planning for the covert rescue mission about to be launched inside the little-talked-about country, Western Sahara. Although recognized only as a semi-autonomous region of Morocco by the United Nations, independence for the half-million or so indigenous people of Western Sahara had been a long and hotly contested issue between its neighbors, Morocco and Algeria.

Planning was just about finished and Broughton and Mills were deciding where AMPHITRITE would be taken after her rescue and extraction, when the Watch Officer at VOCALS interrupted them with a critical update.

"Sorry to interrupt the planning session, gentlemen, but a couple of important developments have occurred that you will want to know about."

"Go ahead. What is it?" asked Broughton. "What have you got?"

"Within the past twenty minutes, AMPHITRITE's wrist communicator has shut down and restarted three times. The last time it shut down was five minutes ago, but it didn't restart."

"What do you think happened?" asked Broughton.

"I think they may have discovered the device."

"How does that explain several stops and re-starts?" Broughton asked.

"We're not sure, sir, but they may have had her remove it in order to examine it and maybe they gave it back to her."

"Twice!" said Broughton. "Why would they return it if they suspected that it was some kind of communications or signaling device? It makes no sense. It looks to me as if they were curious about why it shut down when it was removed, which to my mind doesn't suggest they know what it is. Who knows...? The fact that it didn't restart could mean they're still curious or concerned about it."

"I agree, sir," said the Watch Officer. "But whether they know what it is or not is not our immediate problem. The immediate problem is that the signal didn't resume after the third shut-down. And it gets worse... After the last shut-down, the aircraft plunged suddenly from thirty-seven thousand feet to zero altitude. We've lost all signals from it, sir. All navigation and radar equipment, including the aircraft's Global Positioning System receiver, was either shut down, or the unthinkable happened... they crashed. If they're still airborne, I don't know how they're managing it. The pilot must be hugging the desert floor and flying by visual reference and compass headings only."

"You mean we've not only lost the locator beacon signal from the wrist communicator, but we've lost the aircraft too? You assured me less than an hour ago that we would be able to track the aircraft, even if we lost AMPHITRITE's signal."

"Yes, sir, we did," said the Watch Officer, apologetically. "But no one here expected the Russian to do what any sane pilot would consider suicidal. She has to be skimming sand dunes, sir. We've started maneuvering another satellite with a heat tracking capability to the area; when it is in position it should pick up a signature from the aircraft's engines. These can't be shut down in-flight, so this ought to work."

"How long will it take to get the satellite into position?"

"It's currently over Southeast Asia, which means we can have it positioned over the area in about forty-five minutes."

"That might be too damn late!" Broughton, said, now showing his frustration openly. "If it's still flying, in forty-five minutes it most likely will have reached its destination. Then what do we do?"

"We'll search for and locate it by using the heat from its three engines. They'll provide a good signature, even after they've been shut-down. The signature should be unique, as there are no other Dassault Falcon 900s in Western Sahara. And even if there are others, the chances of finding two with hot engines at this hour are slim to none. We're still convinced they'll land somewhere in the northeast. That's the direction the aircraft was flying when we lost contact."

Once again, Broughton asked sternly, "Why do you think they'll head for the northeastern part of Western Sahara?" His thoughts were flying ahead, mapping the region as he knew it… and a vision of Caroline being drugged and dragged to probable torture and death kept making an unwelcome entry into his mind.

"Because there's an abandoned airstrip not far from Mahbés, at least that's what the Moroccan government claims. But we've had reports from a host of regional and other international intelligence services stating that the area is a virtual hub for drug trafficking and other illicit activities. We'll get the satellite in position and look there first. There's another potentially usable airfield north of Tfaritiy, but that one is not as discrete, but we'll check it out anyway."

"Let's hope you're right, because it's all we've got!" said Broughton.

Simon Mills chimed in. "I've already set up two rescue teams. They'll each be deployed to within twenty miles of the two airfields. I'll be with the team headed for the Mahbés area. A reconnaissance team should be in position at both locations in less than and an hour. We'll get AMPHITRITE out and bring her back safely," Mills said, then added, "You have my word on it, Tom."

"It's all or nothing, Simon. It would be nice if we knew what Ilaivo's next move was going to be," Broughton added.

"It would," said Mills, "but for what it's worth, my thoughts on this are that your visibility with the Foundation and Ilaivo's discovery of your connection to what must have looked like some kind of operation against him, almost certainly cast suspicion on the Foundation. I doubt that he knows about Vanguard, but he's clearly figured out that the Foundation's activities extend far beyond international humanitarian aid and assistance programs. In Ilaivo's mind, anyone linked to the Foundation is now an enemy and therefore a potential threat to his master plan."

"I agree with you so far, but he's still on a fishing expedition. He doesn't know enough about the Foundation to figure out how to disrupt or neutralize its efforts."

"Let's look at the facts," said Mills. "The first red flag was raised by your digging at the Port Authority in Antwerp and taking out a key member of his team."

"You're forgetting an important aspect of that encounter... I was the target, not Dimitar Krastev."

"OK, granted... they identified you as a threat early on, which may have caused Ilaivo to do some back-tracking... to go back and look at where things started, to see what else is amiss. Which brings us to the second red flag and possibly further confirmation of a Foundation operation against him— Caroline's search for Sa'id al-Bashir's former associates and her digging into his activities. Then there's the demise of more than a dozen people, including the Frenchman, all in close proximity or involving Foundation personnel. These incidents can hardly be seen as mere coincidences and they didn't do much to lower the Foundation's profile, either."

"I see exactly what you mean," said Broughton, "but a lot of protocols and procedures had to fall by the wayside. This opened the Foundation up to exposure like never before. We'll have to do damage control later... for now, we'll do what we have to do to get AMPHRITRITE out of their clutches."

Mills acknowledged that risks had to be taken, but continued with his assessment of the situation in the belief that stopping Ilaivo would in effect provide permanent damage control. "At first, Ilaivo may have been just probing," Mills said, "but I would wager that he's now trying to get a fix on a few more things... like the size and focus of our operation. And if he hasn't figured out what we're doing yet, he will do soon. I expect he'll try to use Caroline to draw us out into the open, so he can size us up and deal with the threat without disrupting his plans. If we've gotten too close already, he won't call things off... he'll just adjust the timeline. We know that's how he operates. Thus far, I think his plan is working, but we're in a position to surprise him because he doesn't know anything about how we're resourced."

Let's just hope it stays that way, at least for another twelve hours or so. We're gonna need the element of surprise. If he knows more than we think he does, then AMPHRITRITE will be not just bait... she'll be dead bait by the time we reach her.

Chapter Sixty-One

Northeastern, Western Sahara

The Falcon 900EX's three engines provided perfect control for the slow, steady approach needed to make the landing on the relatively short runway. After making what any competent pilot would have called a perfect approach, the Falcon 900EX's wheels touched down at the disused airstrip. The airfield, which only had a 1,500 meter-long, east-west runway, was located near the Moroccan and Algerian borders, some sixty miles northeast of the town of Al Farciya and twenty-five miles northeast of the small town of Mahbés. It was precisely where the VOCALS Watch Team had predicted it would land.

The airfield had a somewhat checkered history. No one seemed to know, or at least was willing to speak openly about, who had built it, but Morocco was rumored to have used it for military operations, after the opening of its 1979 armed struggle with the Polisario Front for full control of the Western Sahara territory. Other rumors purported that for decades, the airfield was an unpaved, unimproved strip that had been gradually upgraded by smugglers in order to expand their illegal enterprises. Either way, it was officially said to have not been used since United Nations peacekeeping mission troops left it more than ten years earlier.

Aside from the airfield's runway, a hangar, still in fairly good condition, a small make-shift control tower and a fuel bladder were the only evidence that mankind had forayed onto the near featureless and inhospitable landscape. A multipurpose security force comprised of ten heavily armed caretakers and security personnel—four Arabs and six Berber tribesmen—had waited for the aircraft's arrival. They had set out burning oil pots at fifty-meter intervals on each side of the runway to compensate for the lack of electric lighting. In addition to providing security for the facility, the men were also charged with dousing the burning pots, refueling the plane and towing it into the hangar. Their improvised use of a John Deer garden tractor for towing suggested not only their ingenuity, but a frequent need for such a service, given that there was no grass for cutting and almost no agricultural production anywhere in Western Sahara. The content of the small shed adjacent to the hangar was another indication of the frequency of the airstrip's use. Long empty, the shed now housed a new 25 kilo volt amp (KVA) Caterpillar diesel generator.

After landing to the west, Annushka Baikova made a 180-degree turn near the end of the runway and headed back up it to the east. About a third of the way, she exited onto the taxiway and followed it swiftly to the parking apron and brought the sleek executive jet to a gentle stop in front of the hangar. Before shutting down the engines, she flipped the switch for the passenger cabin's public address system and made a final announcement.

"Welcome to Mahbés!" she quipped in her deep, raspy voice. "Or should I say welcome to 'hell on earth!'" If you look out of the window on either side of the aircraft, you'll see a marvelous landscape, replete with a rich variety of peculiar rocky outcroppings and sand dunes. It's an extraordinarily, breathtaking sight for any holidaymaker. The temperature outside is a dry, balmy thirty-nine degrees Celsius. That's just over 102 degrees Fahrenheit for you who do not understand the metric system. We'll be stopping here until… well, until we're done. So, if you feel the temptation to wander off into the desert, I should warn you that there is nothing there to greet you but kilometers of sand and a likely encounter with harsh, sand-infused *sirocco* winds. However, if you do get a case of 'wanderlust' and feel you must explore, I advise you to wear sun screen, preferably SPF 50 or higher, and take along plenty of liquids, as there are no water coolers for miles in any direction. Once again, welcome to hell on earth and we hope you enjoy your stay."

"On your feet!" Farouk Hamdi shouted, grabbing Caroline by her arm as soon as Annushka Baikova's announcement finished. "It's time for us to go have that talk I promised you back at the restaurant. I am sure that before this day is over, there will be many things you will want to tell me. In fact, there may come a time when you cannot wait to tell me these things."

Walking toward the hangar with Hamdi alongside her, Caroline tried to probe to find out what her captors already knew and what they had planned. "You're pretty confident of yourself, aren't you?" she asked, sharply. "You've got to be one of the most egomaniacal men I've ever met!"

"Why, thank you," Farouk Hamdi said. "Coming from you, that's a compliment."

"Don't flatter yourself!" Caroline retorted, scornfully. "What makes you think I have anything to tell you? Or did you even consider that? What happens if I don't?" she added.

"It's quite simple... If you know nothing, then we've lost nothing, except a bit of time. Making sure that this conclusion is true beyond a shadow of doubt and the peace of mind that comes with knowing that, is worth the investment. By the way..." he added. "The answer to your question, what happens if you know nothing of interest, is simple. I will either kill you or set you free in the desert. I haven't decided yet."

"Then why would I talk, even if I did know something, if the outcome is going to be the same?"

"Pain," said Hamdi, grinning. "Trust me... you will want to stop the pain. It will make you want to talk. Perhaps you might even want to talk before the pain begins." He paused, then added somewhat flippantly, "Maybe I shouldn't be too hasty. Foregone conclusions can take the mystery out of a situation. So let's just say that if, after a reasonable amount of time we haven't made satisfactory progress, I will let Miss Baikova have a go at you. The two of you seem to get along so well. To look at her, you wouldn't think she's new at this. But what she lacks in experience, she makes up for in enthusiasm. She's just itching to learn and sharpen her skills. Already she tells me that she wants to develop and refine her techniques. As you have seen, she is dedicated to everything she does. Perhaps some might say she's a bit too eager... too competitive... too impatient, even. Imagine that... wanting to learn, develop and refine all in one day. Now that's what I believe you call in America 'raw ambition.'"

"She's insane and you're an egomaniac. I'm not sure which is worst! So it looks as if I'm screwed either way."

"You might say that."

"Then may I please have my watch back?"

"What for? I've told you already you won't need it again."

"That may be true," she said, "but it was a gift from my late husband and my son. I promised them both I'd never part with it. Besides, what difference does it make if you kill me with it on or off my wrist?" She appealed again, this time more humbly and sounding defeated. "May I please have it back?"

He stopped pulling her along momentarily. "That was very touching. I suppose I could do that," he said, taking the watch from his pocket and pressing it into her outstretched palm. "You're right... it won't spoil what we are about to share."

Chapter Sixty-Two

Northeastern Western Sahara

With the aircraft fully fueled, concealed and ready to go at a moment's notice, Farouk Hamdi pulled Caroline into a closed-off space at the rear of the hangar. It had been converted from a storage space for tools and aircraft parts, to what looked like a gathering place for smugglers and other characters of questionable repute—no doubt to conduct business transactions and arrange transshipment of illicit goods. Three long folding tables, placed end-to-end, with folding chairs strewn around them, stood in the middle of the floor.

Scaffolding, used for changing the long fluorescent light bulbs in the fixtures that hung from the high ceiling and for servicing the room's two wall unit air conditioners, stood near one of the walls. Oddly, several tripod-mounted studio lights had been set up off to one end of the tables. A faint but steady growl could be heard from the large diesel generator. Caroline could see why the generator had been brought in. Whoever was using the airfield wanted to make sure there was enough electricity for lighting, air conditioning units, and a large refrigerator. No electrical runway lighting was installed, because it would almost certainly have attracted unwanted attention to the airfield.

Annushka Baikova followed Farouk Hamdi and Caroline into the room. She was carrying a case containing a satellite telephone in one hand and a laptop computer in the other. Her much-favored Sig Sauer P556 SWAT machine pistols hung by their straps, bandoleer-style, over her back. The Russian placed both cases on the table and said, "Welcome to the devil's workshop!"

Farouk Hamdi pulled a chair away from the table and pushed Caroline down hard onto it. "Get comfortable," he said. "This could take a while… However, how long it takes will depend on you!"

"Go fuck yourself!" Caroline shouted, then spat on him. The vulgarity of her verbal attack brought fire and an as yet unseen level of excitement to Annushka Baikova's widening, deep blue eyes.

"Shut your mouth, you filthy little slut!" the Russian said. "Let me have a few minutes with her. That's all it will take. I'll teach her to show some respect!"

Farouk Hamdi walked to the far end of the table, turned on his heels and said to the Russian, "Be patient. Your time will come. Besides, I'm not concerned about her being heard beyond these walls. She'll have to make a hell of lot more noise than that if she expects someone to hear her. Though later on you may find these little outbursts motivational, especially when we start what will undoubtedly be the most interesting part of our work."

The Egyptian grinned then turned to Caroline. "We are going to arrange for you to speak to your master and a few of your colleagues. We want them to know that we brought you here because your digging into certain matters was far too unusual for an employee of such an organization as yours. We want to know why. We are also going to show them what will happen to you if they don't explain what you have been doing these past few days. We are also going to show them what happens to people like you who misrepresent themselves and violate the provisions and activities set forth in their own charters. Until we are satisfied with the answers you provide, all eyes will be on you."

"This may sound cheesy, even to you, but who died and left you in charge? And what gives you the right to hijack the 'caring for humanity' thesis to justify violence peddled by such a twisted, self-serving philosophy?"

Farouk Hamdi laughed. "Someone has to look out for the weak and the exploited! So I volunteered."

"Don't make me puke! You've never given a toss about anyone but yourself. You're probably enjoying this! Violence excites you, doesn't it? Have you always enjoyed beating up on women when they're tied down, or did you acquire the taste for it on-the-job? I'll bet it turns you on!" Caroline added, angrily. "No matter what you do to me, nothing will change. But that doesn't matter to you, because you're a bully. You're just like your psychopathic friend over there... a subservient sycophant. Both of you will one day get what's coming to you!"

"You know, you talk too much! But thanks for the compliments and for giving me a few fresh ideas. Thoughts of you, violence and my enthusiastic colleague had not entered my mind. But now that you have mentioned it, a close and personal encounter between the two of you might be interesting, if not entertaining. For now, though, I'll set that aside. We can revisit it if what we are doing gets too dull."

"You're as sick as you are spineless!" Caroline shouted. "A disgusting pig!" She may as well speak her mind, she thought. It would make no difference to the outcome.

Farouk Hamdi turned to the Russian and said, "Shut her up! I've had enough of her whining. She is beginning to annoy me. I don't want to hear her voice again until she is told to speak."

Annushka Baikova strode over to Caroline with a roll of duct tape clutched in her fist and stopped in front of her. Smiling sadistically, the Russian looked down at her, then delivered a sharp back-hand across her face. "You've had that coming for a while, you fucking little whore!" said Annushka Baikova. "Believe me, there is lots more where that came from and I am going to enjoy serving it up, every minute of it!" she added, grinning.

The Russian drew back her hand to deliver another blow, but before she could follow through, Farouk Hamdi stopped her. "That's enough!" he shouted. "I don't want her face to be unrecognizable. Tape her mouth and tie her wrists and legs to the chair. You can have her when I am done with her."

Chapter Sixty-Three

The plastic grip-lock straps the Russian put around Caroline's wrists and ankles dug cruelly into her flesh. Annushka Baikova had taken great care to make sure that they were as tight as they could be. After less than ten minutes Caroline could not feel her feet or her fingers. They had gone numb. The ties around her wrists were holding them firmly to the arms of the chair, while the ones around her ankles were attached to the chair's legs—each strap acting like a tourniquet, preventing the flow of blood to and from her extremities. After positioning and turning on the portable studio lights, the Russian moved away and Farouk Hamdi again took up a position directly in front of her. A smile spread across his face. In his right hand he was holding a 50,000 volt Taser.

"Let's see just how compliant you can be," the Egyptian taunted. "These are the rules. I will ask you a question and you will give me the right answer!" he shouted. "We will start the punishment level at 20,000 volts. Wrong answers, flippant or sarcastic responses will count against you and will only make me increase the voltage, which will cause more pain. Nod your head if you understand me."

Caroline nodded and he leaned forward and ripped the tape from her mouth. Caroline licked her bleeding lips where the top layer of skin had been torn off. "I have already told you... I have nothing to tell you!" she blurted. "My work in Algeria and Niger was exactly as it should have been... conducting feasibility studies for irrigation and agricultural projects."

"I see already that I need to remind you of the rules... I ask the questions and you supply the answers... and only to the questions I ask. In order to finish this, I must have your obedience," he said, pressing the Taser against her shoulder and holding the trigger for a few seconds.

Caroline cringed and her body began to spasm. She went limp when he released the trigger.

"That was only 20,000 volts for three seconds. I can increase the voltage and duration, if you wish." He continued, "Your first question... who is Sa'id al-Bashir and why is he important to the Ashmore Foundation? Think carefully before you answer," he warned.

"Until a few days ago, I had not heard of anyone named Sa'id al-Bashir."

Farouk Hamdi struck her sharply across the face. "You are lying!" he shouted. "I can see that this is going to take some time!" He set the Taser's voltage output level to 30,000, pressed it against her shoulder and held it for well over five seconds. Caroline's eyes rolled back in her head and her entire body began to spasm violently. The legs of the chair she was in moved wildly from side-to-side and then tilted forward and backward, clattering against the smooth concrete floor.

"If you continue to defy me," he said, "I will continue to increase the voltage. But before we reach the maximum, 50,000 volts, my enthusiastic friend wants to give you a reprieve from this electrifying experience. She wants to remove a few of your fingernails and perhaps crush a few of your toes to show you just how serious we are. For your sake, I hope it doesn't come to that. So, I ask you again, who is Sa'id al-Bashir and why is he important to your organization?"

Caroline hesitated. Feigning deep fear of further pain, she began, "The Frenchman told me about him... said he was thought to have been responsible for the death of a couple of villagers in the area I would be traveling to. He warned me to be careful because there had been lots of kidnappings and other kinds of crime in the area. He said my project workers would become targets for extortion for thugs like Sa'id al-Bashir and that the Foundation should be prepared to pay lots of money in order to be left alone."

The Egyptian pondered her answer for a moment and declared, "There is some truth in what you have told me, but we will come back to the question later because you have raised another important matter…the Frenchman, Georges Saint-Jacques. How did you come to know him? He is a former French intelligence officer, but I suspect you already knew that. What was the nature of your relationship with him? Study your answer carefully," he warned again. "I have highly reliable information that says there was a relationship between Mr. Saint-Jacques and your boss, Niles Thornton."

This time Caroline did not hesitate before responding. "Of course Niles Thornton and Mr. Saint-Jacques know each other. They know each other for reasons you've just said. As I've told you already, Mr. Saint-Jacques was acting as a consultant for the Ashmore Foundation. My organization paid him to advise us on actual or potential threats to our people and operations in Niger. If we were considering operations anyplace else in the world, we would have sought similar services from an experienced and proven expert."

"This may be true, but Mr. Saint-Jacques was killed… brutally murdered only minutes after talking to you. What did the two of you talk about that was so hazardous to his health?"

"Aside from exchanging views about the ambience and food at the Côte Bleu, we talked about dangers to employees and ways our work might be disrupted by extortionists and other criminals. In his capacity as a security and risk consultant, I am sure that Mr. Saint-Jacque encountered many shady people and perhaps made more than a few enemies. After all, success in his line of work likely meant failure for the people he exposes."

The Egyptian did not believe the explanation and was eager to point to the unusual circumstances surrounding Saint-

Jacques' death. "But he was killed while pursuing you. Wasn't he? Why was that?"

Caroline shot back, "Mr. Saint-Jacques was not the only target! His killers wanted to eliminate me as well. Mr. Saint-Jacques was killed protecting me as well as trying to protect himself. If it were not for him, we'd both be dead! Is that so difficult to understand, or are you too paranoid and stupid to see that?"

Farouk Hamdi leaned in close to her face and shouted, "Why would his accomplices kill their own man? He was their benefactor!"

"Someone offered them more than he was paying?" she asked dubiously. "Who knows... maybe someone made them an offer they couldn't refuse! How the hell am I supposed to know? This place is rife with double-dealing, back-stabbing and double-crosses!"

"Your answers are far too thorough!" he shouted. "In fact, they sound too credible to be true."

"That's your problem, not mine," Caroline blurted, doing her best to ignore the waves of pain coursing through her body as a result of the Tasering and her tight bonds.

"Wrong answer!" he shouted. "On the contrary my dear... It's your problem," the Egyptian said, ratcheting up the voltage on the Taser to 40,000. "Let's try once more." He pulled the trigger, pressed the Taser against one of her breasts and held it there for nearly a full ten seconds.

The electrical current shot through Caroline's body instantaneously, delivering sharp, stabbing jolts to every muscle in her body. She screamed and convulsed wildly until she lost control of her bodily functions and urinated on herself before passing out. After she fell unconscious, Farouk Hamdi placed the duct tape back over her mouth and moved the studio lights and a small, digital, tripod-mounted video camera on the table closer to her. He opened the laptop computer and connected it to a small satellite dish. Afterwards, he tapped in information on the laptop's keyboard and pulled up her image on a temporary website he had created on a server somewhere in Mumbai, India. He then hacked into the Ashmore Foundation's public website and attached the link for the website in Mumbai. He was now ready to send pre-recorded and live streaming video to his intended audience. All he needed now was to wait for a call from another of his accomplices.

PART V

Chapter Sixty-Four

London
St. James's Place

It was nearly 3:30 a.m. and Niles Thornton was still awake, stirring in his Sloane Square flat, located on the Knightsbridge side of the upscale neighborhood. He had left Vanguard's Marylebone headquarters just before 11:00 p.m. to get a few hours' sleep and a fresh change of clothes. Regardless of the crisis, he had to make sure that the Ashmore Foundation was seen to be doing business as usual. Doreen, his housekeeper of nearly twenty-five years, had left only moments after he got home, and only because he had insisted that she take some time off after such a long day.

Robert Riley, Thornton's bodyguard and chauffeur, had insisted on staying until Thornton departed in the morning and had invited himself to the spare bedroom. For the past ten years Riley had been driving Thornton to and from work and to all of his social functions and business meetings. Riley, an operations officer turned bodyguard, had been one of Vanguard's best field officers. He was an intelligent, dedicated, perfectionist—an expert with weapons and in martial arts. But most importantly, Thornton had personally mentored Riley when they were both working for Her Majesty's Secret Intelligence Service, making him a master of tradecraft. Riley had reminded Thornton of himself when he was a young MI6 officer.

As with Tom Broughton, Thornton had come to rely on Riley, but understood his decision when he elected to give up the world of operations to be closer to his wife when she was diagnosed with multiple sclerosis. Riley was devoted to the Foundation. He had moved there from field operations with MI6 in order to be around more often for his wife and to protect the ageing spymaster from his enemies, past and present. Thornton didn't like having a fuss made over him, yet he appreciated Riley's concern about the level of danger Ilaivo's involvement was causing. But instead of letting Riley remain with him, he offered him coffee and insisted that he go home afterwards and attend to his wife.

Thornton had just gone into the kitchen and was putting scoops of French roast coffee into a large *cafetière* when the VOCALS Watch Officer pressed the pre-set button on his emergency alert console, causing Thornton's wrist communicator to vibrate. Like all his operatives, Thornton also wore one of the new wrist communicators. He knew that a message for him, particularly at that hour, would be urgent. He dialed in the obligatory six-number code and shortly afterwards, a message scrolled across the watch's small screen. He returned to the lounge where Riley was waiting. "Sorry," he said. "Something urgent has come up. I'm afraid I have no time to make you that coffee after all. I'll ring you in the morning, to let you know what time to pick me up."

After seeing Riley to the door, he went into his study, pulled out his laptop, and logged into Vanguard's secure web site portal. He authenticated his identity with an iris scan and proceeded to the special access area set up for retrieving detailed emergency communications. VOCALS' Watch Officer appeared immediately on the screen.

"What's the problem?" Thornton asked.

"I knew you would want to see this, sir…" Pulling up the information he was referring to, the Watch Officer announced, "We just received an e-mail via the Foundation's public web-mail from an anonymous sender in Mumbai, India, instructing you to go to the Foundation's home page and view a special link they've attached."

"A link to what…?"

"A video, sir. I've opened the link and I'm sure you'll want to see its contents. It's a video of AMPHITRITE."

"Are you sure it's not a hoax?" Thornton asked, feeling disturbed.

"Our IT folks and the video technicians say it's genuine. It's the real thing. Only thing, though… Mumbai isn't the real point of origin for the feed. It's just a cut-out for anonymity to mask the sender's true location. The e-mail informing us about the link said it was a two-minute video, but there would be a live feed starting forty-five minutes after it ends."

"Put it up!" said Thornton. "Open it up to ZEUS and be ready to pick up the live feed as soon as it starts!" he instructed.

A split second later there was audio between Niles Thornton and Tom Broughton. Broughton had remained in Vanguard's Amsterdam field office the entire evening.

"Tom! We just got this a few minutes ago with no advance warning, so we're both seeing it for the first time. I'm not sure what it contains, but I have a pretty darn good idea what it's about," said Thornton ominously.

A few seconds later, the image of Caroline Dupré appeared simultaneously on the screen in Thornton's London flat and in the secure confines of Vanguard's Amsterdam field office. She was slumped in a chair and unconscious, with duct tape over her mouth. About fifteen seconds into the video, an off-screen voice cut in.

"Mr. Thornton… if you are watching this… and I am sure that you are… this is what happens to people who stick their noses where they are not supposed to be. Don't worry… she's very much alive, but her stubbornness and not the tape over her mouth is why she is unable to speak. If you want to see Mrs. Dupré alive again, you will do precisely as I tell you to do. Here

251

are the instructions… and I encourage you to follow them to the letter. You will be receiving a live feed that will start exactly forty-five minutes after this video ends. When the live feed ends, you are to go directly to the docklands in London's East End. Go alone… no one must follow you. You are to go to Tranton Road… It's a dead-end. There will be a car waiting for you at the end of Tranton Road. There you will meet someone who wishes to see you… someone you should know."

Before the short video ended, the off-camera voice spoke directly to Broughton. "Mr. Broughton, my instructions for you are to sit tight, watch and listen. You are being watched very carefully."

As soon as the video ended, Thornton shouted, "It's Hamdi. I'd know his voice anywhere. He didn't even try to disguise it. In a sick and flippant sort of way, he wants us to know it's him. He seems pretty damn confident about what he's doing. Where are we with the rescue operation?" he asked Broughton.

"Mills and the SAR team launched about a half hour ago. Our satellites located the place where they are holding her. It's an airfield in northeastern Western Sahara, about twenty-five miles northeast of the town of Mahbés. It's out in the middle of nowhere."

"Good!" said Thornton. "We've got to get her out of there as soon as possible. Hamdi is following Ilaivo's instructions, which means that whether he gets the answers he's looking for or not, he has no intention of letting her live. She has clearly been tortured and she obviously hasn't given them anything. Otherwise, they wouldn't be contacting us this way. Ilaivo is desperate! Time is probably running out for him, too and he wants to make sure that no one interferes with his plans. However, with a bit of luck, we'll have a big surprise for him."

"I agree with you," said Broughton. "He's pressed for time and doesn't quite know what's happening. That's why she's still alive, and we have to make sure she stays that way until Mills and the SAR team can reach her."

Chapter Sixty-Five

England, London's East End
Docklands

The darkened windowed, black Mercedes picked up speed as it headed east on Jamaica Road. Niles Thornton was careful not to break the speed limit. He could not be delayed. Every minute counted. Niles Peter Thornton rarely, if ever, drove himself anywhere these days. But after watching and listening to Farouk Hamdi's video message, he slipped quietly from his Knightsbridge flat for the drive to the docklands as instructed. Driving along Jamaica Road toward the rendezvous point, he felt confident, but he also had some trepidation about the intentions of the man he was about to meet face-to-face for the first time in nearly two and a half decades. However, by the time he reached Bermondsey Underground Station, he had expunged all the disturbing thoughts from his head.

At Bermondsey station he turned right and headed south for a short distance on Keeton's Road. After traveling about two blocks on Keeton, he swung into Tranton Road, the dead-end street he had been told to go down. He continued a short distance along Tranton Road and found a parked metallic silver Audi coupé, facing him on the narrow lane. He thought it strange that such a poor tactical position had been taken by the driver. The car was boxed in; because he had taken to the center of the road, there was no room to get past him on either side.

Regardless of any tactical or strategic errors in judgment his opponent may have made, the moment of truth was at hand.

The Mercedes rolled slowly toward the end of the lane and came to a stop about twenty yards in front of the Audi. The driver of the Audi flashed his headlights twice and Thornton responded with a single flash. After a beat, a tall, lean figure emerged from the car and started walking toward Thornton's Mercedes. Thornton opened the door and slid from behind the wheel. The two men approached each other cautiously and in silence. As they drew closer, a dull light at the top of the street illuminated most of the man's face. By now he was only a few feet away. He was not the man Thornton was expecting.

"Where is Ilaivo?" Thornton asked, bemused. "What happened to him? Did he lose his nerve?"

The man grunted. "Old man... you are just as Alexandâr described you... and you talk too much!"

"Where is she? Where is my employee, Caroline Dupré? And who the hell are you?" Thornton barked. "If Ilaivo has hurt her in any way... I swear I'll..."

"You will do what, old man?" he interrupted. "Just shut up and listen! You are in no position to make demands, threats or to give orders."

"Where's the girl?" Thornton demanded again, this time more sternly. "Not another word passes between us until I know she is safe. Do you understand me?"

The man paused briefly as if to ponder the challenge. It was clear that he realized that he had no authority to negotiate terms, conditions or outcomes. After nearly a minute had passed, he spoke. "I am Petrov. Alexandâr instructed me to meet you and tell you that you and your organization must back off or the girl will die."

"I want proof that she is alive, damn it!" Thornton shouted, angered by the ultimatum. He went on, "You tell Ilaivo I'll do nothing of the sort until I see her and hear her voice. Is that clear?"

Without speaking, the man reached into his jacket pocket, pulled out a mobile phone and punched in some numbers. A few seconds later, a voice speaking in Bulgarian came on. "He wants to see the woman," the man said into the phone. There was a slight pause. "One moment," the man said, then handed Thornton the phone. Thornton stared at the phone's screen; seconds later, the image of a woman with dark hair, sitting in a chair with her wrists and ankles bound and duct tape over her mouth, appeared in a large, nondescript room surrounded by portable studio lights. It was AMPHITRITE—Caroline Dupré; it was the same image of her he had seen less than an hour earlier. Except this time she was conscious and struggling to move. She was still alive.

"I want to speak to her!" Thornton shouted into the phone. "Now, damn it!" he shouted angrily.

The line momentarily fell silent and the man at the other end, who never appeared frontally on camera, pushed the camera toward Caroline, zoomed in on her face and stripped the duct tape from her mouth. "Is that close enough?" he growled.

"I want to speak to her!" said Thornton.

"Niles? Is that you?" Caroline shouted. His voice had clearly lifted her spirit, if only momentarily.

"Yes, it's me! Listen to me… I'm going to get you out of there! You hear me?"

Before Caroline could speak another word, the man who had slid the camera toward her pressed a piece of duct tape back over her mouth. "You have seen and heard enough!" he continued. "Don't be so foolish as to try to free her. If you try anything, she'll be the first to die. I will personally cut her throat!" he added with relish and ended the call.

The tall man in the alley took charge again. "You have your orders. Back off!" he said. "Alexandâr said you must follow them, if you want to see the girl alive again. He will contact you again within the next twenty-four hours."

255

"You tell Ilaivo that if any harm comes to her, he'll have to deal with me personally!"

A deadpan smile spread over the man's face and he let out a thunderous laugh. "By the way, Alexandâr sends his regards. I am sure he would welcome the opportunity to personally deal with you."

Before Thornton could move or speak, there was a silvery flash. It was a piece of shiny metal, struck faintly by the distant, subdued street light. The man had produced a stiletto knife. Thornton tried to raise his right forearm to deflect the thrust of the blade towards him, but his attacker halted halfway through the motion and changed the angle of attack. He was now swinging down on his target. A searing pain went through Thornton's upper right arm. The blade had hit him in his right tricep, but he had managed to lean far enough away to stop it from fully penetrating. His attacker was all over him, kicking and punching—going about his work with an artistic yet psychopathic rage.

The man quickly withdrew the knife and again swung it in an efficient arc over Thornton's raised forearm. Thornton's adrenalin surged and he tried to pivot to escape the plunging shard of steel. Already wounded, he was too slow. The point of the blade struck him just below his right collar bone, but he managed again to stop it from penetrating too deep. Another searing pain ensued and he could feel himself weakening. He felt as if he were being attacked by a maniac wielding a red hot poker instead of a knife.

The man withdrew the blade and was preparing to go for a third and potentially more damaging wound when the lights of Thornton's Mercedes started flashing wildly and its horn began to blare. Thornton had squeezed the panic button on the Mercedes' keyless remote. Suddenly, a patrol car from London's Metropolitan Police, which had been cruising along Keeton's Road, screeched to a halt, reversed and turned onto Tranton Road. Seconds later, it was speeding the short distance down

Tranton Road, emergency lights flashing. The man looked up, saw the patrol car and his eyes widened like saucers. He looked back at Thornton, who was crumpling but still on his feet. Thornton could see that his attacker was disappointed that he had been prevented from delivering the full message he had been sent to deliver—a message that surely would have maimed him.

"You were lucky!" his Bulgarian attacker shouted. Then he turned, ran past the Audi toward the end of the narrow lane, jumped up to reach the top of the eight-foot-high wall at the end of the lane and pulled himself up onto it. With his body slung halfway over the wall, he looked back and shouted, "Don't worry! I wasn't going to kill you. Alexandâr wants to do that himself at a time and place of his own choosing."

The man let out another roaring laugh, dropped over the back of the wall and disappeared into darkness. The police patrol car skidded to a halt. As soon as the policemen climbed out of it, the coupé burst into flames and exploded.

Chapter Sixty-Six

The Sahara Desert
Northeastern Western Sahara

The Sikorsky HH-60 Pave Hawk search and rescue (SAR) helicopter raced over the desert, almost skimming the sand dunes. It had been launched from the deck of Vanguard's rescue ship, the Caravel, just two hours earlier—less than sixty seconds after Niles Thornton had given the mission the go-ahead. The Caravel had been a cargo ship, which Vanguard converted by adding an operations and intelligence center, a satellite communications capability, a flight deck, an aircraft elevator and a below-deck hangar to support SAR and covert missions. The Pave Hawk was just one of several makes of helicopters Vanguard had purchased and reconfigured to support its operations.

Simon Mills sat near the door of the helicopter. He had just received an update from the two reconnaissance teams deployed three hours earlier. One of the teams had confirmed what Vanguard's satellite had uncovered earlier through its heat signature sensors—the presence of burning oil pots lining either side of the runway and the brief presence of a recently flown aircraft on the parking apron in front of the hangar. The satellite had also picked up the heat signature from the diesel generator at the facility. But there was more good news. The signal from AMPHITRITE's wrist communicator had resumed five minutes before the report was sent. After receiving the report, Mills looked at the SAR team leader, who had also been listening to the update, and gave the thumbs-up sign. They were right on-target.

The SAR team leader was a lean, energetic and highly enthusiastic former U.S. Air Force Captain. He was young looking, much younger in appearance than the members of his team. After receiving the news, he and Mills sat back in their seats, both stone-faced, concentrating on what lay ahead. The remainder of the team sat quietly, night vision goggles donned and weapons in front of them. They had conducted dozens of exercises for the situation they were responding to and had successfully executed more than a dozen real operations like the one they were now on. They were eager to get down to business.

Chapter Sixty-Seven

The Pave Hawk's whisper-quiet rotors sliced through the warm early morning desert air with precision, pushing the helicopter at a very low altitude toward the objective—the small, isolated airstrip northeast of Mahbés. It was joined at launch by an Italian A129 Mangusta attack helicopter, armed with a chin-mounted, three-barrel 20mm cannon, rocket pods, anti-tank missiles and Stinger air-to-air missiles. The Mangusta's job was to eliminate any threat to the SAR team and the Pave Hawk during the mission.

The Pave Hawk closed to within 500 yards of the hangar, set down and deployed the SAR team. Meanwhile, the Mangusta A129 stayed in a low hover, with its running lights off. Working from up-to-the minute information from the reconnaissance mission, the SAR team identified the location of each member of the eight-man security team that had been posted outside the facility. With synchronized precision, they moved in with silenced weapons and eliminated all of them simultaneously. Although experienced and battle-hardened, the small force of Arabs and Berber tribesman had had no chance to raise alarm. They were taken completely by surprise; it had all happened too quickly.

Accompanied by Mills, two breaching groups from the SAR team entered the hangar and located one more of the last two airport security team members. The man was posted outside the door to the room where Caroline was being held. He was swiftly dispatched by the SAR team leader with a garrote.

However, when he was attacked his weapon fell to the floor. After eliminating the sentry, the SAR team leader slid a fiber optic cable video camera through a slit beneath the door and into the room to identify the number and location of hostile personnel and the subject of the rescue. He could only make out three figures—Farouk Hamdi, AMPHRITRITE, who was strapped to the chair, and the last security guard, who was on the far side of the hangar. The Russian, Annushka Baikova, was nowhere to be seen. She had apparently been the only one alerted by the faint sound of the sentry's weapon clattering when it fell to the floor. After hearing the noise she had stealthily moved closer to the wall behind Caroline to investigate. Giving in to her intuition, she shimmied up the scaffolding and found an old air condition duct. Although the SAR team considered her a serious threat, it could not wait to account for her. It needed to stick to the established mission timeline, and speed was paramount.

The SAR team leader radioed to check that the two members of his team responsible for breaching the sealed door on the other side of the room were in position and they responded, confirming that they were ready. It had been decided during planning that the doors on both sides of the storage area would be breached simultaneously with shaped C4 explosive charges. The two members of the team, whose job it was to set the explosives, quickly completed their work. When they were done, explosives were on all three hinges and locking mechanisms on each door.

The SAR team leader gave the command to detonate. There were two explosions, almost in unison, and both doors flew inward. Members of the assault team swarmed in from both sides of the room, taking everyone inside, except the Russian, by complete surprise. The Berber tribesman positioned as security inside the room swung his AK-47 assault rifle toward the door nearest him, but before he could pull the trigger, three rounds from one of the SAR team members' MP5 submachine guns struck him in the chest and he squeezed the trigger involuntarily as he went down. Several stray rounds ricocheted off the concrete floor. Farouk Hamdi, who had been standing in front of Caroline when the breach occurred, tried to reach for the Sig Sauer P220 pistol lying next to the video camera, but he was too slow. The team leader knew the Egyptian was in charge of the operation and knew he needed to be kept alive for questioning. His response to the threat was swift, but measured —he shot the man in the arm. Farouk Hamdi fell to the floor immediately, writhing in agony. Once the two known hostile occupants of the room were down, the breaching teams did not skip a beat. They set about searching for the Russian.

Annushka Baikova peered out through a hole in the tarpaulin she had hastily dragged over the large air duct that once supplied cool air to the hangar's office and workshop area. She was fairly confident about not being found. She knew they wouldn't linger too long to look for her, as they were on a fixed operations timeline.

"Gentlemen!" the SAR team leader shouted. "We've got exactly three minutes to wrap this up and get to the parking apron for extraction!"

Mills, who had followed closely on the heels of the SAR team leader's breaching group, had raced toward Caroline as soon as the Egyptian went down. He removed the duct tape from her mouth and the blindfold from her eyes. He then cut her arm and leg restraints and pulled her from the chair. Because of the numbness in her lower legs, she collapsed in his arms.

"I sure am glad to see you!" said Mills.

"What took you so long?" she fired back, half jokingly.

Farouk Hamdi was still writhing about on the floor. When Caroline saw him lying there, she broke loose from Mills' clutch and hobbled over to him. She looked at him and spat in his face.

"I told you you'd get what you deserve!" she shouted. "You're no man! You're a worthless piece of shit and a coward. You're a loser! Look at you! All your efforts and arrogance have amounted to nothing... and you're gonna die for what? For nothing!"

The SAR team leader grabbed a handful of the large plastic grip lock ties from the table and handed them to Mills.

"We've gotta' roll, sir..." he said. "Take a couple of these and secure the prisoner's hands behind his back."

Farouk Hamdi had been feigning extreme pain and incapacitation; as soon as the SAR team leader took his eyes off him to signal his team to regroup, the Egyptian made his move. Simon Mills was just starting toward him to tie his hands and lift him from the floor when Hamdi reached down and drew the Sig Sauer P229 he had been carrying in a concealed leg holster.

"Gun!" Caroline shouted and dove for the pistol on the table. She was too late. The Egyptian fired twice. Simon Mills was almost directly in front of him and both rounds struck him in the side, near his armpit, just above his body armor. He was dead before his body hit the floor. After grabbing the weapon, Caroline rolled onto the floor and squeezed off a single round. The bullet struck the Egyptian in the center of his forehead and his lifeless body fell backwards onto the smooth concrete.

Outside, the Mangusta A129 worked with the other five members of the SAR team to secure the hangar against counterattack and protect the SAR helicopter. It circled the hangar continuously, just fifty feet above the ground, looking for threats. The SAR team leader threw Simon Mills' lifeless body over his shoulder, and with Caroline running alongside him, they moved to the parking apron and boarded the Pave Hawk for the trip back to the Caravel, somewhere off the West African coast.

As they flew west, away from the airfield, the SAR team leader reported, "Mission complete... AMPHRITRITE safely onboard... All sighted enemies eliminated... Russian pilot not located, presumed to have escaped into the desert. One friendly casualty... Regional Control Officer." He then said, "Request permission to destroy one Dassault Falcon 900EX on-the-ground in hangar and the facility's major infrastructure."

The reply from Tom Broughton was immediate, "Request denied! I repeat... request denied! Do not take any action that could expose or draw attention to your operation! Is that clear? And get AMPHRITRITE up on the communications net!"

"I read you loud and clear, sir... Take no action that exposes or draws attention to the operation. Understood... and will do! I'll hand you over to AMPHRITRITE."

"It's good to know you're safe," said Broughton, barely masking his emotions. "I heard the communications for the entire operation. It was a threat we should have expected." He went on, "Simon was a good man and a long-time friend of mine. I miss him already... I'm sure we'll all miss him."

"It's good to be back," Caroline said. "If I had been just a bit quicker, he would be here now talking to you as well. He gave his life to save mine. I'll never forget that."

"You shouldn't forget also that Simon fell doing what he wanted to do. He'd have no regrets." He then added, "Now, I need you to help arrange sending him to London as soon as you get aboard the Caravel. I'll contact you aboard ship to let you know what our next move will be and where I need you to be. With Hamdi out of the picture, I'm sure the game will change dramatically. That means it's gonna get even nastier!"

Chapter Sixty-Eight

The two rescue helicopters returned to the Caravel and set down just hours after departing the airfield in northeastern Western Sahara. The Caravel was moving northwesterly at fifteen knots, fifty nautical miles off the coast and moving farther away from Western Sahara, when they were recovered. The ship's captain had already received instructions on his next destination from Tom Broughton and had set a course for Las Palmas in the Canary Islands. From Las Palmas, Caroline would head out on a new assignment and Simon Mills' body would be flown to Boston, Massachusetts, via London.

As soon as Caroline stepped off the Pave Hawk, she headed below deck for an intelligence update, instructions and further guidance from Broughton and VOCALS. After descending two levels below the main deck, she entered the high security and heavily compartmentalized operations center. The chief of the operations center was waiting for her at the door.

"Mrs. Dupré… I have a full update for you, if you're ready. When we're done, you are to await contact from ZEUS. He'll have instructions for you. We've already arranged for Mr. Mills' body to be shipped to London via commercial air. It'll be escorted from London to his home in Boston by his son and a member of staff from the Foundation. I'm not sure where you're headed, but wherever it is, I'm told you'll be departing Las Palmas at the earliest convenience."

Caroline was aware there were critical and quick adjustments to be made, yet she was unable to rid herself of her growing obsession with the fate of the Russian. "What happened to Annushka Baikova back at the airfield?" she asked. "The SAR team couldn't find her. If she escaped, and I'm certain she did, we were foolish to allow that to happen. Why did we let her get away?"

"You're not going to like this ma'am, but it's been confirmed... she did get away," said the Operations Center Chief. "Forty-five minutes after the SAR choppers left the airfield our satellites detected ignition of the Falcon 900EX's three engines. Ten minutes later it was airborne, heading north-northwest toward the Atlantic Ocean."

"Why didn't we destroy the damn aircraft and the whole damn facility before we left?" Caroline's anger was mounting. They'd had it within their power to strand the bitch in the desert and destroy her, yet they'd done nothing. She couldn't understand it. *If it had been down to me...* "We had the firepower to do it! And what did we do? We did absolutely nothing!" she harangued. "We did nothing at all to stop her! She's more than just a loose end, you know... She knows enough about Vanguard's resources and capabilities to cause some serious problems now and in the future. Do we know where she has gone?"

"The answer to your last question is... no, we don't, but the VOCALS Watch Team thinks she'll either link up with Ilaivo or join his two remaining minions somewhere in Central Europe." The Caravel's Operations and Intelligence Chief continued, "Going back to your first question... I agree, and under normal circumstances, the team would have followed standard operating procedures and denied the enemy the ability to retaliate or escape, but ZEUS and the old man himself gave strict orders not to do anything to draw attention to or jeopardize the success of the mission. That meant not attracting any unwanted attention. Destroying the aircraft and the facility would have caused some serious bangs, not to mention creating a few high-visibility fireballs. They wanted the team in and out of Western Sahara without incident."

Referring to Simon Mills' death, he added, "They almost succeeded. And what you mustn't forget is that in this business, secrecy is paramount and plausible deniability keeps you in the shadows. For that reason alone the old man will figure out how to deal with the Russian. He's been at this for nearly five decades," the Operations and Intelligence Chief added, reassuringly confident.

Caroline fell silent. She could see that he had made a valid point, but it did nothing to calm her down. She realized that her desire to see the Russian terminated had gone beyond matters of global safety and entered the territory of fanaticism. It was a personal vendetta now; one that she would do her utmost to see through to the only conceivable conclusion... the death of Annushka Baikova, preferably a violent and agonizing one. But this was a goal she was going to keep to herself—for now, at least.

After receiving field operations and intelligence updates from the Caravel's Operations and Intelligence Center's Chief, Caroline moved to a higher restricted area of the operations center to wait for a special communications linkup with Tom Broughton and VOCALS. In order to prevent unauthorized access to the ultra sensitive brief, each participant had to provide two iris scans—one at the external control door and another at the internal door. This validated not only their clearance and access level, it also determined whether there was a need for them to know what was being discussed.

Two minutes after Caroline had sat down in front of the large monitor, a split screen appeared. Broughton occupied the left side and the VOCALS Watch Officer occupied the other.

"It's good to see your face!" Broughton started.

"It's good to see yours, too," said Caroline. "I have to admit, though... for a while I was really worried. I thought the cavalry might not make it in time."

"I understand your worries, but you should never allow

yourself to think that way!" Broughton admonished. "The old man promised we'd get you out of there and there was no way we were gonna fail you. In case you haven't heard, Thornton was attacked by one of Ilaivo's thugs earlier this morning."

"Is he alright?" asked Caroline. "What happened?"

"He's fine. He was lured out to what he thought was a meeting with Ilaivo—a meeting Ilaivo set up to get us to back off in exchange for your life. He suffered a couple of knife wounds, but nothing life-threatening. They checked him over at St. Thomas's Hospital, bandaged him up and released him a couple of hours later."

"Does Ilaivo know what happened in the desert this morning?"

"He didn't when the attack against Thornton occurred, but I'm sure he does by now. His psychopathic Russian lover has no doubt filled him in on everything," he added, then changed the subject. "What did Moussa tell you he learned from the Nigerien, Agali?"

"Agali told Moussa that Salim Fa'izu Daoud, a criminal cohort of al-Bashir's, said he had helped al-Bashir bury treasure in the desert about fifty miles southwest of Iferouane. Agali said that Daoud called what was buried there 'yellow gold' and said it's worth 'a king's ransom.' The 'treasure', as Daoud called it, is buried in fifty-five gallon drums, 350 of them to be exact. Daoud also said there was a map of where the stuff is buried, but only al-Bashir handled it. He never once let the map out of his sight."

Caroline went on: "Daoud's yellow gold in fifty-five gallon drums, the mysterious map and what Georges Saint-Jacques said about al-Bashir meeting Iranians and a North Korean in Arlit can mean only one thing... It confirms that he stole yellowcake from the uranium mines, buried it and was planning to sell it to the highest bidder."

"That makes sense, but how does Ilaivo fit in?" Broughton asked.

The Watch Officer interjected. "It's Dan here, sir... I think we can add that missing piece of the puzzle. If AMPHITRITE is right, which I think she is, al-Bashir probably was too impatient and too greedy to haggle over price with the Iranians and the North Koreans. More importantly, he almost certainly didn't have the skills or the knowledge to make that kind of deal happen; so he did what any greedy, impatient thief would do... he settled for a knocked-down price, which means he either found Ilaivo and made him an offer, or Ilaivo found him and offered to take the stuff off his hands."

Caroline chimed in. "That seems to track... and it would also explain al-Bashir's trip to Paris and the one and a half million in counterfeit euro notes he had in his possession when he was blown up at Hôtel Esméralda a little over six weeks ago."

"It's beginning to make sense now," said Broughton. "If we're right and we have indeed cracked the code, Ilaivo will be aware that we're fully onto him. He's pretty damn smart." Broughton paused momentarily. "If only Mills had been here to see it all coming together. Snatching you from Ilaivo's clutches and taking out Dimitar Krastev and Farouk Hamdi seriously weakened his perimeter defenses, not to mention his network. Needless to say, it also pissed him off. Believe me... he'll be coming after us, guns blazing! He's no slouch. He'll have already adjusted his schedule. But what's worse is that he's probably desperate now. And that means he'll eliminate anything or anyone who gets in his way."

It was Caroline's turn to share her thoughts about what she had experienced in North Africa, and she immediately changed the subject to Annushka Baikova. "The Caravel's chief of operations and intelligence told me Annushka Baikova got away," she said. "She'll no doubt pass on all the intelligence about Vanguard's capabilities to Ilaivo. He'll realize he's not up against just a few field operatives, but an entire organization and start bringing in reinforcements."

"He may... and he may not," said Broughton. "He may not

have time for that, at least not to recruit anyone of the caliber he needs. He'll have extra eyes and ears working for him and he may bring in a few more foot soldiers, but I think he'll be too busy making arrangements to move his cargo. This means we've gotta move faster than him!"

Once more, the Watch Officer injected his thoughts. "You're both right," he said. "Ilaivo will have to fast-forward his plans. We think he'll make his move within the next twenty-four to thirty-six hours. And if he hasn't been alerted to what happened already, the intelligence report from his Russian girlfriend will soon have him looking for any anomalistic activity. This includes Foundation personnel movement through airports, border crossings, train stations and the likes."

"I'm already under close surveillance," said Broughton, "but with a bit of luck and some serious maneuvering, I should be able to shake free of it. Ilaivo will be expecting us to move swiftly... and we will, but not in the way he thinks we'll move. We'll mix up our transportation... force him to stretch his assets and informants. If I hurry, I can get a flight to Marseille in a couple of hours," he added. "I'll pick up a car in Marseille and link up with you near Porto. It's about a 725 mile run from Marseille to Porto, but as a somewhat low profile location, it's our safest bet. It's under the radar and it's a good jumping-off point to connect with our mission support assets."

"You tell us what's needed, when and where and we'll make it happen," said the VOCALS Watch Officer.

"Thanks, Dan," said Broughton. "Caroline, I need you to take the first available flight out of Las Palmas and make your way to southern Europe... directly to Portugal, if you can; Spain or southern France, if you have to. When you arrive in Europe, avoid any further use of airports. Better to travel by car. VOCALS will arrange a vehicle for you.

"From whatever city they get you to in southern Europe," he continued, "make your way as quickly as possible to Porto. There's a small fishing village south of the city called Vila Nova de Gaia. When you get to Vila Nova de Gaia, go to Hotel Davilina on Avenida da República. It's low profile accommodations... not too swanky, but it's a good place to go if you're not looking to be found. VOCALS will make sure there's a room reserved for you. Check in and stay put. With a bit of luck, I'll meet you at the hotel sometime between twenty-one and twenty-two hundred hours. From now on, only use your secure mobile phone for communications with me and VOCALS. All urgent or critical messages and updates will be received via your wrist communicator. This is extremely sensitive," he declared. "I'll go over the plan with you tonight when I get to the hotel. We're too close to the finish line to screw this up. So, watch yourself," he admonished.

Caroline locked eyes with him in a steady gaze. "Count on me," she said.

Chapter Sixty-Nine

The Air Europa Lineas Aereas flight from Las Palmas, Gran Canaria, to Madrid, Spain, landed at 10:45 a.m. Because all flights from the Island to Portugal had to go via Madrid, there was nearly an eight-hour layover in Madrid. Instead of losing valuable time sitting in the airport, Caroline had elected to make the journey from Madrid to Porto, Portugal, by car. To avoid being identified by Ilaivo's network of killers and informants, she had traveled under the name of Angeline Bertrand, a dual citizen of Spain and France. Recalling what the operations chief, Leonard O'Boyle, had stressed during his briefing in Algiers, she had altered her appearance before leaving the Caraval in Las Palmas. She had skillfully applied prosthetics to extend her chin, giving herself a heart-shaped face and a slightly broader nose. Her new facial features, along with her green eyes, long, brown curly ringlets, butterfly sun dress and straw beach hat, created the perfect image of a sun-loving island resident. The case of art supplies she carried added the final touches to her cover as an artist bound for the picturesque fishing town of Vila Nova de Gaia.

As planned, a car and driver had met her at Madrid's Barajas Airport. The 375-mile journey from Madrid to Vila Nova de Gaia, Portugal, had been more relaxing than she had expected, but it didn't help expunge her most worrisome thoughts. During the seven-hour journey, she had had time to reflect on the events of the past week and to ponder what lay ahead. She was still disturbed by what had unfolded before her eyes in the desert. While the possibility of dying had not frightened her, it did make her more aware of her own mortality. She pondered what would happen to her son, Nicolas, if she were killed. Would he be better off in Paris with her father, or with her mother's family in Virginia? In less than a week, more than a few deaths had occurred in close proximity to her. First there was the informant, Agali; then her driver and guardian angel, Moussa, who had earned her greatest respect; then Simon Mills, without whose selflessness she almost certainly would have been killed. Each of them had made the ultimate sacrifice. Their bravery and deaths reminded her of her late mother, who had died when she was only three years old, and her husband, François, whom she was just beginning to let go of after more than two years.

For the first time since his death, she was beginning to allow herself to form emotional bonds with people other than family and long-time friends. But the disturbing belief that anyone she attached herself to would be taken away violently, had not only lingered, it had become stronger. Her position in Vanguard made the risk of such a scenario all the more likely, but one thing that had become crystal clear during the past week was that all the people in the organization genuinely cared about each other. They were a tightly-knit bunch to work with—from old man Thornton, all the way down to the drivers who moved people and things around for the organization.

Although Tom Broughton was apprehensive about her being given so much responsibility in the operation, along the way he had taken a liking to her. At first, his judgments about her were purely professional, but after a few days there were clear instances when she and others at Vanguard could see that his concern extended beyond the mission and professional caring. Thus it was safe to say that Broughton had developed a soft spot for her and he personally wanted to make sure that nothing happened to her. She recognized what he was doing, but said or did nothing to discourage or encourage it, though she knew it was problematic for him because he was her superior and he needed to manage his personal feelings and emotions. As for her feelings about him, she couldn't deny that she found him very physically attractive. Neither could she kid herself that she felt nothing. The numb shell that had surrounded her emotions since the death of François appeared to be disintegrating. Perhaps it was time to let love in again.

***

At 6:30 p.m., the sedan carrying Caroline from Madrid to Porto entered the town's center, some seven and a half hours after her plane touched down in Spain. In the center of Porto the driver turned and headed the short drive south to Vila Nova de Gaia and the Hotel Davilina. The trip from Madrid to Porto was uneventful. There had been no encounters with Ilaivo's minions and no one had tried to kidnap or kill her. This did not mean that the Chameleon had lost interest in the Foundation, or any of its personnel he thought might be interfering with his plans. The uneventful journey from Madrid merely suggested that the security measures Broughton had put in place and that she had taken had been effective.

After checking into the hotel, Caroline went straight to her room to get some rest. Other than being sedated by her abductors for just over an hour and dozing off for a half-hour on the flight from Las Palmas to Madrid, she had had no chance for restful sleep. She was exhausted. But in order to maintain a low profile, she ordered a large salad from room service and poured herself a scotch from the room's mini-bar instead of going down to the hotel's dining room. When the food was delivered, she removed the prosthetics and makeup she had put on for the trip, then took a shower.

She knew nothing of Vanguard's level of knowledge of Ilaivo's plan, or what it would do to stop him. In fact, she didn't even know if Broughton and VOCALS had succeeded in narrowing down the number of vessels likely to be involved in moving the yellowcake from West Africa to its final destination. All she knew was that the stakes were getting higher and the danger much greater. During the journey from Madrid to Porto, she had managed to clear her head of the thoughts and people that haunted her, but she could not escape the powerful and still growing romantic feelings she had for Tom Broughton. And now that they would soon be close to each other for the first time since they met, she would have to either suppress those desires, or give in to them.

Chapter Seventy

Portugal
Village of Vila Nova de Gaia

The inconspicuous, ten-year-old Peugeot with Tom Broughton behind the wheel rolled into Vila Nova de Gaia just before 9:30 p.m. He had made the 725 mile journey in less than fourteen hours. He was exhausted. He had ignored nearly all of the 50 kilometer per hour speed limit restrictions imposed on vehicles throughout the Pyrenees Mountains. Yet despite his dangerous sprint through the Pyrenees, the tail he had picked up in Marseille—a black sedan occupied by two men—remained in tow. Its occupants probably would have dispensed with him somewhere in the Pyrenees, if they could have caught up to him. But after their car nearly skidded off the side of the mountain twice on hairpin curves, they adopted a safer strategy —one of hanging back to see where he went.

Broughton had stopped only twice during the trip, both times for gas and a quick trip to the toilet. His first stop was in Zaragoza, Spain, and his second was when he entered Porto. He filled up in Porto because he wanted to make sure the Peugeot was ready for the nearly 200-mile trip south to Vila do Bispo. These were the only times his unwanted escort closed to within less than 500 yards of him and on both occasions they were unable to make a move against him. Each time, there had been too many witnesses. He had seen their faces during both stops;

on the last occasion, they had shown little or no concern about concealing their identities. Seeing them, however, raised more concern than being trailed after having been marked for death. He had been expecting at least one, if not both of the Chameleon's protégés to be on his tail, but there was no sign of the Bulgarian, Andrei Chervenkov or the Russian, Branimir Baikov. This meant that they were either laying in wait for him somewhere ahead—ready to leap out at a time and place of their choosing—or they had been given a different and possibly more important assignment.

When he arrived at Hotel Davaline, he drove straight to the car park at the back of the building. He could barely keep his eyes open. He went straight to reception, collected his key and went directly to the fourth floor. Upstairs on the fourth floor, Caroline lay on her bed, wide awake. Once again, she was thinking. Except this time it was not about what lay ahead for the mission. She was thinking instead about what would happen during the few hours she would spend in close proximity to Tom Broughton.

Her thoughts were suddenly interrupted by a faint knock at the door. "Yes?" she said. "Who is it?"

"It's me... Broughton," he replied in a low whisper.

"Just a minute," she said, sliding her feet into her slippers.

When she opened the door, he was leaning against the door frame looking tired, but he still managed to smile.

"It's good to see you," she said.

He walked in and stood in silence, looking down at her face. "It's good to see you, too," he said. "I was worried that your first time out might be your last. I have to confess... Although I was attracted to you, I didn't have much confidence in you. But now I can see why Thornton recruited, trained and made you a part of this team. You're smart, imaginative and determined. And good-looking!" he added bluntly.

She smiled a wide, warm, welcoming smile. "Why don't you tell me how you really feel about me?"

Broughton felt embarrassed. "All day I've been thinking of ways to tell you that, and believe me… just blurting it out wasn't one of them," he said. "I've never been so drawn to someone I've only met briefly. I felt the chemistry immediately, and I have to admit it was powerful… it still is. And right now, at this very moment, I could be making a real fool of myself for telling you all of this."

Caroline threw off her slippers and sat on the side of the bed. He came over and sat down beside her. She was wearing pale blue silk pajamas. Her dark brown wavy hair was pinned up in a *chignon* at the nape of her neck. "You haven't made a fool of yourself. Believe me, you haven't. I know and I understand," she said. "I, too, have a confession to make… For the last few days I've been thinking about my feelings for you and whether or not I should tell you about them. I was very tired this evening, but I couldn't get to sleep. I lay awake for several hours, trying to understand and describe the feelings that I experienced when I first saw you, feelings that have been growing inside of me ever since…"

She paused, took a breath then went on: "Do you think our feelings for each other and our desire to get things off our chests have anything to do with what's been happening this past week? You know what I mean… thoughts of mortality and imminent danger tend to propel feelings forward, sometimes faster than we can deal with them. What I mean is that it's a 'do or die' situation and one or both of us might not make it out of this. Along with that, there's the thought that if only one of us survives, that person will be dogged forever by the question, 'why didn't I allow myself to give into a bit more emotional recklessness?'"

"You mean, not allowing the cliché 'it's better to have loved and lost than never to have loved at all' define and guide our situation?" he asked, knowing the answer already. "If that's what you mean, you're probably right. In fact, I know you're right," he added.

She looked at him wantonly and said, "Yes, that's precisely what I mean."

He continued. "You know... I became fully aware of the depth of my feelings for you when you left Algiers for northern Niger. I knew it was a dangerous situation and Thornton knew it as well. I told him that if you were the only person who could do this, then we had to find discreet backup for you—someone unknown, but someone who could be trusted to look after you. I assigned the job to Moussa. Moussa and I had known each other for years and he had earned my complete trust. I knew you wouldn't like it, and I knew it would probably make you angry, but I didn't care. I didn't want to lose you before I got to know you."

"It worked," she said. "And yes, it pissed me off because it made me feel like a child," Caroline said jokingly.

"I also pressured Simon Mills to go in with the SAR team," he added. "I wanted to make sure you got out without a hair on your head being hurt."

"Stop..." she said. "You don't need to tell me anything else. I've known... well, at least *felt* this all along. Call it women's intuition," she added, smiling. "But now I know for sure that you care deeply about me. I think it was my intuition about you that nudged me over the line and brought me back from a two-year emotional flat-line."

"I'm pleased that you understand and don't mind me caring about you, because tomorrow morning, we're probably going to face more danger than either of us have ever faced before. That danger stems from something dark... something that's at the heart of all this deception, killing and double-crossing."

Broughton paused, wondering whether or not to tell her about the car that had followed him all the way from Marseille. He decided not to; not now. Why spoil the moment? He went on: "Our job and the mission are pretty straightforward. We've gotta get out of Vila Nova de Gaia and make our way south to the Portuguese coast. If we succeed, the job waiting for us just might stop the next world war from happening, or at least delay it. To do that, we've gotta board a ship sailing from West Africa bound for the Persian Gulf. I'm here with you because you're part of that mission and also because I want to make sure that nothing happens to you. I have to protect you—and not only that, I *want* to protect you!" He smiled. "Forgive me if that sounds paternalistic. It's not meant to be. It's just plain old-fashioned selfishness."

"I know," Caroline said. She turned toward him, stroked his chest and kissed him on the cheek. "I know you'll look out for me and I'm sure we'll look out for each other. In the meantime, you should get some sleep. You haven't slept for over twenty-four hours. Have a shower and come to bed... this bed. I'll wake you when it's time to leave."

Ten minutes later, Broughton emerged from the bathroom with only a towel around his waist. She threw back the covers and in the light that spilled from the partially opened door, he could see the firm and well-defined, womanly shape of her *café au lait* body against the white sheets. He moved over to the bed, let the towel fall away, slid into her arms and dissolved in her warmth. At first, they caressed and embraced awkwardly, but hesitation and uncertainty soon gave way to passionate and intense lovemaking. Afterwards, she lay awake for what seemed like hours, watching him as he slept in her arms. For the first time in a long, long time, she felt truly safe.

Chapter Seventy-One

It was just past midnight when Broughton awoke. It was a soft kiss on his forehead and the aroma of black coffee passed under his nose that roused him from a short but deep sleep. When he opened his eyes, he was surprised to see who had kissed him. It was not Caroline Dupré. For a moment, he was shaken and disturbed. Then he realized she was wearing a disguise. She had short, bobbed, brunette hair and dark brown eyes. Her nose was slightly longer, with a bulbous tip and her cheekbones were higher and rounder than her natural ones. The disguise was incredibly convincing—even to the man with whom she had made love a few hours earlier—thanks to the enhanced makeup techniques she had learned from Cayce, Vanguard's makeup artist, only days earlier.

"It must be my lucky day!" he said, still groggy. "Two women in one night!" he added teasingly, pulling her toward him. "When I saw your face, it gave me a shock. You shouldn't make drastic changes like that to your appearance without telling me. It could be dangerous!" he added jokingly.

"I didn't want to wake you," said Caroline. "You needed the sleep. We have quite a journey ahead of us. Besides, this way, if we're seen together, Caroline Dupré won't suffer from 'guilt by association'!"

"Maybe not for the remainder of this operation, but I suspect that'll change!" he replied, putting on his clothes.

When they stepped outside the hotel, the night air was pleasant and still. On the small green across from the hotel, glistening dewdrops clung to the foliage. The village of Vila Nova de Gaia was quiet. All of its inhabitants were fast asleep; the only signs of life were nocturnal creatures. In the distance, the musical hooting of a lonely owl could be heard, while a chorus of cicadas provided background percussion. Shrouded by darkness, the old Peugeot 504 rolled cautiously, headlights off, over the short driveway leading to the main road. After leaving the hotel's driveway, Broughton turned north on Avenida da República and drove along the one-way street for one block before making a U-turn and heading south. Even though she was wearing a disguise, Caroline nevertheless crouched on the floor between the front and rear seats.

With the events of the previous day still weighing heavily on his mind, Broughton nosed the car toward the edge of the village. The streets of Vila Nova de Gaia at night were colorless. There were a few fancy neon signs, but the town was not completely pitch black. A few scattered street lights helped to expose some of the places that might have otherwise been good cover for an ambush. Thus far, there had been no sign of the black sedan that had tailed him all the way from Marseille to Porto. Much to his surprise, it had broken off and disappeared before he entered Vila Nova de Gaia, most likely to turn the job over to a new and as yet undetected surveillance team.

The Peugeot continued its slow crawl south toward the edge of the village. Broughton had hoped to pick up speed before joining one of Portugal's motorways, the A1 Estrada Nacional, heading south toward Lisbon. But near the edge of the village and without warning, a pair of high beam headlights from a rapidly advancing car pierced the night from a side street and shone directly inside the Peugeot, nearly blinding Broughton. The advancing lights stopped with a bone-jarring crash. The car had rammed the Peugeot on the right rear side, pushing it around nearly 45 degrees.

"Damn it!" Broughton shouted. "They're onto us!"

He turned the Peugeot's headlights on, dropped it into low

gear and pushed the accelerator to the floor. The car fish-tailed and its tires clawed at the road for traction then sped away. The car that had rammed them quickly straightened up and fell in behind. A few streets later, another vehicle, a 4x4, skidded out of a side street onto the main road and fell in behind them. The second vehicle was cause for bigger worries. *There'll be nowhere to go if one of them overtakes us*, he realized.

"They're going to try to box us in!" Broughton shouted. "Hang on!" he instructed, almost yelling to be heard above the Peugeot's whining engine.

The drivers of the two vehicles had picked the ideal spot for an ambush. For several blocks the street narrowed and snaked its way tightly between the village's old buildings. Before Broughton and Caroline could figure out what was happening and come up with a plan to gain the advantage, the situation deteriorated—it suddenly went from bad to worse when they heard the tat-tat-tat-tat of a submachine gun. Seconds later, the Peugeot's rear window exploded.

"Shit!" Broughton yelled, leaning toward the passenger side. He began to serpentine—scraping the buildings on the left and right with the car in order to avoid being hit by bullets coming from the car behind them.

"Keep your head down!" he told Caroline. "I'm gonna try something!" *This tunnel of a road has to be nearing its end.* Fighting the wheel with one hand, he jammed his 9mm Beretta pistol under his thigh and declared, "Here we go!" As soon as the buildings on both sides came to an end, he hurled the Peugeot into a J-turn, grabbed the Beretta from under his thigh and squeezed off four shots at the first trailing vehicle, now coming toward him head-on.

Two of his bullets hit the car's windshield and another must have hit a front tire because the right front side pitched downward sharply. The car swerved wildly to the right, then flipped and rolled several times before landing on its side, engine still revving.

"One down, one to go!" Broughton shouted. "I like these odds much better!"

"You can say that again," Caroline said, climbing onto the back seat. "That was far too close for my liking!"

Chapter Seventy-Two

It was pitch-dark along the road outside the village, which made the surrounding terrain almost indiscernible. There was intermittent cloud and only a spattering of faint stars hung in the night sky. Speeding south, away from population centers, Broughton looked up at Caroline in the rearview mirror. "We still have a ways to go to make the rendezvous at the old fort in Sagres," he said calmly. "We can get there by 3:30, maybe earlier, if we can maintain this speed and keep well out in front of our tenacious friends."

For the next half hour, the Peugeot pitched and swayed along narrow roads. It was the second time they had briefly left the motorway to evade their followers. Before long, they were passing remote dwellings, threading through narrow lanes and passes that cut through the steep hills of northern Portugal like human veins. But unlike human veins, enclosed pathways carrying a life force to all parts of the body, these narrow lanes were open and had no guard rails to stop an out-of-control vehicle from leaving the road and plummeting hundreds of feet into the gullies below.

Just after 1:30 a.m. activity on the roads began to increase, evidenced by the appearance of logging trucks making the trek up the mountain to harvesting areas. The trucks came from Lagos, Lisbon, Sintra and other cities and ports, to take on loads of bark for cork from trees harvested in the hills of central and northern Portugal. Less than twenty minutes after meeting the first truck, they had had to squeeze past three more. Several of the encounters had forced them dangerously close to the edge of narrow roads. Silt and loose gravel on the road had made passing with any speed impossible. Each time, Broughton was forced to slow the car to a crawl. The truck drivers clearly recognized the advantage of size and seemed determined not to cede a single foot of roadway to smaller vehicles.

After squeezing past the fourth truck, they approached the next hill and Broughton could see what looked like a herd of animals, silhouetted in the distant glimmer of the Peugeot's headlights. The animals looked to be the size of sheep or goats. Before long, they could also make out the figure of a man, a shepherd or goat-herder. He was moving the animals down the side of the hill and across the road. As they drew nearer, he could see that the animals were goats.

"What's this? A herd of goats and a goat-herder at this hour in the morning…?" Caroline asked rhetorically. "What's wrong with this place? Aggressive truckers, goat-herders! Doesn't anybody sleep? What's next… a jumbo jet?"

Chapter Seventy-Three

The early morning dew and the oily asphalt made the car's tires feel as if they were sliding across the surface of the road. Broughton could see the direction in which the animals were moving, yet he didn't slow down. "Let's hope this damn herd is only a couple of dozen animals." he mumbled. As the car headed up the next hill, its headlights pitched upward and Broughton could see a herd of over fifty animals, all goats. He eased off the accelerator, braked slowly and brought the Peugeot to a modest roll and stuck his head out of the window. "Can you please hurry? We've got an emergency!" he shouted in broken Portuguese.

The lanky figure herding the animals, who was dressed like a *lavradore* in white shirt, waistcoat, long-waist trousers and oddly, cattleman's boots, said nothing. He had a woolen blanket thrown over his shoulder. After Broughton had spoken, he halted and shielded his eyes from the car's lights, but still said nothing. Instead, he tapped the staff he carried more rapidly on his thigh and made a high-pitched kissing sound. As he went about changing the tempo of his tapping and kissing, the tempo of the clanging bell around the lead goat's neck increased. After hearing the new pace, the entire herd quickened its step. The lanky shepherd tapped his staff again, this time intermittently, and repeated the kissing sound he had been making. The entire herd responded. It turned and flowed at an oblique angle, slightly toward the Peugeot, then at a much less sharper angle as it crossed the road.

"What the hell is he doing?" Caroline asked. "It looks as if he didn't understand you. Unless...." she paused, "unless he's deliberately doing this to piss us off!"

Without any additional coaxing from Broughton, the shepherd quickened his steps and took up a position alongside the road, as if he was a spectator at a parade. The quick change in his demeanor was perplexing. But it soon became clear why he had behaved the way he had done—without warning a sharp, jarring impact was felt at the rear of the car. A vehicle had slammed into the back of the Peugeot at a good speed. The force from the collision nearly sent Caroline flying forward onto the front seat. Before she could right herself, the driver of the large 4x4 that had rammed them threw the vehicle in reverse, turned on its headlights and plowed into them again. What remained of the Peugeot's rear window shattered, spraying a shower of glass throughout the car's interior.

"Damn the goats!" Caroline shouted. "Get us the hell out of here!"

Broughton gave several blasts on the Peugeot's horn and waded into the herd. The animals parted and the lead goat's bell clanged steadily; other animals in the herd sang out and began to scatter nervously, going to the left and right of the car. The shepherd was still standing by the side of the road, looking on in a trance-like state. A second later, he threw the blanket from his shoulder and leveled a machine pistol at the Peugeot and fired. More windows exploded, and more glass sprayed all over the car's interior.

"Get down!" Broughton shouted. "There's an MP-5 and an ammo satchel under the right front seat."

"Got it!" Caroline shouted and swung the weapon's short barrel through what was left of the shattered right rear window. The 4x4, still on their tail, came closer and spat semi-automatic weapons fire. Bullets whizzed, sparked and ricocheted in every direction.

"Our friends finally caught up and it looks like they mean

business!" Caroline yelled.

More bullets spat from the 4x4. They had only just narrowly escaped a crossfire from the shepherd and the trailing 4x4, then two more vehicles joined the fray—heavy 4x4s which descended from the hillside ahead of them at a dizzying speed. A new threat was no more than fifty yards in front of them. But one of the 4x4s did not enter the road. Instead, it stopped to wait for Broughton and Caroline to go past.

With his eyes still fixed on the road ahead, Broughton yelled, "It's about to get worse! We've got more company! How's the ammo holding up?"

"Six more clips!" Caroline replied.

"Make every round count!"

"Don't worry, I intend to!"

Caroline swept the MP-5's barrel from left to right and a high pitched wail came from the side of the road where the shepherd had been standing. Gunfire from the side of the road stopped. With her head still below the back of the rear seat, she swung the barrel to the rear of the car and through the glassless window and squeezed off three efficient bursts. The lights of the 4x4 tailing them suddenly went out and the vehicle began to serpentine, twisting wildly from one side of the road to the other before flying off it into the pitch black night. A few seconds later it exploded and an orange fireball rose from the gully below.

"Good shootin'!" Broughton yelled as he straightened out the Peugeot's direction of travel on the narrow road.

Just as Broughton expected, the second 4x4 in front of them waited for them to go past it on the road. As they passed, the vehicle already in front of them slowed down.

Broughton down-shifted, floored the accelerator and shouted, "We've got a squeeze play in the making! I'm gonna try to get around the joker in front of us. Grab onto something and hold tight!"

Broughton approached the lead vehicle with all the speed

the undulating and winding road would allow the Peugeot's engine to muster. As soon as he closed on the lead 4x4, the other 4x4 that had waited at the bottom of the hill dropped onto the road in pursuit. The Peugeot was less than ten yards from the lead 4x4's bumper. Broughton stayed in tight on the vehicle for several minutes, waiting for the right opportunity. Then, without warning, he dropped back a few meters, down-shifted, floored the accelerator and swung sharply to the left of the 4x4. The Peugeot went high on the uneven embankment, narrowly avoiding large boulders and straddling or dodging pits nearly as wide as the car.

For several minutes the two vehicles jockeyed for the lead. Unlike the heavy 4x4, the engine of the Peugeot strained under the demand for more power; its soft suspension gave way to repeated encounters with crevices, dips and rocks on the embankment. Despite the advantages of the off-road vehicle, he refused to concede.

He down-shifted and floored the accelerator again. He was about to overtake the 4x4 when its rear passenger window dropped and small, fiery stars appeared from it. The star-shaped flashes were from a semi-automatic weapon. Bullets peppered the side and rear fender of the Peugeot.

Broughton snatched the steering wheel to the right and slammed into the side of the 4x4. The collision threw the passenger with the automatic weapon away from the open window and interrupted the assault. Sparks flew between the two vehicles. The Peugeot surged forward and slid back onto the road in front of the 4x4.

"Now you're on my turf..." Caroline said. "You're right where I want you!"

She switched the MP-5 to full automatic, swung the barrel to the rear window once more and raked the vehicle's front grill, its wheels and windshield. The vehicle's headlights went out and the driver jammed on the brakes to avoid going off the road.

His reaction was too slow. A screeching sound came from

the vehicle's wheels; then screams pierced the night air above the whining engines. Seconds later, there was a loud crash.

Their odds for survival had just improved. They were one-on-one again.

Chapter Seventy-Four

It was nearly 2:00 a.m. and the deadly contest had continued for nearly three hours and across more than 200 miles. Leaving Portugal's motorway in an attempt to shake off their pursuers had cost them yet more valuable time. They were now more than thirty minutes behind schedule. The old fort at Sagres was still more than an hour away and the last 4x4 was still trailing, though it seemed to be deliberately lagging behind. Caroline pondered. *What are they up to? Devising a new strategy or calling for reinforcements?*

"How are you holding up back there?" Broughton shouted above the whining engine and loud rush of air passing through the windowless car.

"I'm OK! Just get us to Fortaleza de Sagres in one piece. I'll take care of our friends."

Suddenly, the headlights of the trailing vehicle surged forward and closed the distance between them.

"Here they come!" Caroline bellowed. "I guess they were cooking up a new strategy after all."

The heavy vehicle fell in behind the Peugeot and started a dogged pursuit that lasted for twenty minutes. But instead of following directly in their wake, it swerved from side to side until the Peugeot reached the foothills of the mountains. Every half mile or so and around each sharp bend it pulled closer and spat bullets from the right front and rear passenger windows. The occupants were exercising more caution than that used by the occupants of the first vehicle.

Three times the 4x4 approached and rammed the rear end of the Peugeot, causing it to fish-tail. Each time the old Peugeot nearly skidded off the road and into the valley below. The second time it rammed the Peugeot, Broughton had braked sharply then sped ahead again to interfere with the timing of the collision. When the Peugeot's brake lights came on, Caroline could make out three figures inside the 4x4. The man on the front passenger seat had jeered as he tried unsuccessfully to fire through the glassless rear window of the Peugeot. The sneer on his face made her pulse with anger. *Right*, she thought. *You'll die first.*

The duel continued until after they passed through the village of Tunes. After passing through Tunes, Broughton turned and headed west on *Estrada* N269-2, off the motorway once more. About five miles onto the narrow road, he swung the Peugeot onto its shoulder, just before a sharp bend. For a split-second, the Peugeot's right rear wheel hung suspended in mid-air over a dark valley below. After he rounded the hair-pin curve, he could see the taillights of a large truck in the distance and those of another large vehicle approaching. The approaching vehicle was just starting its climb into the hills. He knew that the two large vehicles passing in opposite directions would be the perfect time to make his move—a move that could eliminate his pursuer.

Having seen the tactics of the 4x4, Broughton slowed down. He knew the driver would back off and come closer at high speed when he came to the next bend in the road. Their adversary would use the bend to prevent Caroline from gaining a direct line-of-fire and to stay out of the most accurate range of her weapon.

"We'll soon have a chance to get rid of them, if you can hang on a couple more minutes!" Broughton shouted. "There's another large truck ahead of us going down the mountain and another one coming toward us!"

"More trucks?" she yelled. "You've gotta be kidding me!"

"Yeah, more trucks! But this time it's to our advantage. We'll wait until the trucks are about to pass each other and we'll overtake the one in front of us."

Just as Broughton predicted, when they came to the next bend in the road, the 4x4 trailing them sped up. It closed to within seventy-five yards and its windows lit up again with muzzle flashes, except this time even more furiously and more sustained. The muzzle flashes and tracer rounds looked like roman candles on the fourth of July.

The truck in front of them was now less than a hundred yards away; when it went around the next bend in the road, it swung wide and obstructed the view ahead. The driver of the 4x4 could not see the oncoming truck ahead at the foot of the steep hill. Broughton made his move. He down-shifted and pushed the accelerator to the floor, swerved to the left abruptly and overtook the truck in front, just after it came out of the bend. The 4x4 followed instinctively, but halfway along the log-laden long trailer, the oncoming truck was nearing the crest of the hill. Broughton had just managed to swing the Peugeot out of the overtaking lane and back onto his side of the road before the two trucks met. He had had only a few yards to spare. When he cut back in, there was nowhere for the 4x4 to go.

The driver of the oncoming truck gave two long blasts on its horn. With the large truck bearing down on him, the driver of the 4x4 braked sharply and tried to slide back into his lane behind the truck he was overtaking, but he had reacted too late. For several seconds, the sound of skidding tires from both vehicles filled the air. Then it was replaced by a crash and a huge explosion and both the truck and the 4x4 burst into flames.

As they raced ahead, Caroline saw the truck come to a shuddering halt nearly on top of the 4x4 just before the explosion. She had also seen the driver of the truck climb from his seat and stagger away from the inferno. A few seconds later, the truck's fuel tanks exploded and set off the fuel tank of the 4x4. The explosions sent a tremor along the road; a cloud of dark smoke bellowed upward from the crash and an orange plume of fire grew larger and danced at its center. For the first time since she had lain in Tom's arms at the hotel in Vila Nova de Gaia, she felt safe, if only for a few moments.

***

Less than half an hour after shaking off their pursuers, Broughton turned the Peugeot onto Portugal's auto route A22 motorway and headed west. Twenty minutes later, they turned off the auto route and headed south, moving more cautiously in their battered vehicle toward *Fortaleza de Sagres*. A few miles earlier, the Peugeot had begun to lurch, its engine had started to knock and the smell of burning oil had begun to saturate the passenger compartment. When they turned off the main road, Broughton looked at the oil pressure gauge. It had plummeted, but he continued for several hundred meters before the engine died. He let the car coast to a stop. Blue smoke bellowed from underneath and soon enveloped it.

"Looks like we did some serious damage to the oil pan during our little joy ride," Broughton said light-heartedly. "There's not a drop of oil in the oil pan or the engine."

"How far are we from the fort?" Caroline asked, looking worried.

"About a half mile… a mile at most… You can practically see it from here," he added, pointing south.

"So, what do we do? There's no way this thing is going to move from here. It's had it!"

"I suggest we hoof it, if we intend to make the rendezvous." He stared at the illuminated hands of his wrist communicator. "We've got seventeen minutes."

They clambered from the smoldering car, gathering their weapons and the ammunition satchel. Broughton opened the trunk and they took out small black backpacks, slung them over their shoulders and broke into a brisk trot. Ten minutes later, they were standing in front of the heavy wooden gates of Fortaleza de Sagres. Because of its location and construction, which featured a rear wall that dropped to the sea, the fort provided sanctuary and masked their rendezvous and pickup. Caroline could see why the decision to go over the walls had been made. It was far easier to scale Fortaleza de Sagres' thick concrete walls than to waste time trying to breach its heavy doors, or make a rendezvous on an exposed beach or over the rocks.

Working in silence, they moved along the right front face of the thick wall. They removed the packs from their backs and took out climbing ropes with collapsible grappling hooks attached. Standing a few feet from the base of the thick wall, they used their semi-automatic rifles to launch the grappling hooks over the wall. Seconds later, they began scaling the twenty-foot high obstacle. Once on top of it, they reaffixed their hooks to the opposite side, and scurried down the back side. They scampered across the rough cobblestones, past the fort's chapel, toward the rear wall. Still working in silence, they repeated the same procedure at the fort's rear wall.

The back wall of Fortaleza de Sagres dropped almost directly onto the Atlantic Ocean. There was no moon, but the ambient light that fell from the faint, star-lit sky onto the pale cobblestones, cast enough of a shadow for them to detect movement. The surroundings were still. They were alone in the old fort.

Alongside the back wall, in total darkness, their contact waited aboard a Rigid Hull Inflatable Boat (RHIB). As soon as the boat's coxswain spotted them, he started the engines and signaled all-clear with two short flashes from a red lens flashlight. Caroline acknowledged with a single flash of her red light. Seconds later, they were onboard the RHIB, headed out into the Atlantic Ocean.

As the boat moved away, the lights along Portugal's coastline began to twinkle and grow fainter. The inflatable picked up speed and was soon skipping and bouncing over the crests of modest waves at nearly 45 knots. Surprisingly, the sea became calmer as they moved farther away from the coast. As the glowing lights along the coastline became fainter, the night sky slid opened like a curtain, revealing a blanket of twinkling stars against the vast blackness of space. Caroline gazed upward in silence, contemplating the challenge that lay ahead and the dire ramifications if they failed. The thought of failure, however, was short-lived because she knew that too much was riding on her doing her job. Failure was not an option.

The RHIB continued heading southwesterly at top speed toward a position ten miles off the Portuguese coast. There it would rendezvous with the *Aphrodite*, a large, ocean-going trawler of Greek registry, which was sitting dead-in-the-water. The boat's coxswain, who also commanded the RHIB, broke the silence, leaning over from his position at the center-mounted console and shouting above the noise of the engine and the waves slapping against the boat. "We should arrive at the rendezvous point in about forty-five minutes. You'll be fully briefed when you get aboard. I know you are already familiar with the details of the mission, but I was instructed to inform you that there has been a slight change in the timeline. The whole operation has been moved forward by forty-five minutes."

"What's the reason?" Caroline asked, concerned. Had there been a new event that they hadn't been informed of?

"Nothing's wrong! They want to make sure you have sufficient darkness for cover," the coxswain replied.

Caroline went silent for a moment as another thought occurred to her. "Are all of you Vanguard?" she asked.

The crew of the small boat exchanged looks of surprise. "I'm not supposed to divulge that information, ma'am. But seeing what you two are about to do, I reckon' it won't affect operations security," the trim, tall, leathery-skinned coxswain chuckled. "We all are!" he shouted. "The engineman, the guy up there on the 50 caliber machinegun, and the two guys armed to the teeth at the front end of the boat! We're all with the Foundation. I'm a retired U.S. Navy Chief Petty Officer. Spent six years with Special Boat Units... drivin' Navy SEALS around." The man grinned widely, showing nearly all his teeth, then added louder for the benefit of all onboard, "I love this job! I can't think of anything else I'd rather be doing!"

The boat suddenly began to encounter larger waves, and the coxswain turned his attention back to operating the craft. When the crests subsided a bit, he turned again to his two passengers. "Right now, though, my job is to deliver you two safe and sound to this position," he said, pointing to a blip on the boat's small radar screen.

Chapter Seventy-Five

Captain Bill Tremont held the *Aphrodite* in position at the rendezvous coordinates by using the boat's main engines and its thrusters. The *Aphrodite* was no ordinary fishing trawler. Not only was it larger than most, it was loaded to the gills with the latest navigation, sounding and weather equipment. It could also receive down-links from Vanguard's various arrays of satellites, including its global positioning satellites like those of the United States' Global Positioning System (GPS). The covert vessel also had several removable antennae that allowed high frequency direction finding and use of satellite phones—encrypted and unencrypted.

Bill Tremont stood leaning over a large map spread out on a transparent chart table. His chiseled features, particularly his square jaw and thick eyebrows, were amplified in the greenish-blue light that shone upward from beneath the table. He was a man deep in thought. Suddenly, the radio near him erupted with a crackle and a crisp, clear voice broke through.

"*Aphrodite* base, this is *Aphrodite Two*!"

It was the call from the inbound RHIB. Captain Tremont lifted the handset. "This is *Aphrodite Base*. Go ahead, *Aphrodite Two*."

"Estimated time of arrival, ten minutes... Repeat, E-T-A one, zero minutes..." The voice on the radio continued. "As notified earlier, we are plus two. I say again, we are plus two. Copy...?"

"Roger, *Aphrodite Two*. I read you loud and clear! Plus two... Standing by for your arrival... Base out..."

Captain Tremont hung up the microphone and dispatched his second-in-command to the trawler's accommodation ladder off the port quarterdeck to prepare for the RHIB's arrival. He then left the bridge to welcome his special passengers aboard.

Chapter Seventy-Six

The RHIB's coxswain swung the small craft alongside the *Aphrodite's* accommodation ladder and Caroline and Broughton ran up to the main deck.

"Good to have you safely aboard," Captain Tremont said. "We haven't any time to waste. We have to get underway straight away. We've got only two hours of darkness, maybe two and a half at best, to get within range of the targets. We have two vessels, approximately ten miles apart, heading in our direction at about 24 knots. We are going to need every minute of cover we can get if you are to have any real chance at making this a surprise assault." He paused, then resumed. "I suggest we go straight down to the Operations Center. VOCALS provided everything they've got. It may not be everything you're going to need, but that's where we are. I'll explain when we get below."

Caroline descended two levels below the main deck and headed forward down a passageway, with Captain Tremont leading the way and Broughton bringing up the rear. After a short distance, they reached a door with *MAINTENANCE ROOM* stenciled on it in bold black lettering. Tremont opened the door and they walked into a space with work benches, tables, band saws, lathes and tool-and-dye equipment. They passed through the workshop to the back of the space and stopped at what looked like an ordinary bulkhead. A cabled hoist control with a generous number of colored buttons hung suspended near the wall. Tremont took the control and pressed five of its seven buttons. A section of the bulkhead receded several inches, then slid to the right to reveal a heavy, vault-like door. Tremont peered into an iris scanner and after a few seconds, a computer-generated voice declared 'subject recognized.'

Captain Tremont pushed the heavy door and it swung open easily. Inside, there were about a half-dozen personnel working at consoles. On the far right bulkhead there were several large flat screen monitors; in the middle of the space stood a six-foot square interactive display screen. Two men stood in front of the large screen, moving several images around with their fingertips. Moments later, Vanguard's first officer entered carrying a small, highly polished canister, clearly of considerable weight. Caroline stared at it, trying to guess what it held. She had a fairly good idea.

"Ah, that's good!" Tremont beamed. "Let me formally introduce you to Mr. Mumford, my first officer," he added excitedly, reaching for the canister. "Mr. Mumford has just handed me something that's very important to your mission. In fact, it's why you are here."

Mumford exchanged pleasantries and smiled at Caroline and Broughton. Captain Tremont turned to the first officer and nodded, then added, "Once we get underway, he'll keep us moving toward our target while I fill you in on the details." The first officer read the Captain's body language, excused himself and made his way back to the bridge to take charge of the ship.

Tremont slowly released the pressure latch on the canister and tilted the open container toward Caroline and Broughton. "This is what it's all about! Looks kind of innocent in its natural form, doesn't it? Actually, like this, it poses virtually no danger to handle. Too bad it becomes so deadly when enriched and turned into weapons grade uranium. Thanks to the two of you and a few faceless and nameless others, we are hot on the trail of what may be the largest load of this stuff that's ever been illegally amassed and shipped," Tremont declared. "I know you've been digging hard and living dangerously for the past several days to put the pieces of this puzzle together, but I'm afraid you didn't know before you left North Africa that we managed to get a sample of the stuff that was stolen. We got it rather unexpectedly. It was acquired by a little-used agent run by one of Vanguard's North African operatives—Simon Mills— a friend and long-time colleague of yours, I believe," Captain Tremont added.

Caroline's mind flashed back to the room where he was killed, the room where she had been tortured and held prisoner, and she winced inwardly at the bitter memory of that day.

"I'm very sorry about his death," Tremont said, turning to Broughton. "From what I've heard, he was a damn good man and a top-notch operative."

"He was one of the best," Broughton replied. "And when you're in charge, you're responsible for everything… successes and failures."

"Tom, you've been at this business as long as I have, maybe a bit longer, but take it from me, you can't be in several places at once. Thornton also said you didn't have direct contact with Mills because his cover was too sensitive for face-to-face meetings. If it's any consolation to you, Mr. Mills knew that if he stepped out of the shadows and revealed himself, he ran the risk of being killed, if not immediately, then later. However, it seems he made the decision to do that; it was a brave and selfless thing he did."

Tremont's soliloquy seemed to fully capture Mills' persona. His comments about Mills' self-sacrifice in particular hit home and Caroline's eyes began to well up. After Tremont finished, a hush fell over the small Operations Center. It had happened intuitively—an undeclared moment of silence for a fallen comrade.

After the pause, Tremont shifted the subject back to what lay ahead. Holding the shiny canister out in front of him, he declared, "It's all from the uranium mine in Arlit!" Shifting his eyes from the canister to Broughton, then to Caroline, he continued. "Your team succeeded in identifying the origin of this stuff, but what they didn't learn was that nearly three tons of it was stolen in just over two years by the Algerian who got himself blown up in Paris. Little by little, he managed to squirrel the stuff away in the desert. Its theft was never detected or suspected because he moved it in such small quantities and hid it a good distance from where it was stolen. And during the past twenty-four hours, we've learned a bit more. Unfortunately, VOCALS couldn't get the information to you or Caroline because the two of you were making your way here."

"What else has come to light and how was that possible?" asked Caroline. "I thought Vanguard had pulled all of its productive assets out of the area."

"Nearly all…" Tremont said. "Tom knows better than I do, but there were a few low-level assets we could still connect with. By the looks of it, we got lucky, because it was one of those that paid off."

Caroline asked, "What kind of luck?"

Tremont looked at her pensively for a few seconds. "I'll get straight to the point… Yesterday, while you were both making your way to Portugal, the chief cook of the *Montserrat Star* fell ill… something to do with the ship's supply officer having procured some poisonous mushrooms from a vendor in The Gambia, which he cooked and sampled. The ship's captain and most of its crew refused to sail with two young apprentices in charge of the galley. So the ship sent out an urgent call for a replacement chief cook."

"How do the *Montserrat Star's* culinary woes affect our mission?" Broughton asked.

"I was coming to that," said Captain Tremont. "A relatively new and somewhat inactive agent in Banjul, a local, got wind of the opening and took the job. He had had no time to notify Vanguard, so he took the position and made contact after he was onboard the vessel. Within a few hours of reporting aboard, he contacted VOCALS and informed them that the ship's first officer had bragged to him that he would be well off after the voyage and would be able to retire and spend more time with his family. When the agent asked the first officer why the voyage was paying so well, the first officer told him that some rich men in the Persian Gulf urgently needed the ship's services and were paying ten times the going price and bonuses for the ship's crew if the cargo was delivered on schedule."

"How do we know we can trust this agent?" asked Caroline. "He's virtually untested. Besides, our last dealings with Vanguard's old friend, the Frenchman, Georges Saint-Jacques, showed us that honesty and integrity fly out the window when there's an opportunity for someone to get their hands on an extraordinary sum of money."

"She's right!" Broughton cut in. "Besides, we figured that when the time came to move the yellowcake to its buyer, it would be split up and moved overland to several West African sea ports, loaded onto small coastal vessels and then onto a couple of the oceangoing merchant ships. VOCALS identified the *Montserrat Star* and the *Northern Celeste* as the two vessels most likely to transport the cargo to its buyer. As you are no doubt aware, VOCALS tracked the movement of the *Louis Breavard*, the *Montserrat Star* and the *Northern Celeste* and eliminated the *Louis Breavard*. That left the *Northern Celeste* and the *Montserrat Star*, which are both heading our way."

"I must admit, I thought they would do something similar, if not the same thing," said Captain Tremont. "And for a while, I also thought they'd play a shell game with the shipment, but I am now confident that I was wrong."

"How can you be, if we can't be certain about the information from the agent in Banjul?" asked Caroline. "And if we're still not sure about the target then we're putting all of our eggs into one basket, solely on a report from an agent who may have fabricated it for his own benefit."

It wasn't just Caroline who was feeling frustrated by the Captain's apparent reliance on shaky information. Broughton's frustration was beginning to grow, too. "Look," he said. "I wish we had time to collect more information and analyze it in more detail, but we don't have that luxury. The *Northern Celeste* and the *Montserrat Star* are headed in our direction and we'd better know which one we've decided to target before we make contact. So... confirmation or not, we've got to decide which vessel we're going to hit."

"Have we received anything more from the agent aboard the *Montserrat Star*?" asked Caroline. "If we get newer reporting that says it's the *Montserrat Star*, then we have no choice. But without confirmation, we have to decide which ship to strike and we need to do it soon." *And God help us if we make a mistake*, she thought.

Captain Tremont looked at Broughton. "There is no further information, I'm afraid. But you do realize that if the agent aboard the *Montserrat Star* passes on anything substantive within the next hour, which is quite possible, you'll have to be the one to decide whether to accept or disregard it."

"You're absolutely right!" said Broughton. "We've been operating in the blind since the day this operation started. There's a lot of ocean out there and we don't have enough resources or time to go after both vessels, especially if they put more distance between each other. But believe me, when the time comes, I won't hesitate to make the call."

Chapter Seventy-Seven

London, England
Balcombe Street, near Regent's Park

Niles Peter Thornton sat at the end of the large conference table inside Suffolk House's ultra-secret facility at 28 Balcombe Street, watching and listening to unfolding events. His bodyguard and former operations officer, Robert Riley, was seated near him at the large table. It was Riley's first time inside Vanguard's operations nerve center. Thornton was in good form, despite his encounter with the Chameleon's messenger less than twenty-four hours earlier. The wounds the man had inflicted to the right side of his chest and arm were only lightly bandaged and all that remained from the encounter was some stiffness and a headache. Only one of his wounds, the one on his upper right arm, had needed repair; the young doctor on duty at St. Thomas's Hospital had managed to do that with only five stitches.

Thornton was monitoring the movement of the *Montserrat Star* and the *Northern Celeste* as they closed on Vanguard's mission ship, the *Aphrodite*. At the rate of speed the vessels were traveling, the *Aphrodite* would be within five nautical miles of the *Montserrat Star* in less than ninety minutes. He and Riley had both heard the briefing Captain Tremont had given Broughton and Caroline and they knew a decision had to be made soon about which ship to target.

Thornton turned away from the large screens at the end of the room and looked at Riley. "Bob, I brought you here because you've been steadfast in your support for the organization for more than a decade now. You, Tom and Simon have been my best field operatives. Correction..." he added, "you still are. You have personally given a lot to this organization and you haven't complained at all since you left the field. You accepted what needed to be done and you did it. It's been three years since Maureen's diagnosis and you've stood by her and done all you could for the organization as well. I want you to know how grateful I am... we're all grateful for your sacrifices. I know what it feels like to give up something you love, but I also know that your love for Maureen is greater than it is for any of this... as it should be. You are a devoted husband and father." He paused, then resumed. "I brought you here because I wanted you to be involved... and if we pull this off, I want you to take over the day-to-day running of VOCALS. You'll have the support of a deputy, so you won't have to worry about being able to get away to look after Maureen when you need to."

"I'm flattered," said Riley. "I'm honored that you still have that kind of faith in me, but I like what I'm doing now. Maureen has gotten used to me being where I am." He paused and looked away for a moment. "I must admit that I miss being in the thick of things, but that time has passed, at least for the time being. But if anything should happen to Maureen... and it will at some point... What I mean is... when she deteriorates to the point where the nurse and I can no longer manage looking after her at home she'll have to be moved to some place where she can get help around-the-clock. Maybe then I'll come back and try to pick up where I left off."

"I understand," said Thornton. "Give it some more thought, but in the end, I'll support whatever decision you make."

Thornton had just returned his gaze to the large screens when a retractable screen rose from the conference table with the VOCALS Watch Officer's face on it.

"Sorry to interrupt you, sir," said the Watch Officer, "but we've had another anonymous web-mail sent to the Foundation's website. This one has an internet provider address in Manila, Philippines, but it looks just like the one we received yesterday morning. We opened it and it says that there'll be a personal message for you on the Mumbai site in two minutes and you shouldn't miss it."

Thornton instructed the Watch Officer to pull up the message on the Mumbai site as soon as it was accessible and restrict viewing to his screen. "I want this one to be private," he told the Watch Officer. "Restricted access... No broadcast to any other work stations beyond mine. Understood?"

"I understand, sir. I'll bring it up for you as soon as we capture it," the Watch Officer assured him.

As soon as the Watch Officer's image disappeared, it was replaced by that of a blonde, deep-blue-eyed woman. It was the Russian, Annushka Baikova, Alexandâr Ilaivo's lover. "Before you say anything, old man," she started in her husky voice, "you should know that you are not being contacted for a question and answer session. There are only instructions... no questions and no answers. So, I advise you to listen carefully, as I won't be repeating myself." she commanded. "Alexandâr wants a meeting with you exactly two hours and thirty minutes from the time this message ends. There's an abandoned warehouse off Shoreditch High Street in London's East End... even you should be able to find it. If you head north along Shoreditch High Street, you will see it off to your right. That's where he'll meet you. Come alone and don't be late!"

"How do I know Ilaivo is going to show up?" Thornton asked. "He lost his nerve and didn't show up for the last one... sent one of his minions, a young Romanian, named Petrov."

"I told you there would be no questions!" the Russian snapped. "You need not worry, he will be there! He has chosen the place and time, just as Petrov told you he would. Be there!" she said sternly before her image faded.

When the webcast ended, Riley looked at his watch then turned to his boss. "What was that all about? Surely you're not going to meet this madman!" he said. "Have you forgotten what he tried to do to you less than twenty-four hours ago?"

"Alexandâr Ilaivo is the least of my worries," Thornton replied. "You heard Captain Tremont's briefing. There's something much bigger in the making. Besides, I think he wants to distract us… pull our efforts away from what's happening off the coast of Africa. Yes, he has a score to settle with me, but I don't think he's really interested in settling it today. I'm willing to bet he won't show up this time, either. I'm willing to take the risk. Besides, even if he succeeds in dealing with me, the last thing he'll want to do is get trapped in London. No… Ilaivo will want to see that his precious cargo makes it to the buyer. And if it does, he'll want to take the paycheck and vanish as quickly as possible."

"So, are you saying that you're going to go through with it?" asked Riley.

"Yes, of course I am," said Thornton. "And if he does turn up, it'll mean keeping one more member of his team occupied."

"I see…" said Riley. "There's nothing I can say to change your mind then?"

"Not at all," said the elderly spymaster. "This day had to come sooner or later."

Riley knew that Thornton had been under immense pressure during the past week. He was concerned more than ever that the pressure and stress may have caused him to make what could be a fatal error in judgment—one he could not stand by and watch from the sideline.

Chapter Seventy-Eight

Atlantic Ocean
North African Coast

It was approaching 3:45 a.m. when *Aphrodite's* starboard lookout contacted the bridge and reported visual contact with the *Montserrat Star.* The *Montserrat Star's* port and starboard running lights were barely recognizable, as it had just come over the horizon on a northeasterly heading. *Aphrodite's* operations officer confirmed the vessel's distance at 43,000 yards and its speed at 23 knots. Given both ships' courses and speed, they would pass within two nautical miles of each other in just over forty-five minutes. Broughton and Caroline were still below deck in the special operations center with Captain Tremont, discussing how they would board both vessels, when the VOCALS Watch Officer interrupted with an urgent message. He had just received a report from the Gambian agent onboard the *Montserrat Star.*

"Sir, I apologize for the interruption," the Watch Officer said, "but we've just received some information that should help you. The agent aboard the *Montserrat Star* just reported that the entire shipment of yellowcake is onboard the vessel. All 350 barrels are in the aft cargo hold. Confirmation is based on visual inspection and four high resolution digital photographs. Technical analysis of the date/time stamp on the photographs and the trace signal confirm the authenticity of the photographs and the agent's current location. He also reported that there are eight European men onboard, providing security. He never saw all eight at once, but he was instructed to prepare four 'European' meals for each twelve-hour watch shift. The ship's deck officer also said there were eight onboard. He said that of the four European watch standers, one is posted at the entrance to the cargo hold, one on the stern, one on the bridge and another patrols the decks."

"Just in the nick of time! I just hope that the report is accurate. If it is, it's exactly the break we need." Broughton declared.

"If the *Montserrat Star* stays on course," said Captain Tremont, "we've got exactly thirty-two minutes until we intercept it. We'll have to work quickly," he announced, raising the handset to contact the bridge. "Have the deck officer lower the go-fast boat over the side!" he ordered. He then turned to Broughton. "Your high altitude low-opening (HALO) parachute rigs are already onboard the go-fast."

"Good." said Broughton, turning to Caroline. "We'll run this just like it's written in the textbook," he added. "It'll be just like a training exercise. The go-fast boat will get us up to an altitude of 500 feet. It'll approach the *Montserrat Starr* from the stern and close to 1,000 yards. At that point, we'll release and steer our chutes aboard from the stern. The agent reported one guard posted on the stern and a total of eight European security personnel throughout the boat. They should be easy to identify among an all-African crew. The Europeans no doubt accounted for the extra mouths the agent had to feed. With these solid facts, we'll have to accept the report." Broughton then turned to Captain Tremont. "What about wind conditions?"

"You're in luck… wind conditions are pretty darn good! There's a light three-to-four-knot northeasterly. The high altitude-low opening chutes should make your thousand-yard glide onto the deck fairly easy. If the stealth design of the go-fast boat conceals its presence, they won't be expecting you," he declared. "You'll take them completely by surprise."

"That's just what we need," said Broughton. He looked at Caroline, showing a hint of concern. "Are you alright? You've been rather quiet the last half hour."

Caroline smiled at him. "I'm fine," she said. "It's just my way of organizing my thoughts... focusing on the task ahead. I like to think of it as meditation." Then she added, "If you think I'm having second thoughts, you're off your rocker! I wouldn't miss this for anything in the world!"

Chapter Seventy-Nine

Fifteen minutes after the *Aphrodite's* deck crew lowered the black, stealth-design, go-fast boat into the water, it was speeding away, heading southwest on the Atlantic Ocean at 60 knots— en route to a rendezvous with the *Montserrat Starr*. The choppiness of the Atlantic was the only thing that kept the boat's coxswain from demanding 90 knots from the boat's powerful engines.

Caroline and Broughton sat in back in a small compartment, directly behind the coxswain and a crewman whose job it was to get them aloft. They sat in total silence as the boat's black, angle-plated, dart-like hull sliced through three foot swells. Although Broughton did not speak or make eye contact with Caroline, the look on his face obviated the need for words. He was pensive and she knew what was on his mind. She had seen the same look when they had laid side-by-side in the darkness of her room at Hotel Davaline. She looked at him, stroked his hand and smiled. It was a message of reassurance. *Don't worry. I'll be fine. We'll be fine. Soon it'll be over and all behind us.*

The lashing of waves against the boat's fiberglass hull and the roar of its combined 1,200 horsepower engines were the only sounds that disturbed the quietness of the night. Overhead in the sky, stars twinkled and Venus was visible well above the horizon. The blackness of night-time was still with them, but in an hour or so, the first hint of sunlight would arrive on the eastern horizon. Behind where Caroline and Broughton sat, two large winch-controlled reels had been mounted on the boat. Each of the large reels had 700 feet of static nylon rope spooled on it. Two HALO parachutes and two harnesses rested in front of the winches, ready for attachment to their users.

Just under thirty minutes after they launched, the coxswain turned the boat west and made a wide arc that brought his craft onto a northeasterly heading. The sleek boat was now five miles astern of the *Montserrat Star*. This was only the second time the new stealth-design had been used in a Vanguard operation, and for the second time the design seemed to be working perfectly. They had approached the target completely undetected—no radar signature at all had been picked up by the *Montserrat Star*.

After falling in behind the *Montserrat Star*, the coxswain throttled back the engines. He reduced the boat's speed to 35 knots and closed on the large vessel. He had positioned the boat smartly in the middle of the *Montserrat Star's* wake and directly in line with its huge, churning propellers. As soon as the go-fast was in position, its crewman signaled to Caroline and Broughton that their launch would occur in ten minutes. Both rose to their feet, donned their harnesses, shouldered their rucksacks and weapons, and checked each other's rigging. They each carried two Sig Sauer 9mm pistols, a Sig Sauer P556 SWAT machine pistol, eight thermite incendiary charges, and three four-pound C4 explosive charges. Four of the C4 charges were rigged with timers and two for remote detonation by Caroline and Broughton or, as a contingency, the crewman aboard the go-fast.

A few minutes after their harnesses were connected to the nylon tethers, the coxswain throttled-up the boat's engines and the two rectangular canopies filled with air and rose aloft. Caroline felt like an eagle soaring on a thermal as they climbed steadily and moved smoothly through the air until they reached 500 feet. At 500 feet altitude and a distance of 1,000 yards from the *Montserrat Star's* stern, they released the ropes from the harnesses and the go-fast broke off, then took up and maintained a position three nautical miles to the west of the *Montserrat Star*.

With Caroline in the lead, they approached in tandem, their black parachute canopies advancing on the vessel at staggered altitudes. At three hundred feet from the vessel's stern, they split up and floated wide of the stern on either side, maneuvering their parachutes above and outside the arc of illumination cast by the vessel's white stern light. At an altitude of one hundred and fifty feet and a distance of two hundred feet from the vessel, Caroline could see the guard on duty. He was European. The information provided by the agent onboard was accurate. The man had his back toward them, leaning against the lifeline, smoking a cigarette. She was relieved to see that he was alone.

At a distance of seventy-five feet, Caroline executed a highly dangerous maneuver with precision and swiftness. She released the parachute's controls and in a matter of seconds, she raised her silenced Sig Sauer P556 SWAT machine pistol and fired at the lone figure. Her first shot missed. It hit the metal deck and ricocheted in front of the man, sending sparks flying. *Damn it!* she thought. *That was a bad move.*

***

Roused by the ricochet, the guard instinctively raised his weapon and gazed through the darkness toward the vessel's forward upper decks. Seeing no movement, he spun on his heel and looked out over the stern into the darkness, but the ship's stern light reduced his night vision. After a beat, he caught a flicker of movement above, just to the left and aft of the ship. His eyes quickly shifted to the right. For an instant, he was shocked and paralyzed by the sight of the two parachutes moving toward the vessel. But before he could raise his weapon toward either of them, Caroline fired a second and a third shot. Both tore into the man's chest and Caroline was the last thing he saw as he fell backward onto the deck.

Chapter Eighty

Shortly after taking out the guard, both parachutes floated down onto the vessel's aft deck. Caroline and Broughton quickly threw off their harnesses and made a communications check. After dragging the guard's body into the shadows, Broughton's voice broke radio silence.

"Are you alright?" he asked.

"Couldn't be better!" Caroline replied, her breathing rapid. "One down, three to go!"

"Correction… One down, seven to go," said Broughton. "Keep your eyes open and stay alert!" he added firmly, then switched to using hand signals to instruct her to don her night vision goggles, move up the starboard side of the vessel and eliminate the guard posted at the ladder leading below deck.

It took less than a minute for their eyes to adjust to the infrared goggles. As soon as visual acuity was acquired, Caroline moved toward the middle of the vessel, sticking close to the superstructure to avoid detection. As she approached mid-ship and the entrance to the ladder, she could smell Turkish tobacco. *Turkish tobacco… What is it with the stuff? Every self-styled rogue intelligence operative these days seems to be smoking the crap!* The guard was standing outside the hatch, looking out to sea. He was unaware of the intrusion. He gave one final deep drag on his cigarette and flicked it over the side. He started to turn in her direction and she froze, pressing her body against the metal structure. He turned quickly toward her, stared for a few seconds and then started walking in her direction. Thinking quickly, she took a 9mm round from a magazine and flicked it forward of his position. The man raised his weapon and spun around to investigate. As soon as he turned, a bullet spat from Caroline's silenced Sig Sauer pistol and pierced his right temple. She moved quickly to where he lay and dragged his body over to the rail and left it behind a lifeboat. Then, panting from the effort of dragging the heavy corpse, she descended the ladder two decks and found the main hatch to the aft cargo, where Broughton was waiting for her.

"You OK? What took you so long?" Broughton asked, displaying what was clearly a mock grin.

"What do you mean, what took me so long? I couldn't shoot him before he finished his cigarette, now could I?" she said, smiling.

Broughton signaled that they had five minutes to set all the charges, then went about undoing the hatch dogs that secured the large hatch to the cargo hold bulkhead. When the hatch was open, they slipped through. Inside the huge hold they found the 350 drums containing the yellowcake, just as the agent had reported. They were also handed an extra bit of luck. The drums containing the yellowcake had been conspicuously marked, but rearranged so as not to draw attention to them. They had been strapped tightly against the bulkhead, but were tucked away behind dozens of drums containing light, sweet crude oil.

"This is better than we could have hoped for," Caroline whispered into her highly sensitive throat microphone.

"Set the incendiary charges to go off in ten minutes," Broughton instructed. "Spread 'em around the entire area. We'll get a good burn that way. When this oil gets to burning, everything in here will go up in flames."

"What about the C4 charges?" Caroline asked.

"The lower part of the hold is a few feet below the waterline. Use four charges. Set two on the port side and two on the starboard side. Keep 'em close together and set the timer on each for twenty minutes. We wanna give the fire enough time to consume everything before this tub goes down. We don't want to leave anything that can be salvaged."

"What about the other two C4 charges? What do we do with them?" she queried.

"Leave that to me. I've got a special place for them. Just make sure you get everything in place here," he added. "I'm gonna give our friends up forward a little present. A few more holes at the other end of this tub will guarantee that it goes to the bottom quickly. Remember," he admonished, "when all the charges are in place, get the hell out of here and make your way topside."

Caroline grinned. That was one order she was certainly going to carry out with no delay!

"Wait for me where we came aboard," Tom continued. "Start the timers on the incendiaries and the C4 by remote as soon as they're all in place. Remember, you'll have just ten minutes to get clear of the cargo hold before the incendiaries detonate. Don't mess about! Here... take this," he said, thrusting the remote toward her. "When the incendiaries detonate, you'll have ten minutes before the C4 goes off. You're wearing your inflatable life vest and wrist communicator, so as soon as the incendiaries go off, go over the side. At this speed, the ship should move a good distance beyond you before it goes up. The go-fast should have you out of the water within fifteen minutes."

Caroline frowned. "Shouldn't I wait until you come topside before I activate the C4 timers? We both have to get clear of the ship before they detonate, don't we? Look... we've got enough charges in place to do the job already," she added, frustrated by his intransigence. "Remember what you told me... 'Never take chances if you don't have to.' Well, this is one of those times. You don't have to do this! There are already enough explosives planted to blow this boat to kingdom come!"

He lifted his night vision goggles, kissed her forehead and then planted a gentle kiss on her lips. "Go on," he urged. "I'll be topside by the time you get there. This is the wrong time to have a debate about this. If we're gonna finish this, you've gotta get moving. Contact VOCALS and have them send the agent onboard a message instructing him to go over the side when he hears the first explosion."

She grabbed him and kissed him passionately. "You had better come back to me!" she said quietly. "Do you hear me? I was just starting to get used to you, and that's not an easy thing for me to do. Don't you dare disappoint me!" she scolded. But as she turned away from him to carry out his order, she felt a chill of anxiety prickle down her spine.

***

Broughton smiled, pulled away from her and made his way back to the main deck. He made it all the way forward without being detected. All the off-duty crew members were still in their bunks. He slipped down the ladders to the forward cargo hold and placed one of the C4 charges on each outer bulkhead. With all of the charges in position, he raced up the ladder toward the main deck, but as soon as he stepped through the hatch, he heard the unmistakable *tat-tat-tat-tat* of an AK-47 and saw sparks from ricochets to his right and just above his head. The shots were coming from the forward end of the ship. He looked in that direction and saw muzzle flashes. They were coming from a weapon held by a European man who was also wearing night vision goggles. He must have been the roving guard. He had apparently discovered the lifeless bodies of his comrades, but for unknown reasons had not raised alarm.

The man was closing steadily on Broughton's position. He was also firing in Broughton's direction, but he was clearly not trying to hit him. Suddenly, and for no apparent reason, he removed his night vision goggles and started laughing. Broughton recognized his face. It was the Russian, the ex-KGB officer Branimir Baikov—one of Alexandâr Ilaivo's henchmen.

The Russian seemed to be expecting him.

"Mr. Broughton," he said in thick, Russian-accented English. "Come out! I've been expecting you. I know why you are here. Let's talk. You didn't think you would get away with what you are trying to do so easily, did you? You will never succeed on your own, you know," he said. "You will need help! I don't want to kill you, but if you don't come out, you will force me to kill you or we will both die! Come out! You're trapped! There is only one other way to the main deck… the starboard side hatch, and I have locked it."

"Why should I trust you?" asked Broughton.

"You don't have a choice. But if you must know, three weeks ago my sister Annushka died in one of Alexandâr Ilaivo's safe houses. Raped and gutted by one of his sadistic goons while she slept. He showed her no respect. Even in death he still abuses her name and her honor," the Russian added.

Several seconds of silence passed after the Russian finished speaking. He had halted his advance just twenty feet away from where Broughton was crouched inside the hatch. Remaining somewhat cautious, he had taken the opportunity to change magazines. He remained silent. Moments later, the Russian resumed firing. This time, his shots went inside the hatch above Broughton's head. Broughton knew he had to eliminate Branimir Baikov if he was going to get off the ship before it went up. But he was perplexed. He couldn't ignore what the Russian had said. Suddenly, he had to consider an unexpected and potentially plausible change in the scenario. *What did he mean when he said I couldn't succeed on my own and that I need help? Was he offering his services? If so… why? To avenge his sister? But could he be trusted?* There was no time to find answers to these questions. By now, everyone on board would have heard the shots and would be getting out of their bunks. It would only be a matter of seconds, or minutes at best, before the entire crew flowed onto the main deck. If they did, he and Caroline would be trapped. They would be doomed.

Broughton dropped as low as he could, dove over the bottom of the open hatch and fired a burst from his silenced Sig Sauer machine pistol at the Russian's feet to force him to seek cover, but one round hit the man in the foot and he swore loudly in Russian. Instead of finding cover, he lowered his weapon and started to limp toward Broughton.

He had to decide in a split second... Was it a trap or was the Russian serious? Broughton signaled to the man to come forward carefully. The Russian smiled, but before he could take a step, a shot rang out and he fell, face forward. Broughton rolled to his left and took cover behind a lifeboat pod. After a beat, a volley of shots was fired. This time they were bursts of automatic weapon fire. He looked around the lifeboat pod and there he was. Thirty-five feet away... another European, descending the port side superstructure ladder, headed toward Broughton. The man wore night vision goggles, but they were swung upward and not over his eyes. His face, too, was familiar. It was the Bulgarian, Andrei Chervenkov... Alexandâr Ilaivo's most loyal and most fanatical minion.

Chapter Eighty-One

It was still pitch dark, and with only the *Montserrat Star's* running lights on, concealment on deck wasn't difficult. Broughton glanced at his wrist communicator. Only five minutes until the incendiary charges detonated. The past fifteen minutes had gone by far too slowly. It seemed as if hours had passed since they had parasailed onto the ship's main deck. Crouched low, he moved cautiously from behind the lifeboat pod and darted aft, taking cover behind the next pod he came to. Caroline had heard the gunshots. But rather than waiting for him as she had been instructed, she headed forward to help him. She was soon to realize that she had made a grave tactical error. Before she could reach the halfway point along the main deck, a man sprang out and grabbed her around her neck. He had been waiting behind the lifeboat pod, presumably to intercept Broughton.

"Where do you think you are going, young lady, and how the hell did you get aboard this ship?" the man whispered in her ear then beckoned an associate who had just emerged from a nearby open hatch. "Look what I've found! A *mulatto!*" he said, grinning.

"Where did she come from?" the man's associate asked.

"I don't know. She's probably a stowaway, running away from the shooting," he replied. "Does it matter?" he asked, unconcerned. "She's a hot one! Nice firm body... Nice tits and ass, too... She'll bring a good price when we reach Port Bushehr. But in the meantime, she'll be a delightful distraction during the rest of the voyage. We'll put her in one of the gear lockers," he added, with a wide grin.

Caroline didn't respond to any of the man's questions. Instead, she remained silent and calm. She knew that belligerence or resistance would lead to more forceful restraint. Her attacker was distracted; he had interpreted the lack of resistance from her as submission and left both of her hands free. Despite the gunshots, the man's mind was fixed on money and carnal pleasures. Excited about his good fortune and Caroline's compliance, he loosened his forearm grip around her neck. If his hand had traveled down beyond her left breast, he would have discovered her weapons.

It's now or never, she thought. Taking advantage of his mistake, she slowly raised her left hand and eased it across her body until it reached the silenced Sig Sauer 9mm pistol in one of her shoulder holsters. Without removing it, she tilted the barrel to the rear and upward and fired two shots behind her into the man. The man stumbled and fell backward against the lifeboat pod. His associate, who had moved off toward the gear locker to prepare a place to inspect their find more closely, turned and was moving toward her. She released the 9mm pistol and grabbed the silenced Sig Sauer P556 SWAT machine pistol from its holster.

"This ought to break up the monotony you find so mind-numbing!" she said, through clenched teeth. "Too bad you won't be around to see what happens next. But you can believe me when I say 'it's gonna to be a hot time in the old town tonight!'" she declared, as she released a burst of bullets into the figure charging toward her. The rounds hit the man like a sledgehammer, knocking him backward off his feet. He grunted loudly and his body hit the steel deck with a thud. Six of the eight-member European security force aboard the vessel had been eliminated. The final two would almost certainly be the deadliest.

After disposing of her attackers, Caroline continued

forward, in search of Broughton. As she passed the next lifeboat pod headed forward, a hand reached out and grabbed her. She gasped, but before she could reach for a weapon, she realized that this time it was Broughton.

"Am I glad to see you," she whispered.

"What the hell are you doing here?" he demanded. "I thought I told you to stay aft and wait for me!"

"You did, but I heard shots... a lot of them and I thought you might need some help. I thought you might be pinned down."

"That was brave of you, but very foolish!" he said through clenched teeth. "They're pretty pissed off and I can't say that I blame them. With the two you just took out, that makes six down. One of them was Branimir Baikov, but I wasn't the one that killed him."

"Who did then?" she asked.

"His associate, Andrei Chervenkov... It seems Branimir Baikov wanted to settle a score with Ilaivo... said he wanted to help... that is, before the back of his head was shot off."

"We've got to get off this boat!" Caroline declared. "Where's Chervenkov?"

"Over there somewhere," Broughton said, pointing to the opposite side of the lifeboat pod. "He's the one that's been shooting at me for the last minute or so!"

Before Broughton could finish speaking, a hail of bullets raked the lifeboat pod.

"We've got to move and we've got to do it now!" Caroline whispered sternly.

"No shit! It'll start getting light in a few minutes and we've got less than three minutes before the incendiaries go off." He flipped his night vision goggles down over his eyes and said, "Let's go. Follow me."

As soon as Broughton stepped from behind the lifeboat pod, Andrei Chervenkov punched him in the throat and fired a burst of bullets, two of which caught Broughton in his right leg.

Broughton had made a dangerous mistake. He had taken his eyes off Chervenkov's position and Chervenkov had crossed the deck and crept in closer. But Chervenkov had not seen Broughton pull Caroline behind the lifeboat pod; therefore he didn't know of the distraction she had caused his target when she turned up. He had simply gambled by moving, and he had won.

Caroline's hand flew up to her mouth, but she remained silent. She didn't know where the eighth member of the security team was, nor if she would be next. She had gone tense; her fingernails were digging crescents into her palms. Chervenkov's attack had been lightning-fast; she could only look on as the Bulgarian produced a stainless steel fighting knife, seemingly from nowhere, and thrust it into Broughton's stomach. She knew she had to try to stop what was happening, even if Chervenkov wasn't alone.

Chervenkov pulled the knife out of Broughton's stomach and was about to slash his throat when a kick from Caroline lashed across his face and spun him around. The Bulgarian was surprised and stunned, but he recovered quickly. Despite the bone-jarring kick to the side of his head, he held onto the knife.

"I'm going to slice you to pieces, you little bitch!" he declared, thrusting the blade toward her.

As he thrust the knife at her the second time, her left leg swung across in a roundhouse and the knife flew from his hand. "You are pretty good!" the Bulgarian declared, smiling coldly. "Looks like I'm going to have to kill you with my bare hands. But before I do, I want a taste of what's underneath those clothes. Who knows... afterwards, maybe you will want to run away with me," he said, with a chuckle.

Caroline was pumped with adrenalin. Realizing that time was running out and that Broughton's condition might be fatal, she went for both of her Sig Sauer pistols. "You're no man, you're just a bag of hot air!" she declared angrily, firing a volley of rounds into the Bulgarian's chest. Before the man's body had even hit the deck, she had turned to assist Broughton. As she was crouching to assess Broughton's condition, another white man, the last European onboard, sprang from a hatch, some thirty feet behind her, and leveled his assault rifle on her. But before he could pull the trigger, Broughton drew his pistol and fired two rounds past her. One struck the man in the chest and the other in the center of his forehead. The man stumbled and back-pedaled as he fell, muzzle flashes streaming uncontrollably from his weapon as he went down.

"You alright?" Caroline asked, staring down at Broughton through her night vision goggles. "How bad is it? Can you move?" she asked, trying not to show her deep concern. Blood had pooled on the deck beneath him and he was beginning to shiver. She knew it would not be long before he went into shock. Her breathing quickened and she could feel her hands growing cold. *What if he bleeds out and dies here? What do I do after all this... all we've done... all the obstacles we've overcome... and before we've even had a chance to explore a relationship? It's happening all over again. Everyone I give my heart to dies I'm bad luck.*

"It's pretty bad," said Broughton. "You had better go," he commanded.

"I won't leave you behind," she said, staring down at him.

"You've got to go!" he added, glancing at the second hand on his wrist communicator. "There isn't a choice. The cargo hold is gonna go up in about fifty-five seconds."

"I'm not going without you," she told him.

Grabbing hold of the rescue ring on the thin horse-collar life vest he was wearing, she dragged him as fast as she could to the aft part of the ship. As soon as they reached the stern, an explosion rocked the entire ship and the large outer doors of the cargo hold blew open, breaking the dogging latches and sending the heavy doors high into the air. Bright orange flames followed the doors and climbed past them in the night air. After the explosion, the entire crew of the *Montserrat Star* poured onto the decks. A handful of the crew raced toward the inferno, dragging fire hoses. A few charged the flames with portable fire extinguishers. But most of them headed for the rails, launched the lifeboats and jumped into the water.

Caroline looked up at the huge fireball. "Aren't you glad that sometimes I can be a stubborn, hard-headed broad?" Flashing a smile, she added, "You don't have to say anything, you can thank me later. Hang on!" She inflated his life vest, then rolled him under the lifeline and over the side.

The *Montserrat's* captain and a couple more of the ship's officers, who had collaborated with their European passengers, spotted her and fired wildly in her direction. It was time to go. Caroline climbed between the lifelines and jumped over the side. The *Montserrat Star* continued its northeasterly course, with barrels of crude oil exploding in its aft cargo hold. As soon as she was in the water, she looked for the flashing white light on Broughton's life vest. She quickly spotted it and swam over to him. A few minutes later, multiple explosions rocked the *Montserrat Star* and the flames from its cargo hold illuminated a wide area around it. The ship's stern dropped quickly below the waves and its bow pointed toward the sky. Less than ten minutes later, the sea had devoured it. Except for the eleven lifeboats bobbing about on the ocean, which had been launched by its unwitting crew to escape imminent catastrophe, it was as if the *Montserrat Star* had never existed.

Only minutes had passed, but to Caroline, it seemed as if it had been ages before the go-fast crew spotted them and the Gambian agent, who was in the water some three hundred meters from them. The first signs of daylight were just beginning to appear. Broughton looked to the eastern horizon then back at Caroline and smiled.

"You'll be alright," Caroline said. "I told you we'd look out for each other."

"Yes, you did," Broughton said and fell unconscious.

As if cued, the go-fast boat bulled up beside them. The coxswain and the crewman plucked them from the water, picked up the Gambian and headed full-throttle back to the *Aphrodite*.

Chapter Eighty-Two

Niles Peter Thornton stepped into the street from the doorway of the abandoned warehouse, just off Shoreditch High Street in London's East End. He had been standing there, hiding in the shadows at the back of an alcove, away from the dim but still revealing street lights. He had expected Alexandâr Ilaivo to be laying in wait for him, so he arrived twenty-five minutes early. But he had been wrong. There was no sign of the Bulgarian. He was alone. When the car he was expecting finally turned up, it was not his nemesis that it delivered. It was Annushka Baikova, his Russian lover. Upon seeing Thornton, the Russian killer's normally steely composure gave way to uncontrollable excitement.

"You foolish old man!" she shouted scornfully as she clambered from the car and walked toward him. "Who do you think you are, turning up like this in your condition?"

"What is it with Ilaivo this time?" Thornton lashed out, tauntingly. "After all the threats and promises, he sends a woman to do his work. I never thought I'd see the day when he hid behind a woman's skirt tail," he added.

"You disgust me, old man… You are always poking your nose where it shouldn't be. It's time for your meddling to end! It's time for you to die like the emaciated, decrepit old windbag that you are. Alexandâr said he should have killed you a long time ago."

"Why didn't he?" asked Thornton.

"He would have, but he would have had to do it from a

distance, and that would have been unsatisfactory to him."

"Then why isn't he here? Why did he send you?" Thornton quipped.

"He thought about killing you himself. Believe me... he wanted it to be up close and personal. He wanted to see the fear in your eyes and smell the putrid breath seeping from your fossilized, decaying old body. But I came up with a better idea and he agreed to it. I convinced him that there would be nothing more undignified for you than having your life extinguished by me. That pleased him as much, if not more, than doing it himself." Thornton remained silent, refusing to rise to her bait. "You pride yourself as an English gentleman... you and your sickening, antiquated, chivalrous ways," she went on. "He knew that having your manhood and your life extinguished by a woman against whom you were defenseless, would be the ultimate undignified death."

Thornton sighed. "Well... here I am. And by the sound of it, Ilaivo seems to still be angry about that rather nasty mark I left on his face. I suppose it makes him think of me whenever he looks at it. Quite frankly, I think it added a bit of character to an otherwise banal profile. After all, it did make him look more menacing. I suppose for that he should be thanking me." Thornton paused. "I'm sorry. I forgot for a moment that his victims never see what he really looks like because he never reveals himself to them. He's always hidden behind some disguise. It all seems like cowardice to me. What do you think?" Thornton's last remark seemed to infuriate the Russian. "Enough! I've had enough of your drivel!" she shouted. "It's time for you to die!"

Annushka Baikova moved in closer toward Thornton. He reciprocated and closed the distance between them further. Soon, only a few feet separated them. After a beat, they began to move clockwise in what seemed like a well-choreographed circle pattern, almost like figures on a carousel. Except theirs was a pirouette of death. Without warning and without taking her eyes off her target, Annushka Baikova reached behind her back and drew a Glock 9mm pistol. Her movement was so fast and fluid that Thornton almost didn't see it. The Russian raised the pistol and leveled it at Thornton's forehead then broke into laughter. Before he could say a word, she pressed the magazine release and the fifteen-round magazine fell to the ground. She then pulled back the Glock's slide and ejected the chambered round. Her laughter ceased and a taunting smile consumed her face as she tossed the pistol onto the ground.

Thornton breathed a quiet sigh of relief. But before his fear could subside, she drew a large, highly polished, stainless steel knife. "I am going to slice you to pieces. But before you die, I'm going to cut off your balls and send them to your office so they'll know how you died."

Thornton smiled and drew his own weapon, a 9mm Sig Sauer pistol, and began waving it from side to side. "That's the problem with today's youth…" he said. "You're all slow learners! Didn't anyone ever tell you that you should never bring a knife to a gun fight?"

The ageing spymaster's voice crackled with a faint spark of energy. He was doing his best to put on an air of confidence. But before the last word rolled off his tongue, the Russian's wrist darted forward like a lizard's tongue on unsuspecting prey and the blade in her hand slashed across his forearm.

"Now you, too, are marked for life!" Annushka Baikova quipped, then launched her body forward. She was all over Thornton, landing punches and kicks to his face and stomach.

The succession of blows and their rapidity took Thornton by surprise, but he managed to stumble away. He steadied himself and stepped ungracefully to one side. He had managed to evaded most of the barrage of blows.

After shaking off the cobwebs, he circled his arms in front of his body and moved into a martial arts stance. Annushka Baikova responded to the challenge and charged him, this time with a flurry of fists and elbows. Thornton blocked every one of them and swept her legs from under her. The Russian flew backward and landed on her back. But before he could descend on her, she arched her back inward, threw her legs underneath her and sprang to her feet, using her well-toned arms and large hands to propel herself back onto her feet. Now back on her feet, she circled left, then right and launched her body into her opponent once more.

A windmill of fluid motions from Thornton's arms ended in a fist that thrust through her defenses and smashed her nose. Blood splattered all over her stunned face.

"That's good!" she said in a raspy, deep voice. "You're deceptively talented. But you punch as if you are striking a woman!" she declared furiously. "Now fight me like you are a man, not a decrepit old woman! Give me your best, because you know that no matter how gallantly you fight, I am going to kill you. You know that, don't you?" she taunted.

A split second later, she delivered a roundhouse to the left side of his face, snapping his jawbone, instantly causing dizziness. The elderly spymaster had no time to recover before his legs were swept from under him. He fell backward like a tree that had met a lumberjack's chainsaw. The fall caused a surge of air to escape from his lungs. Time slowed. He tried to roll over to escape the lean-cut figure that seemed to hover suspended in full flight above him, but his movement was labored. Annushka Baikova landed on him on all-fours. She rammed her knee into his groin and delivered a sharp blow to his diaphragm with her fist that almost caused him to black out. The Russian was preparing for two more deadly blows—the first to his throat to crush his larynx and the second, the coup de grace, to his ribs, which would be smashed and their jagged edges sent into his heart. Her full frame, which was holding him pinned to the ground, was surprisingly heavy for a woman. In excruciating pain and barely conscious, Thornton managed to move his head to one side, a split second before her right fist came down, causing her to drive it into the pavement.

"You son of a bitch!" she screamed and raised the knife high in the air with her other hand. She struck Thornton in the right temple with the butt of the knife and shouted, "I am going to cut your throat from ear to ear! But before I do that, I'm going to cut your balls off and scalp you like the Apache Indians scalped their victims. You will be alive and I will make sure that you are conscious." She threw her head back and laughed. "I promise you old man, it's going to hurt you a hell of a lot more than it's going to hurt me!"

Straddling Thornton's weakened frame, she raised the knife in the air, but before she could bring it down, a sharp pain pierced her left side, just below her rib cage. Thornton had taken her by surprise. He had stabbed her with a stiletto knife he had pulled from his jacket sleeve. He had plunged it into her spleen and pulled downward sharply on it.

"Damn you!" Annushka Baikova swore then let out a wail.

Thornton's eyes brightened. He twisted the slender blade and pushed it toward the center of her back. With blood gushing from the flap-like wound, she fell sideways, writhing in agony. She tried to reach the knife to remove it, but could not get a grip on its slippery, bloody handle.

Suddenly, the headlights of a car appeared. It had turned off the High Street and was moving rapidly toward them. Seconds later, it screeched to a halt, just a few feet away. As soon as it stopped, the door flew open and a tall, slim, silhouetted figure, bathed in backlight from the car's headlights, rushed over and bent down over them.

Annushka Baikova was almost unconscious from the loss of blood, but she managed to raise her head and look up at the man whose face was still consumed by the shadows. "You are too late! The old bastard is dying, if he isn't already dead!" she said, laughing between bouts of coughing.

She then turned to the man on the ground beside her and raised her hand to her head. She grabbed hold of the skin just below her hairline, pulled the hair away from her head and let it fall to the ground. She then gripped the skin at the top of her forehead and peeled away the prosthetic mask to reveal an angry scar that ran from the hairline in the middle of her forehead, down to her left eyebrow.

The man standing above her did not speak. Instead, he knelt down and peeled away a prosthetic mask from the older man's face. As he knelt, he turned sideways and stared into the eyes of his nemesis, but his face remained in partial darkness. The man lying on the ground beside Alexandâr Ilaivo was Robert Riley, his faithful bodyguard and chauffeur.

Startled by what he had seen, Thornton turned to his chauffeur. "Riley? What on earth have you done? You damn fool. You could have been killed!"

"I know," Riley said, grinning through pulverized lips and bloody teeth. "So could you."

When Thornton turned to look down on Ilaivo, he was directly in the car's headlights.

"And you thought you were invincible," he said to the Chameleon, his face impassive. "You've lost, Alexandâr. You've lost everything. Do you know that? Less than fifteen minutes ago, the *Montserrat Star* went to the bottom of the Atlantic Ocean, but not before all of its precious cargo was destroyed by fire."

Ilaivo looked up through squinting eyes. He was surprised to see the ageing spymaster, very much alive. He became furious. "You…? It can't be!"

Thornton smiled a self-congratulating smile and bent towards the dying man. "Alexandâr, I've always known you to be a ruthless killer without scruples, but a simple killer nevertheless. Up 'til now, you've been lucky. You've managed to claw your way back from every situation that should have been terminal. But this time there's no coming back! You chose to play a game that couldn't be ignored by any self-respecting nation or society. It was a game we simply couldn't allow you to win."

The Chameleon stared coldly and silently into Thornton's eyes. Raising himself painfully, he grabbed Thornton by the collar and mumbled, "I'll see you in hell!"

A few seconds later, a sharp blast of air rushed from his lungs and his head fell to the pavement.

Chapter Eighty-Three

Caroline Dupré and Niles Thornton strolled arm-in-arm along Queen's Walk. Spring had finally arrived and was in full-swing, bringing with it a fragrant mélange of horse chestnut and cherry blossoms that filled the air. To the casual observer, they might be seen as a loving father and daughter, or even a love-struck, elderly man, smitten by a younger lover. In this place and at this time, however, others' perceptions didn't matter, because they were oblivious to them. They were enjoying the sunshine and tranquility of their surroundings.

A week had gone by since the sinking of the *Montserrat Star* and the demise of Alexandâr Ilaivo and his network of killers. Thornton had acknowledged that what Vanguard had accomplished was due to a combination of talent, determination, sacrifice, and a great deal of luck. Not only had the demise of the Chameleon stopped a plan with unthinkable consequences for millions of people, it had also preserved the organization's anonymity, enabling it to continue its mission of disrupting and eliminating threats, without the constraints of constitutions and treaties. But success had carried a tremendous price tag, and that worried Thornton. He was also still exhausted, but there were signs that he was returning to his unflappable self.

Thornton was uncharacteristically silent and Caroline could tell there were things on his mind. She peered at his face to see what was in his eyes, but he lowered his head to avoid eye contact and caressed her hand. He was collecting his thoughts.

"Do you know what I find disturbing about all of this?" he suddenly asked.

"No. I don't," she said. "Tell me."

"For a week, we played a costly game of catch-up. And all the while Ilaivo was operating in our midst—moving about freely, collecting information and killing with impunity. It wasn't until a few days ago that we realized he was the security guard that killed the woman at the Port Authority in Antwerp. My God! He was there while we were there, gathering information, looking over our shoulder, seeing how close we were getting to him." He paused then continued. "I have to admit it, I was impressed. I was especially impressed by his assumption of his dead lover's identity to get to the center of our operation. But what disturbs me most is that we wouldn't have known any of this, at least not in time to stop him, if he hadn't let his ego get the better of him. He damn near pulled it off, and in the process he took out some of my best operatives."

He could see that his last comment troubled Caroline, so he moved quickly to assuage her concerns. "Don't worry," he said soothingly. "Tom's going to be alright."

"Where is he?" she asked.

"He's in Davos, Switzerland, convalescing… getting lots of rest—rest he's going to need."

"When can I see him?" she asked eagerly.

"I'm afraid you won't be able to, at least not right away. But I can tell you that he wants very much to see you."

"I'm pleased to know that," she said. "I almost got him killed."

"That's not true," said Thornton. "According to him, you saved his life. He said Chervenkov would have finished him off if you hadn't been there." He stopped walking and looked into her eyes. "I know Tom. He's not one to exaggerate."

"But it was my selfish desire to help him that almost got him killed. I didn't stick to the plan. I let my feelings get in the way.

I was afraid I'd lose him, just like everyone else I have loved…
my mother, my husband…"

"I know," Thornton said. "I suspected that all along, and so
did Tom. That's why he tried his damnedest to complete the
mission without you. He knew what was going through your
head and it wouldn't surprise me if he wanted to prove you
wrong." A twinkle suddenly appeared in the ageing spymaster's
eyes and he smiled. "If that's what he intended to do, it looks
like he succeeded!"

"Yes. I believe he did," she said, feeling a bit more upbeat.
"Maybe I'm not cursed after all," she added, smiling.

"No, I don't think you are," he replied, then tactfully
changed the subject. "You're going to visit Nicolas in a couple
of weeks, aren't you?"

"Yes, I am," she said. "Why do you ask?"

"I just wanted to confirm your plans," he said. "You've
earned some time off and Nicolas will no doubt be happy to see
you. I believe Tom will be able to receive visitors by then as
well. You should drop in after your visit with Nicolas and see
him. I'm sure he'll be excited to see you. Who knows…? Seeing
you might help speed up his recovery. He could use that and so
could Vanguard. After all, I have big plans for him, and for
you."

Fantastic Books
Great Authors

Meet our authors and discover our exciting range:

- Gripping Thrillers
- Cosy Mysteries
- Romantic Chick-Lit
- Fascinating Historicals
- Exciting Fantasy
- Young Adult and Children's
  Adventures

Visit us at:
www.crookedcatbooks.com

Join us on facebook:
www.facebook.com/crookedcatpublishing

Lightning Source UK Ltd.
Milton Keynes UK
UKOW03f2016130814

236869UK00001B/21/P